I0663524

Manhunt: Return to Justice

Book 5 of An Adventure of the Old West series

Gary L. Pullman

Campbell and Rogers Press

CR

Campbell and Rogers Press

Copyright © 2024 by Gary L. Pullman

All rights reserved. No part of this book may be reproduced in any form or by any means without the prior written consent of the publisher, excepting brief quotes used in reviews. For permission to use material from the book, other than for reviews, please contact campbellandrogerspress@gmail.com.

This is a work of fiction. Characters, names, events, places, incidents, business establishments, and organizations portrayed in this novel are products of the author's imagination or are used fictitiously.

E-book ISBN 978-1-887402-39-2

Paperback ISBN 978-1-887402-40-8

First Edition

Published by Campbell and Rogers Press

https://www.campbellandrogerspress.com/

Manhunt: Return to Justice is dedicated to my beloved wife Paula Darnell, author of the two cozy mystery series **A DIY Diva Mystery** and **A Fine Art Mystery** and the stand-alone historical police procedural ***The Six-Week Solution***.

Chapter 1

The Monster of White Pine County

"He who wishes to be rich in a day will be hanged in a year."
— Leonardo da Vinci (1452–1519)

Excelsior, Nevada
September 1884

The White Pine County Courthouse was an imposing edifice, standing as a silent, but stately, testament to law and order or, at least, to the penalties for violating the same. Neoclassical in style, the elegant structure, which featured an impressive, triangular pediment supported by four pillars, seemed to have been transplanted from ancient Greece itself. It looked about as out of place in this mountainous region of the Wild West as Zeus might appear, were that deity to visit Excelsior in this day and age.

In Judge Harry Hawthorne's courtroom, however, the scene taking place contrasted sharply with the building's external grandeur.

Spencer Rowelings was on trial for "allegedly" robbing a Woodruff & Ennor's stagecoach, near Mineral Hill, during which crime he had "allegedly" murdered the driver, the shotgun messenger, and the four passengers inside, one of whom was a woman.

The end of the court proceedings was at hand now, and District Attorney Robert Benson presented his closing argument, as only he could.

"Ladies and gentlemen of the jury, look upon him!" Benson cried, half-turning to glower at the defendant.

If Rowelings cared a whit about the outcome of the trial, which could very well cost him his life, he betrayed no such concern.

"He is an anomaly; indeed, an abnormality. The accused is guilty of each of the crimes with which he is charged, and he is guilty, too, of a state of existence for which he cannot, but ought to be, charged: monstrosity! The man is a freak of nature, a spawn of the devil himself!"

Throughout the trial, the jurors had remained impassive, letting neither their expressions nor their attitudes convey even a hint of their thoughts or feelings. But, now, several of them tensed, stiffening in their chairs, as they darted glances at the seemingly inhuman figure they'd been called upon to judge.

They seemed to see the evil in the accused and in his soulless indifference to all that was good and decent. How else, Benson asked himself, *could* they see him, but as a monster who, besides having committed the other crimes with which he'd been charged, had murdered a woman?

The district attorney waited, studying their faces as they deliberated upon the scarred visage of the monster on trial and looked, however briefly, into the cold eyes of the fiend whose presence seemed, now, somehow to dominate the courtroom. Yes, he thought, the jury was intimidated by the brute; they were afraid, but, even more, they were disgusted.

"I won't again recount the deeds of this villain; they were horrible enough to relate during my examination and cross-examinations of him. Let me leave you with only two thoughts.

"First, Spencer Rowelings deliberately, and with malice, fired a bullet through the brain of Lois Martin, who was traveling home, blowing her brains out and splattering them against the interior of the coach—all for the sake of stealing the gold and silver carried by that conveyance. Rowelings had *already* assassinated the coach's driver, the shotgun messenger, and the three male passengers, thereby rendering the woman completely unprotected." He paused, looking from one horrified juror to the next.

"Second, I ask you, ladies and gentlemen—indeed, I *implore* you,—to find this monster guilty of the crimes he has committed against God and man; he cannot, he *must* not, be allowed to rob and kill again!"

Looking from one juror to the next, into horrified eyes, a fear-filled gaze, or a teary stare, Benson said, his voice soft, "I have the duty to do justice by the living and the dead. So do you, ladies and gentlemen."

The defense's closing argument then commenced, but, judging by the jury's expressionless faces, the attorney's words went mostly unheeded.

Then, Judge Hawthorne ordered the jurors to deliberate upon the evidence presented to them during the course of the trial. "Court will reconvene once a verdict is reached," he announced. "Until then, court is adjourned." He rapped his gavel, rose, descended from the bench, and exited the courtroom through a door at the rear of the chamber.

As the spectators began to leave the courtroom, one of them, remaining in his seat, asked the well-dressed stranger beside him, "What do you think?"

"Should be a short deliberation."

The other man shook his head. "Killing a woman in cold blood like that!" He shook his head. "It's hard to believe anybody could *do* such a thing."

"Not for me."

The spectator seemed surprised. "Really?" He presented his hand. "Don Madison, by the way."

They shook hands.

"Bane Messenger." He looked closely at his new acquaintance. "You're not from these parts."

"Nope. I'm an Arizona man myself, here to visit a relative."

"What brings you to Judge Hawthorne's courtroom?"

"The trial. Newspaper's been full of nothing but the robbery ever since it happened. When I read that Spencer Rowelings's trial had been scheduled, well, hell, I just had to see it for myself; it's history in the making. What about you, Bane?"

"Professional interest."

Taken aback, Madison frowned. "What do you mean?"

"I'm a U. S. marshal."

Madison looked impressed. "Damn!"

As Madison and the marshal conversed, the lawyers for the defense and the prosecution entered the courtroom, taking their seats at their respective tables.

Although both men affected neutral expressions, it seemed to Bane that the attorney for the defense looked resigned, as if he expected bad news.

The jury filed into the chamber, taking their seats in the two rows of chairs cordoned off by a low, ornate railing.

As other spectators sat beside or behind them, Madison remarked, "Something's up, sure enough."

Bane nodded. "Verdict."

Judge Hawthorne entered the courtroom, ascended to the bench, and took his seat in the high-backed, upholstered chair. Rapping his gavel, he announced, "Court is reconvened." Looking to the jury's foreman, he asked, "Has a verdict been reached?"

The gentleman stood. "Yes, Your Honor. We find the defendant, Spencer Rowelings, guilty as charged, on all counts."

The judge nodded. "Thank you, Mr. Foreman. Please be seated."

He resumed his place among his peers.

Regarding the convicted felon from the height of his bench, obvious disgust in his fierce, glaring eyes, in his stony demeanor, and in his scathing tone of voice, Judge Hawthorne said, "The defendant will rise."

Rowelings remained seated.

At a nod from the judge, the bailiff hooked his hands beneath the defendant's arms, lifting Rowelings from his chair.

With a shrug of his shoulders, the defendant twisted out of the other's grip.

A tense moment passed before the judge spoke. "Mr. Rowelings, you have been convicted of the most heinous crimes that anyone who has ever stood before me in this courtroom has committed. Your atrocious actions set you apart from many other criminals whose crimes are likewise of the most flagitious character.

"The gratuitous murders of five men and a helpless young woman are unspeakable! If I could sentence you to hell, that is the prison to which I would condemn you for eternity, but, since such a punishment is beyond the purview of this court, I must be content to order you to hang by the neck until dead, within the next fortnight. For that purpose, I hereby direct that you be taken immediately to the State Prison. May God *not* have mercy upon your wretched soul!"

Rowelings sprang forward. Glancing at the district attorney, he cried, "I'll kill you, Benson, you bastard, same as I'll kill the foreman of this kangaroo court's jury!"

Then, directing his glare at Judge Hawthorne, who'd raised his gavel to adjourn the proceedings, the murderous robber screamed, "You're a dead man, too, Judge!"

From his seat among the horrified spectators, Bane called, "You won't have time to kill anyone else, before you swing, Rowelings!"

Rushing forward, the city's deputy grabbed the prisoner, grappling with him. Rowelings delivered a savage punch that sent the officer of the law flying headlong into the low railing separating the front of the courtroom from the spectators' seating at the rear.

The bailiff cut off the fleeing prisoner.

Judge Hawthorne beat his gavel. "Order!" he commanded. "Order in the court!"

The deputy tried to rise, but fell.

Rowelings struck the bailiff a vicious blow, and the officer of the court collapsed, lying motionless on the floor.

Bane leaped from his seat, jumped the railing, and struck Rowelings, knocking the man's head back sharply, following this initial blow with two others, one to the side of the killer's head, another to his midsection.

Rowelings went down like a felled tree.

Landing a knee in the small of the sprawled criminal's back, Bane jerked Rowelings's right arm to the rear, before slipping the smaller "C"-shaped end of his handcuffs around the convict's wrist and snapping its ends shut so that the cuff formed a loop. Then, he fastened the end of the larger, attached "C"-shaped cuff closed. Taking hold of the larger ring, Bane hauled Rowelings to his feet. "By assaulting an officer of the law and an officer of the court, you've just committed two more crimes," Bane snarled.

The deputy rose, looking confused for a moment. Then, he scowled at Rowelings, remembering his altercation with the outlaw.

"And contempt of court," Judge Hawthorne called from the bench. "Deputy Lane, I see you've recovered consciousness. Will you be so good as to convey this refuse to the city jail?"

"It will be my pleasure, Your Honor."

Bane said, "I'll give you a hand."

"Thanks, but I can handle the likes of Rowelings easily enough."

"I'd like the marshal to accompany you," the judge told the deputy.

"All right, Marshal; thanks."

"Just doing my job."

"Thanks, just the same."

Bane nodded. "You're welcome."

The bailiff, who had also recovered, watched them leave. "I hope we don't have any more like him on the docket," he said.

From the bench, Judge Hawthorne replied, "Not today." Rapping his gavel, he decreed, "Court adjourned!"

As Bane and the deputy conducted their prisoner toward the back of the courtroom, the marshal saw the look of awe and reverence on Madison's face, as he stared at the lawmen.

Bane nodded at him.

The man from Arizona shook his head. "Wait 'til I tell Myrtle about *this*!"

Bane had no idea who Myrtle might be, but, he reckoned she'd be pleased to hear that Madison hadn't been hurt or killed by the Monster of White Pine County.

Chapter 2

A Special Day

There are men who rise refreshed on hearing of a threat . . . ."
— Ralph Waldo Emerson (1803-1882)

Excelsior, Nevada

"It's been a long day," Judge Hawthorne said, as he rubbed his brow, "so I'll get right to the point."

Bane nodded, thinking that the judge *did* look tired. Dark circles accentuated his large, owlish eyes.

Although there was enough illumination to see by, the judge's chambers were dim. The flames in the lanterns burned low, and the curtains were drawn at the windows.

"District Attorney Benson's birthday was two days ago. The same day, he received *this*." The judge slid an envelope across his desktop.

There was no return address, just the recipient's. Bane removed the envelope's contents—a birthday card. Ornate lettering read, "*Enjoy your special day!*" Under this text, a handwritten addendum warned, "It may be your last."

The card was unsigned.

"Rowelings," Bane said.

The judge nodded as he slid another envelope across his polished desktop's surface.

Again, the envelope bore only the recipient's address. Inside, another card, this one suitable for all occasions, bore a similar message: an amateur's rough sketch of a tombstone inscribed with the warning, "You'll get what's coming to you."

"That one arrived the same day as Benson received his. It was addressed to the jury's foreman."

"I remember Rowelings's threats," Bane said.

"He's in prison, awaiting execution," Judge Hawthorne remarked. "Apparently, he has accomplices who *aren't* incarcerated. I want you to investigate this matter, Marshal. I want the man or men who sent these threats in my courtroom as soon as possible."

Bane nodded.

"That'll be all, Bane."

The judge's use of Bane's nickname wasn't typical, but it also wasn't exceptional. Those who did not know the judge well might not suspect it, but, despite his somber comportment, Harry Hawthorne was as much a man of flesh and blood as anyone else. From time to time, with people he trusted, he'd act as such.

Bane slipped the cards back into their envelopes. "I'll do my level best, Harry, and I'll be sure to hold onto these envelopes and cards; they're evidence."

"I'd expect nothing less."

Chapter 3

Home, Sweet Home

"There is nothing so confining as the prisons of our own perceptions."
— William Shakespeare (1564–1616)

State Prison, Carson City, Nevada

State Prison wasn't *all* bad.

That was Spencer Rowelings's assessment after he'd had a chance to get to know the lay of the place.

It wasn't much to look at, of course. A large building, built of limestone blocks cut from the prison quarry, it stood in an open yard that was devoid, for the most part, of trees, shrubs, and other vegetation. Tall wooden fences, along which guard towers were spaced, surrounded the site. Not far away, the Sierra Nevada Mountains reared against the sky.

The upper floor of the long two-story structure was home to Nevada's lieutenant governor, who also served as the prison's warden; to the deputy warden; to the officers who guarded the prisoners; and to their families.

The lower story was occupied by the two tiers of prisoners' cells and by the kitchen, laundry, offices, storerooms, armory, and other necessary facilities.

Naturally, the cell-room, or hall, in which the prisoners usually congregated during the day, until 6:00 p.m., when they were returned to their individual cells, was also located on the first floor.

Tedium was one of a prisoner's worst enemies, but, unlike some other correctional institutions, Nevada's State Prison provided at least a few opportunities for its inmates to while away the hours.

There wasn't a library; a fire a few years back had destroyed what little there *had* been of one, and nobody seemed to think a replacement necessary for convicts. After all, everyone knew what uneducated, ignorant savages prisoners were. How could reading improve the minds of murderers, robbers, rapists, and other specimens of humanity's dregs?

There was the quarry, though, a place of back-breaking labor for nine hours a day, except during the summer, when workdays lengthened to ten or twelve hours. It was hard labor, sure, but, even so, it beat the hell out of being penned up in a cell all day.

The kitchen, the laundry, and the vegetable garden also needed workers, most of whom were selected by the officers, from among their favorites and from older men for whom productive work in the quarry was impossible.

Trustees were rewarded with jobs in the warden's, the deputy warden's, or the guards' living quarters.

Overall, the prison was clean, too, and well-ventilated; nothing—and nobody—reeked. The warden also made sure that the prison was well-lit. There were no shadows to hide an inmate who might lie in wait for a fellow prisoner or a guard.

A prisoner who behaved himself was rewarded by being allowed to carve stones from the quarry into whatever shapes he fancied—well, within reason, of course—and, even in the short time that Rowelings had been among the inmates, he'd seen some truly fine carvings.

Among them were match safes—cases in which to store matches to keep them dry—carved with images of naiads leaping from lakes or rivers; miniature limestone suitcases, complete with handles; and angels playing harps. Other works were etched with emblems of Free Masonry. One of the bastards had even carved himself a plaque inscribed "Home Sweet Home," but the guards had forbidden him to hang the damned thing in his cell on the grounds that its creator might use his work of art as a weapon.

These items could be sold by their sculptors, for the purpose of buying tobacco, fruit, or other treats. Tombstones, it turned out, fetched a goodly sum from relatives of deceased prisoners who wanted their errant loved ones' final resting places in the prison yard to be marked for eternity. Sometimes, grieving parties who lived free, outside the walls of the State Prison, also purchased the markers.

The quarry that had produced stone for the building of the state capitol also delivered some prisoners from months and years of mind-numbing incarceration.

The officers even kept a conduct roll, recording good and bad behavior. If a man behaved well for a month, he received five days off his sentence. If he misbehaved at any time during a month, whatever time he'd earned in the reduction of his sentence in exchange for past good behavior during the year would be reduced by five days. It was a fair system, and, by obeying the prison's rules and avoiding fights with other inmates, a man could earn two months off his sentence during each year of his incarceration.

Yes, sir, Spencer Rowelings had served time in places a lot worse than this one.

The problem was, he wasn't going to be around to enjoy the prison's privileges for very long.

His execution date was only a week away, when repairs to the gallows would be complete.

Then, by order of Judge Hawthorne, the gallows' trap would be sprung, and the condemned man would hang by the neck until dead. If the hangman figured the length of the rope wrong, the execution would be a ghastly spectacle. If it were too long, the fall would rip Rowelings's head off; if too short, it would strangle him.

Since he didn't have much time left to live, he hadn't bothered to make any friends among the prison's hard cases. He knew only the names of some of them, and the reasons for their sentences, just as they knew his own. In prison, no one could keep a secret for long.

The crimes of the men whose names Rowelings had come to know were bad enough to have earned them a reputation as people it was best not to offend. His own notoriety also more or less protected him from injury or insult. With luck, he'd be able to get by without any trouble until it was time for him to climb the steps onto the gallows.

Until then, he'd enjoy the fringe benefits that his status as a guest of the Silver State afforded him.

Chapter 4

Another Day in Paradise

"Neither snow, nor rain, nor heat, nor gloom of night stays these couriers from the swift completion of their appointed rounds."
— Herodotus (c. 484 – c. 425 BC)

Excelsior, Nevada

"Good morning, Marshal," Sally Tyler said, smiling, as Bane approached the enclosure projecting from the rear wall of the post office, between the door to the postmaster's office on its left and the money order sales window on its right. "How may I help you?"

"Need to see Chester."

"I'll let him know."

"Thanks."

A few moments later, Sally returned to her station as the door to the postmaster's office opened.

"Come on back, Marshal."

Stepping through the doorway, Bane asked, "How goes it, Chester?"

"Another day in paradise. What brings you here? Not something we did or didn't do, I hope."

"Nope."

Chester rounded his desk and sat in his padded swivel chair. "Have a seat," he invited.

Accepting his offer, Bane cautioned his host, "My visit's confidential, Chester." He laid the envelopes on the postmaster's desktop.

"What have we here?" Chester asked, even as he drew them toward him.

"That's what I'm hoping you can tell me."

Chester frowned. "No return address on any of them. What's inside?"

"Take a look—and, remember, this is confidential."

Nodding, Chester removed the cards, read them, and, frowning again, more deeply, looked across his desk at Bane.

"Recognize the handwriting on any of them?"

Chester studied the handwritten recipients' addresses, then shrugged. "Can't say as I do."

"How about the writing on the cards inside?"

After examining the writing, Chester shook his head. "Nope."

"You sure?"

Again, Chester considered the scripts. "Yep."

Bane sighed. Leaning forward, he scooted the envelopes toward himself. "Well, it was a long shot."

Bane had started to stand, when Chester's eyes widened. "Wait a minute, Bane."

The postmaster rounded his desk. "Be back in a bit."

Stepping through the rear door of Sally's office, he spoke to her.

Afterward, he took her place.

Walking up to Bane, Sally looked somber, even a little scared, as she declared, "Mr. Reynolds said you wanted to ask me a confidential question, Marshal."

"That's right, Sally. What I say and what you tell me has to remain strictly between us and can't be repeated to anyone else."

She nodded.

"Have a seat."

She took the swivel chair her supervisor had vacated.

Bane showed her the envelopes and cards. "Thought you might recognize the writing."

After closely considering each item, she nodded, pointing to one of the cards. "That one," she said, "was written by Donald Lombardo."

"You sure, Sally?"

"Yes. The card inside was, too," she confirmed.

"Recognize the handwriting on the other?"

She considered it again. "No, sorry, Marshal."

Bane smiled. "Thank you—and remember: tell no one."

"I won't, Marshal."

He nodded. "Better get Chester out of there before he misdirects somebody's mail," Bane said.

She chuckled. "Right, Marshal!"

They were switching places when Bane, nodding at them, took his leave.

Chapter 5

A Loner by Nature

"Whoever delights in solitude is either a wild beast or a god."
— Aristotle (384-322 BC)

State Prison, Carson City, Nevada

Those who were new to the life of the desperado, especially those who had taken a life at the outset of their criminal careers, sometimes did not sleep well at night. Visions of the dead haunted their sleep.

The men and, on rare occasions, the women, whom they had killed visited their dreams. Again and again, the killers witnessed the agony and the shock in the eyes and upon the faces of their victims in the moment that, following the fatal blow of a cudgel, the deadly stab of a knife, or the mortal shot of a six-shooter, the wounded suspected that they might die.

These fledgling killers did not escape such memories during the daylight hours, either, but their diurnal duties, whether in the quarry, the kitchen, the laundry, the vegetable garden, or elsewhere, distracted them to some degree.

For most, it was a terrible thing to kill another man, and a worse one, yet, to murder a woman.

That's what several novice killers had told Spencer Rowelings, anyway. He wouldn't know himself, first-hand. Killing a man, or even the woman he'd murdered in cold blood during his stagecoach heist, hadn't troubled him a whit. What horrified other men, even many a hardened killer, had never disturbed Rowelings.

Some said that such men as he had no conscience. Rowelings supposed that this was true, but he found the lack of troublesome scruples a boon, not a curse. It was empowering. Unlike most other men, he could kill without hesitation, without remorse, an ability that made him even more dangerous than others of his kind.

Another uncommon feature of his personality, he had learned from the observations and declarations of others, was his passion for inflicting pain and suffering upon other people, especially those who were vulnerable or helpless. Such power, like the ability to extinguish the life of another, was godlike.

Those who wielded it were superior; they were a law unto themselves, which made them a danger, of course, to other, weaker men. The sheep looked to the few among them who had the courage and the ability to resist the wolves, who were not afraid to fight them, who were courageous enough to die, if need be, to protect the woolly lambs. What motivated such men was beyond Rowelings's ability to discern. They were fools, he had decided, years ago, and had let the question go at that.

A loner by nature, Rowelings cultivated no friendships, although he was capable of cooperating with others of his ilk, when it was advantageous for him to do so, and such a time had come, or would come soon.

His natural inclination to keep himself to himself didn't mean that he wasn't observant. Quite the contrary. He was always on the lookout, and he was ever ready to overhear a conversation meant for the ears only of those involved in it. He never gave himself away, though. He heard without appearing to listen, just as he saw without seeming to observe. These actions had served him well on more than one occasion.

Although his stay at Nevada's State Prison had been brief and would remain such, since his execution was set for a week from now, when repairs to the prison's gallows would be complete, his habit of watching and listening had paid off.

He'd learned a thing or two about some of the prison's more notorious inmates. Jack Davis, E. B. Parsons, and John Squires had played a hand in the West's first train robbery at Verdi, Nevada, in November 1870. The roles that Parsons and Squires had played in the crime had ended in an almost comical way, a fact that tarnished their reputations.

After the robbery, three of the bandits took refuge in the Sardine Valley House in Sierra County, California. The proprietor's wife, Mrs. Pearson, suspected them of some sort of chicanery almost immediately.

Two had arrived well after midnight. The third showed up even later, conferring in whispers with the others. Thereafter, the three men had only continued to behave oddly.

The next day, the two who'd arrived first left at dawn. The third man did not accompany them, and, when hunters from Truckee, California, arrived, the man panicked, taking to his heels to hide out in the barn.

Fortunately, Mrs. Pearson knew James Burke, one of the hunters, and she told him of her suspicions. As a result, he and his associates apprehended the suspect, James Gilchrist, believing him to be one of the Verdi train robbers.

James Kinkead, a deputy tracking the bandits, was next to arrive at the Sardine Valley House, and Gilchrist, who'd confessed to the robbery, described his confederates, Parsons and Squires.

Kinkead and his posse, tracking the fugitives, found Parsons sacked out, asleep, in a Sierra Valley, California, hotel; took possession of the suspect's six-shooter, which Parsons had stashed beneath his pillow; and arrested their quarry.

Kinkead, aware that Squires had a brother, Beau, who resided only a short distance away, in Sierraville, rode with his men to Beau's house, where they found Squires, asleep in the guestroom. After confiscating the sleeping robber's gun, they apprehended him without so much as a skirmish.

Now a prisoner in the Truckee jail, Gilchrist made further statements to the lawmen, which led to the arrest of the mastermind behind the train robbery, Jack Davis himself.

Yes, sir, Rowelings thought, a man could learn a lot just by keeping his eyes peeled and his ears cocked. Although Davis could be a man to be reckoned with, both Parsons and Squires were apt to be more of a danger to themselves than to anyone else. The manner of their capture indicated as much.

While he respected Davis, Rowelings had nothing but contempt for the other two men. It helped a man to survive to know who his potential enemies might be. Davis could be one; Parsons and Squires, despite the reputations their participation in the great train robbery had won them, were not.

Watching and listening without other people's awareness that they were being watched and listened to paid off in other ways, too, Rowelings knew.

A man imprisoned cannot help but to hear of conspiracies, as they arise among the other convicts with whom he is caged, especially when he has been let out of his cell to mingle with other prisoners.

Most of the captives had been here, with him now, in the cell-room, or hall, where they'd been free to mix and converse since eight o'clock this morning, as they were every day. In whispers passed, again and again, from one man's lips to another man's ear, the secret had been repeated until word had finally reached Rowelings. He, in turn, had passed the word to the man nearest him: *The break's tonight, at six o'clock, when Collins arrives.*

By nine a.m., all within the yard knew when the moment would come.

Rowelings had heard that such an event was scheduled, but he had not been informed of its details. The particulars didn't matter to him, though. Let others plan, he thought; let others take the risks. He was content to stand ready to act when the time came, as it would, any moment now, for the hour of six p.m. was nigh.

Like clockwork, Quinton Collins, the captain of the guard, entered the hall, calling to the prisoners to return to their cells. As Rowelings had learned from experience, the doors to the cells closed and locked automatically upon a prisoner's entrance into the small, barred rooms.

Then, the guard on duty threw the brake associated with each tier, which locked the doors a second time.

Finally, making his rounds, the guard locked the doors manually, thereby thrice ensuring the prison's security. The facility, the warden, boasted, was escape-proof. He himself had helped to make it so by inventing the mechanism that automatically closed and locked each cell door upon its resident's entrance. He stood, he'd declared, to make a fortune from its sales.

On previous occasions, the prisoners had offered no resistance to the guard's command, returning to their respective cells obediently, if not meekly, and were locked in for the night. As planned, this evening was different.

"Return to your cells!" Collins repeated, raising his voice.

The prisoners lingered.

"*Now!*" the guard shouted, an undercurrent of threat in his voice.

Chapter 6

Sleeping on the Job

"It's hard to make hay while sawing logs."
— Badger Thompson (1846-)

Near Excelsior, Nevada

Lanky Don Lombardo was asleep in a hammock when Bane walked up on him.

Without bothering to greet the farmhand, Bane tipped the hammock with the heel of his boot, and the suspended sack spilled the sleeping man onto the ground.

"What the *hell*?" Lombardo cried.

"Sleeping on the job?" Bane asked, eyeing the layabout coldly. "Wonder what Walt would think about that." He glanced at the hammer, the pail of nails, the rolls of barbed wire, and the rough-hewn poles of wood stacked on the bed of the wagon parked alongside the fence.

"I wasn't asleep, Bane—"

Bane tapped the star on his chest. "That's 'marshal' to you, Lombardo."

"I was just resting."

"Some 'resting.' I heard you snoring twenty feet away."

"I work for Walt Myers, Marshal, not for you." Lombardo had sneered the lawman's title.

"I'll be sure to tell him what I saw—and heard."

"Something on your mind, Marshal, besides *my* business?"

Bane held up the card he'd taken from one of his saddlebags. "As a matter of fact, there is: this card you sent to District Attorney Robert Benson."

"Why the hell would I send a card to the district attorney? I don't even know him."

"You know as well as I do why you sent him the card."

"I didn't send him any damn card."

"Why's your handwriting on it?" Bane read the card's text and Lombardo's added note: '*Enjoy your special day!* It may be your last.'"

"I never wrote that, and I never sent that card. I never saw it before you showed it to me just now."

As Bane rounded the hammock, Lombardo ran.

He was fast, but Bane was faster. After a ten-yard dash, Bane tackled him, and the men struggled on the ground—but for only the few seconds that it took for Bane to fully subdue the suspect.

Bringing Lombardo roughly to his feet, Bane shoved his prisoner forward. "Run, and I'll shoot you."

"You have no right—" Lombardo protested.

"Tell it to the judge."

Chapter 7

Prison Break

"His fate had made him fugitive."
— Virgil (1st century BC)

State Prison, Carson City, Nevada

From behind, a prisoner struck the captain of the guard atop his head with a bottle. As the thick glass shattered into shards, a deep, long gash appeared in the victim's scalp. Quinton Collins staggered forward, a look of shock and pain on his twisted features.

Another prisoner swung a slung-shot at him. The metal or stone inside the pouch of cloth attached to the loop around the convict's wrist—most likely stone, Spencer Rowelings suspected, given the proximity of the quarry—opened a wound in Collins's brow, just above his left eye.

The twice-wounded man stumbled, the blood streaming from the new gash probably blinding him. Most likely, the cut had gone clear to the bone.

Collins fell, and half a dozen inmates rushed toward him, murder in their eyes. Most of the other prisoners, except Rowelings himself, were caught up in the frenzy of the mob. They acted, now, with an animalistic spontaneity born more of instinct and passion than of reason.

One of them, though, a con named Curt Hardesty, grabbed Collins, heaving him into a nearby cell, and its door closed of its own accord, before the others could get to the man. This one convict, uninfected by the wild passion of the mob, had saved the captain's life.

Although Rowelings respected the man's courage, he scoffed at his actions. Saving a screw's life was nothing more than a waste of energy; it was better, for criminals, that men like Collins were dead.

Armed with slung-shots and makeshift knives, the six convicts who'd rushed Collins now climbed to the top of the upper tier of cells. Working together, they cut through one of the walls.

Rowelings had climbed with them. Uninformed as to the escapees' plans, he'd thought it best to follow the lead of the half-dozen who seemed to be in charge. Apparently, so had a couple dozen or more others; the sheer number of them was more than impressive—it was astonishing.

With no idea where they were going, what they were doing, or what to expect, Rowelings was ready for anything. A man who lived by his own rules, rather than by the law, had to be.

Following the other men's lead, he rushed through the gaping hole they'd cut through the wall. They emerged inside a well-furnished room, in which Rowelings was surprised to see two women, one older, the other younger, and a girl, maybe six years of age.

A bell tolled; the prisoners' attempt to escape had been discovered!

A door slammed against the wall, as a man in a suit, a white shirt, and a black bow tie appeared in the doorway at the top of a steep flight of stairs. The tall, authoritative man with unruly curly hair and a scruffy beard and mustache glared coldly at the intruders, his eyes narrow, before firing at one of the advancing convicts, a horse thief from White Pine County named Fred Clyne. According to the prison scuttlebutt, Clyne was serving a ten-year sentence. He seemed to be the other men's leader—in this incident, at least.

Clyne grimaced, as a wound opened in his upper chest, but, behind him, more prisoners rushed into the room. One of them managed to get behind the shooter, who'd stepped farther into the room, and swung a crude weapon at the back of the defender's head.

Almost at the same moment, a second assailant struck the man in the forehead, above the eye, and blood poured down the hero's face. He swayed on his feet for a moment, before toppling.

The crowd rushed toward him, as other men had sprung at the captain of the guard in their earlier attack, in the cell-room below, and it was plain to Rowelings that they intended to kill the man who'd shot Clyne.

It was certain to Rowelings that the man would be slain, but another man, who'd rushed upstairs behind the downed combatant, grabbed a chair. Swinging it left and right and jabbing it forward, as the occasion demanded, he knocked down five of the inmates, one of whom fell over a balustrade.

He might have taken out another five of them, had someone not knocked *him* out.

"Finish him!" one of the villains cried.

"Forget him; the bastard's already dead," Clyne answered. He nodded in the direction of the bearded, mustachioed man who'd been the first to arrive in the room. "Just like the lieutenant governor. Now, follow me!"

"You mean the warden?" one of the men, newly arrived from Lander County, asked.

"In Nevada, one's the same as the other," someone else educated him.

One of the convicts leered at the women. "What about them?" He licked his lips. "They could be useful as hostages and—."

"Leave the women and the girl alone," Clyne ordered. "Let's go!"

As the horse thief scrambled down the steep flight of steps, the others followed, Rowelings included.

"Where we headed?" one of them asked.

"Armory," Clyne replied.

Rowelings cast an eye on the man. Maybe Clyne wasn't as stupid as he'd first thought.

The armory was a treasury not only of weapons and ammunition, but also of clothing and other supplies. Their raid upon the arms room provided them with two Henry rifles, four double-barreled shotguns, five six-shooters, and something like 3,000 rifle cartridges, not to mention a few sets of the guards' plain clothes.

To protect them against prisoners' theft, the armory also stored such medical supplies as bandages; bellows, to resuscitate breathing; splints, to mend broken bones; saws, to amputate arms or legs; and chloroform, to anesthetize patients, but Clyne told the men to leave them. "It's easier to let a choking or injured man die, or to kill him, than it is to treat him," he said. Such cold calculation earned the prisoners' leader Rowelings's grudging respect, as did the man's escape strategy.

Clyne's plan had succeeded admirably—so far, at least—partly, Rowelings knew, because of its timing. It was Sunday, which, the stagecoach robber's short stay as a guest of the state had taught him, meant that most of the guards would be unarmed, believing that their charges had been locked in their cells for the night. For the same reason, no guards would be in position atop the main building's walls.

Although the alarm had sounded—the damned bell was still tolling its warning—the guards outside the yard would be unable to get inside. Maybe, Rowelings allowed, the horse thief *was* smarter than he'd looked or had acted until now.

Unknown to the convicts, outside, G. N. Ives, one of the guards, awaited them.

Chapter 8

A Fount of Knowledge

"It is better to eat the carrot than to taste the stick."
— Luke Meadows (1850 -)

Excelsior, Nevada

Back at the local sheriff's office, Bane sat outside the cell that Don Lombardo now occupied.

His prisoner lay on the narrow bunk inside the cell, facing away from his captor. His arms bent, his hands under the back of his head, and his fingers interlaced to form a cushion, he stared at the stone wall before him, his mood somewhere between sullen and angry. It wasn't as if Lombardo had never occupied this cell or one of those adjacent to it; he'd been in one or the other several times for various offenses, although, at trial, he'd been acquitted.

Sooner or later, his luck would run out. Maybe this time would be the occasion. Bane certainly intended to do all that he could to encourage this outcome.

"You've avoided a cell in the State Prison a few times already, Lombardo," Bane pointed out. "Maybe this time, you won't."

His captive said nothing.

"Threatening an officer of the court, *especially* an officer of a district court, isn't a petty crime. It's best you confess that you're the one who threatened District Attorney Benson. That way, I can put in a word for you with Judge Hawthorne."

His prisoner remained silent.

"I'm *trying* to help you out here, Lombardo."

"You're wasting your time, Marshal," the prisoner said, "and mine."

Bane stood. "I reckon you're right." Approaching the cell, he unlocked its door. Stepping inside, he hauled Lombardo to his feet. "Let's go."

"Where?"

"Judge Hawthorne's courtroom."

"For what? I ain't done nothing."

"Maybe you can convince the judge of that," Bane said, "but I doubt it."

The courthouse was only a couple of blocks away, but Lombardo dragged his feet, pulled against Bane, and otherwise resisted every step of the way, despite the fact that the scrawny miscreant was no match for his captor's greater size and strength.

The pedestrians they passed had various reactions to the marshal's half-dragging his reluctant prisoner down the middle of the street. Some of the men laughed or grinned. The women mostly looked disgusted or disapproving—of Lombardo's behavior, not his own, Bane hoped.

Since there was no trial scheduled for this morning, the judge was in his chambers.

Bane rapped at the door.

"Come in," Judge Hawthorne called.

"I'm sure glad I'm not in your boots, Lombardo," Bane said, as he opened the door and shoved his prisoner into the judge's presence.

"What's this you've brought me, Marshal?"

"Donald Lombardo, Judge."

"I'm familiar with the reprobate, Marshal. I meant, what's the charge?"

"Threatening an officer of this court."

"And which officer is that?"

"District Attorney Robert Benson."

"Ah! Mr. Lombardo, I must say, that, when you commit yourself to breaking the law, you do so on a grand scale, undaunted, it appears, by the consequences, which, in this case, amount to a thousand-dollar fine and a three-year prison sentence."

Lombardo seemed to shrink as he turned pale.

"Of course, such penalties would be imposed only after you have been convicted of posting threatening correspondence to an officer of this court, such as District Attorney Benson." The judge eyed the accused. "What have you to say for yourself, Mr. Lombardo? And I caution you against perjuring yourself in this, or any other, matter."

The culprit looked more miserable than ever. "I never threatened nobody!"

Judge Hawthorne continued to glare at him. "You threatened District Attorney Benson. It might help you to confide in me, here and now, as to who encouraged you, by whatever means, to commit such a serious crime."

His confidence not merely shaken, but shattered, Lombardo said, "What's in it for me, if I do?"

"I can be merciful on occasion, when someone's expression of remorse is supported by his actions."

"Ratting out somebody else? Is that what you mean?" Lombardo demanded.

The judge shrugged. "That's for you to decide, Mr. Lombardo, but I caution you again: my patience—and my willingness to extend mercy—are finite."

"That means 'limited,' Lombardo," Bane explained.

"All right! All right! It was—" he paused, took a deep breath, and plunged ahead—"Andy Sanders. Spencer Rowelings set it up."

"And just how did Mr. Rowelings communicate with Mr. Sanders on such a matter from his cell inside the State Prison?" Judge Hawthorne asked.

"He didn't," Lombardo explained. "Rowelings, uh, arranged for it ahead of time, before his trial. Even gave Sanders the birthday card that Sanders gave me."

Judge Hawthorne nodded. "Take him back to jail, Marshal."

"But, but we have a deal!" Lombardo protested, "You said, you *promised*, Judge—"

"I said, Mr. Lombardo that 'it *might* help you to confide in me.'"

"I *did* confide in you!"

"Yeah, you've been a fount of information, Lombardo," Bane said, as he hauled his prisoner toward the door.

"It might help you yet," Judge Hawthorne called, "provided that Marshal Messenger can verify the truth of your statement."

Chapter 9
Like a Stone Wall

"... Move swiftly, strike vigorously, and secure all the fruits of victory. ..."
— Stonewall Jackson (1824-1863)

State Prison, Carson City, Nevada

As soon as the convicts appeared in the yard, G. N. Ives commenced firing.

His aim was true, more often than not, and his gun brought down three of them. One was dead when he hit the ground. The other two, though spared death, had suffered disabling wounds and could fight no further. They'd be left behind, to be returned to their cells, no doubt with longer sentences, now, to serve.

As smoke drifted across the yard, Ives faltered, his right knee bending awkwardly. His other leg splayed beneath him, broken, it appeared. A convict's shot had struck true, shattering the guard's right knee. Almost falling, he managed, by some miracle, to straighten himself.

Throwing his weight upon his other leg, he fired again into the mob that had closed to within a distance of thirty or forty feet of him.

The convicts pressed relentlessly upon him, despite the guard's own gunfire, raising a cloud of dust and smoke as they returned Ives's shots.

Finally, a bullet tore through one of the guard's hips, and Ives went down. He struggled to rise, to gain his feet again, but to no avail.

Now, a shot caught the valiant defender in the arm, leaving him grimacing in pain.

The prisoners rushed forward, seized his revolver, and hesitated, each and all, their rifles and handguns aimed to kill.

Without a word, in unison, they lowered their arms. A man with the grit that this guard had displayed, they seemed to reckon, did not deserve to die.

Some of the prisoners compared Ives's valiant actions to those of Thomas Jonathan Jackson, the Confederate general who'd earned the nickname "Stonewall" for his courageous refusal to surrender, even in the face of insurmountable odds, during the Battle of First Manassas.

Jackson's officers had repeatedly brought word to him that their positions were in danger of being overrun by Union troops.

"Give them the bayonet!" Jackson had advised Gen. Barnard Elliott Bee, Jr.

Returning to his men, Bee had shouted, above the din of battle, "There is Jackson standing like a stone wall. Let us determine to die here, and we will conquer!"

Rowelings had to admit that the comparison was a valid one. The nature of the guard he'd seen in the yard that day, among the smoke and hail of bullets, puzzled him, though, as did the behavior of soldiers, lawmen, and others who braved death for little or no personal gain.

He couldn't understand what prompted men to act in such a manner when, by looking out exclusively for their own interests, they could amass a fortune, fleecing the sheep—and most men, when it came right down to it, *were* sheep, rather than wolves—of their hard-earned pay, or, better yet, unburden banks, stagecoaches, and trains of their stores and cargoes of gold, silver, and paper currency.

At the cost of nothing more than the lives of the driver, the shotgun messenger, and the passengers, who'd included a young woman, Rowelings himself had earned a fortune from the stagecoach robbery he'd committed a few weeks back, and he'd hidden the gold and silver far from the crime scene so that he could retrieve it another day.

Most other outlaws would have drawn a line at murdering a woman, but not Rowelings. His willingness to kill anyone, anywhere, at any time, if their deaths could benefit him in any way, separated him from other criminals, including even Clyne, who, otherwise, was a man to be reckoned with.

Oh, Clyne had strengths, it was true. He could appear less intelligent than he was, which could come in handy, and he was adept at planning. Clyne was also a man of courage, but he'd refused the opportunity to kidnap the women and the girl, when he'd had the chance to do so, and they could have been their tickets out of here, without the need to fire a shot, had the outlaw had the heart to take them prisoners. Rowelings would have done so in an instant.

While it was true that his own killing of the woman during the stagecoach robbery had resulted in a death sentence, it was also true that fate, or the devil, or chance had appeared, instead, to have delivered him from execution.

A man didn't know, and couldn't know, what the future might bring, and threats of death should never give him pause. How many times had Lee or Grant or any other soldier come under fire during the war? Had Alexander the Great, or Julius Caesar, or Charlemagne, or Napoleon, or Washington surrendered to doubt or fear, even of death?

No, win or lose, live or die, they had persisted, and that was the secret of their ultimate successes. They did not fear death; therefore, they did not fear living. In fact, they had lived, as Rowelings himself did, with the knowledge and the acceptance of the fact that, at any moment, whether now or later, they could die. Despite this certainty, they, like Rowelings himself, lived each moment of every day, willing to tempt fate, to challenge death, to be extinguished, for all time, in an instant, during a duel, in an ambush, or at the end of a rope.

But men like Ives were, and Rowelings supposed, would ever be, a mystery unsolvable to him. That's one of the reasons he hated them. Men who could not be read were dangerous. They couldn't be intimidated, and they couldn't be bought. They could only be killed—or kill.

Chapter 10

The Cabin in the Woods

"The chase is among the best of all national pastimes; it cultivates that vigorous manliness for the lack of which in a nation, as in an individual, the possession of no other qualities can possibly atone."
— Theodore Roosevelt (1858 -)

Near Excelsior, Nevada

Bane, Badger Thompson, Luke Meadows, or one of his other deputies—on the occasions he'd had more than two—had arrested Andy Sanders more than a few times, just as they'd hauled Don Lombardo to jail on a fairly regular basis. Some men never learned, it seemed, the simple lesson that crime doesn't pay.

Oh, it might, on occasion, but the risks were always high: fines, imprisonment, or even death, in some cases. A criminal could also be executed or could be killed by a lawman, a posse, a bounty hunter, or someone the outlaw wrongly took to be an easy mark. Rarely, crime—usually a lifetime of it—might enrich a man financially, while it bankrupted him morally, but, most often, the wages of lawlessness were a prison cell or a grave.

Still, some men remained intent on trying—Spencer Rowelings, it seemed, even after he'd been sentenced to hang. The fact that the outlaw had set in motion plans to avenge himself even before his trial made Bane reassess him.

Bane had taken him, at first, to be a typical criminal, more evil than most, and more violent, no doubt, but not especially intelligent. Certainly, the man was a monster. But Rowelings hadn't seemed any cleverer than most of his sort.

Still, the gold and silver he'd stolen had never been found, and he had apparently set his plans to avenge himself, should he be found guilty—and maybe even if he hadn't been found guilty—in motion before his trial had even begun. That showed foresight and had taken preparation.

He'd either paid Lombardo and Sanders to mail threatening messages to District Attorney Benson and the jury foreman or had intimidated them into doing so. He could have used the same man to send both threats, but he'd chosen to employ two, maybe to hedge his bets against a single man's being caught or the less likely event of one of his couriers' backing out of the undertaking.

Yep. There seemed to be more to Spencer Rowelings than Bane had thought. He didn't like that.

Underestimating a man, especially one like Rowelings, could get a lawman killed.

It was a good thing the bastard would hang soon.

His musings had passed the time as Bane rode into the hills beyond his adopted hometown.

Although he'd been born and reared in Kansas and had seen a lot of the country during his enlistment in the Union Army during the Civil War, Bane felt more at home in northeastern Nevada in general and Excelsior in particular than he ever had anyplace else.

He'd resided here since he'd begun his bounty hunting days after the War. He'd lived just outside of town during the period that he'd been—or imagined himself to be—a rancher. He'd lived in Excelsior again as its sheriff, too, and he lived here now, as a U. S. marshal. Although he and Pamela had a place near Lightning Hill, they preferred Excelsior, as did the rest of their family, Lizzie, Ben, Bane's Aunt Flossie, and Bane's father Bradford.

His love for the town and its people, like his love for his family, were parts of the reason he wore a badge. His love for law and order, he guessed, had been born of the lawlessness he'd witnessed during the War and during its aftermath, and this love was strengthened, daily, by the violence and outlawry he continued to witness, if not every day, frequently enough.

There were other reasons, too, but he seldom spoke of them to anyone but Pamela. Other people might not understand, he thought, and what folks didn't understand they often mocked, or, worse yet, vilified.

The high country offered spectacular views. Ahead of him, beyond tall firs and aspens that seemed to burn like trees aflame, were a succession of steep hills, each tier giving way to the next and the next, until their ascent was blocked by a range of tall gray mountains surmounted only by thick, gray-white clouds and the wide, blue-gray sky.

Always, such sights took Bane's breath away. Nature was a work of divine art, a masterpiece—or a gallery and a treasury of masterpieces—that only God could have created.

A man felt small in such an environment, but, paradoxically, also big—huge, in fact.

Bane shook his head. What musings a man will entertain when he's alone, in a wilderness.

As Bane spotted his prey's rude cabin in the distance, something changed about him; something seemed to come alive inside him: the instinct of the predator, a feeling akin to that of the stalking panther, the lunging wolf, or the diving eagle. His senses on alert, it seemed to Bane that he could see farther and more clearly; hear at a greater distance and more acutely; feel the heat of the sun as if he wore it; smell the scents of the forest and the field as only a wolf or a cougar could experience such fragrances and odors; and taste the very essence of life itself.

He was quiet as he trained his senses on the cabin in the woods, inside of which, going about his daily affairs, was the man who'd used the U. S. Postal Service to threaten the foreman who'd announced the jury's unanimous verdict of "guilty, as charged," concerning defendant Spencer Rowelings, stagecoach robber and killer of six.

Just as Rowelings had, through AndySanders, convinced Lombardo to mail the threatening birthday card to District Attorney Benson, so had Rowelings persuaded Sanders to post a threatening message to the jury foreman.

In riding toward a man's home, whether it was a house, a cabin, or a tent, it was customary to hail the resident from afar, especially when the dwelling was situated in a remote location. Bane did not do so on this occasion, however. He rode past the cabin, in the concealment of a draw, and into the forest beyond the clearing in which the cabin stood.

After hitching his mare to a tree, he studied Sanders's backyard, before making his approach.

Crouching low or crawling, as the terrain demanded, Bane made his way slowly across the property, availing himself of the cover and concealment that the uneven land, the trees, the bushes, the clumps of brush, and the occasional rocks offered.

When he was within ten or twelve feet of the cabin, he hazarded a sprint that took him to its back wall. He crawled along it, below the cabin's window, around the right rear corner, along the featureless right side wall, and around the right front corner, to the front of the place.

Here, Bane paused, noting the low, slightly bowed porch, the timber columns supporting an overhang of the roof, and the front door between two small windows, both shuttered.

Judging by the column of smoke that rose against the sky, Sanders was home, but the shut door and the shuttered windows made it clear that he neither expected nor wanted company.

There was no way that Sanders would see him with the door closed and the windows shuttered. Only a misstep on Bane's part or the groan of a loose porch floorboard could give him away.

Drawing his six-shooter, Bane crept gingerly across the porch. His luck held. None of the warped boards creaked or groaned.

He tried the doorknob.

It turned easily, and Bane hit the heavy door with his shoulder, bursting into the cabin.

"What the hell!" Sanders threw himself toward a rifle hung on the wall, near the stone fireplace.

Bane fired a shot through the ceiling, and Sanders dropped to the floor. When he realized he was unhurt, he demanded, "Who the hell are you, and why did you break into my cabin?"

"I'm U. S. Marshal Bane Messenger, and I have a warrant for your arrest."

"On what charge?"

"Threatening a jury member."

"I've done no such thing!"

"There's a witness in the Excelsior city jail who says you did."

"He's a liar!"

"Maybe he is; maybe he isn't. That's one of the things your trial will sort out, I expect."

Chapter 11

Biding His Time

"Agamemnon is a fool; Achilles is a fool; Thersites is a fool;
and . . . Patroclus is a fool."
— William Shakespeare (1564-1616)

State Prison, Carson City, Nevada

As the lopsided gunfight continued in the prison yard, Joe Williams, who was doing time for burglary, was on the lookout for additional targets. It wasn't prudent, he'd thought, for all of them to have trained their gunfire on a single man when other guards or, perhaps, the sheriff or volunteers from Carson City, could present themselves at any moment. They could be killed or their attempt to escape could be ruined.

As the gun smoke drifted apart, he spied just such a target!

Upstairs, in the main building, the warden's wife, Mrs. Dawes, was gazing out one of the windows of her quarters, through a narrow gap in the curtains.

Terrified, she was watching the action below, in the yard, Williams thought.

Shoot her! he told himself, and turn the attention of the guards from the prison break to the lieutenant governor's family.

Aiming along the barrel of a stolen Henry rifle, he fired. The glass in the windowpane level with his target's face shattered, and Mrs. Dawes and the figure standing beside her, a visiting gentleman, perhaps, spun away from the window and ducked for cover.

Damn! He had missed!

Just as Ives had fallen, another guard, Jesse Norton, had managed to find a way into the compound, and he immediately began exchanging fire with the convicts. His first shot took down one of the prisoners, but he didn't get a chance to wound or kill another; the swing of a prisoner's slung-shot brought him down, and he lay unconscious on the ground.

Sokol, a guard who hailed from Slovakia but lived in Carson City, rushed into the yard, firing a six-shooter—he had borrowed it from the bartender at the Warm Springs Hotel, the prisoners later learned, where he'd ridden after hearing the commotion in the prison yard.

And Sokol wasn't the only man to respond to the alarm bell that still sounded from the prison. Mark Peters, the hotel's proprietor, rushed to the scene as well, arriving while both Sokol and Norton were yet on their feet.

Spotting prisoners who, having taken refuge inside the guard room, were firing at Norton and Sokol, Peters rushed their position. As he raised his pistol to fire, he was shot, instead, by Chuck Jennings, one of Clyne's henchmen. The bullet struck Peters below his eye, splattering his blood and brains down the wall and over the yard, and he fell dead before ever firing a shot.

Outside, in the yard, three of Sokol's bullets found their marks, and as many convicts writhed in the dust, before Sokol himself was brought down by a convict's bullet to his left hip.

Spencer Rowelings had run to the guard room with the other cons, considering it a safer place to be, especially for an unarmed participant, as he was, not having been given a rifle or a six-shooter when the weapons had been passed about following the armory's robbery.

Now, he dashed outside, claiming Peters's pistol.

For a moment, he thought of joining the fray, but he dismissed the idea as quickly as it had come to him and ran back to the relative safety of the guard room.

There would be time enough to fight—after the prisoners in the yard out-lasted the guards and volunteers.

Initially, the opposition had been small, almost nonexistent. Then, two guards and one of Carson City's townspeople had come to the aid of the embattled guards.

It was all but inevitable that, despite the danger, others would come as well. In frontier towns, men depended upon the help of friends and neighbors, and the citizens of Carson City were no exceptions. If help were needed, they would come, and the alarm bell suggested that such aid was required, and quickly.

He might as well wait for the battle to take its course, revealing whether it would be profitable for him to lend a hand.

Certainly, he was no coward, but he was no hero, either. He'd risked his life many a time, and he was handy both with his fists and a gun. But he'd always acted with deliberation and purpose, never recklessly, and only when he believed that doing so would benefit him personally.

Only a fool risked his life for no reason or to protect someone else, which added up, to his way of thinking, to the same thing. What was it that Alexander Pope had written? "Fools rush in where angels feared to tread"?

Rowelings would act, all right—when the time came.

But now was not the time.

Not yet, not quite. . . .

Chapter 12

Judgment Day

"Know how to listen and you will profit even from those who talk badly."
— Plutarch (c. AD 46-c. AD 119)

Excelsior, Nevada

With Donald Lombardo and Andy Sanders cooling their heels in separate cells in the Excelsior jail, Spencer Rowelings's threats against those whom he saw as having been responsible for his conviction for robbing the stagecoach and killing its passengers, driver, and shotgun messenger stopped.

Complimenting Bane on his speedy investigations of these incidents and the arrests of their perpetrators, Judge Hawthorne exercised equally swift justice.

In exchange for District Attorney Benson's offer to allow the suspects to accept plea agreements, both Lombardo and Sanders had opted for the judge to hear their cases, rather than having them tried before a jury.

In both cases, during the defendants' hearings, Judge Hawthorne had pronounced the culprits guilty. He had also rescinded the plea agreements and sentenced both convicts to three years in State Prison.

A week later, the judge summoned Bane once more to his chambers.

Handing the marshal an envelope, Judge Hawthorne announced, "It's happening again."

"Threats?"

Judge Hawthorne nodded. "Just this one."

Bane recalled Spencer Rowelings's vow, after his conviction, before Bane and Excelsior's Deputy Lane had hauled him to jail to await his transfer to State Prison. Rowelings had threatened to kill not only District Attorney Benson and the jury foreman, but also Judge Hawthorne himself.

Sure enough, as he read the message on the sheet of folded stationery that the judge extracted from the stamped, addressed envelope, Bane saw the judge's name:

> Consider this judgment day, Hawthorne! You have just received the same sentence as the one that you decreed for another: *you will be hanged by the neck until dead!*

The judge hadn't looked nervous when he'd met Bane's eye with his own somber gaze, nor had his hand shaken. The judge retained the same calm manner as always, without any hint of fear or anxiety on his countenance.

Bane wasn't surprised. In addition to having himself once been a prosecuting attorney, before he'd become a federal judge, Harry Hawthorne had worked at half a dozen other jobs, each of which had been more dangerous than presiding over defendants' fates. His earlier lines of work included his being a lawman in the Dakota Territory; a shotgun messenger for Wells Fargo; a teamster who'd driven through some of the most lawless regions of the West; and a scout for the Army. In between, he'd been a professional boxer and a gambler, occupations also fraught with danger.

It wasn't likely that a man with such a resumé would be frightened by a threat from the likes of Spencer Rowelings or whoever Rowelings's current go-between happened to be.

The judge handed Bane the envelope. "Take this and the note that arrived inside it to the post office and see whether either the postmaster or a mail clerk can identify the person who wrote either or both."

"Yes, sir."

* * *

At his destination, Bane was in luck. No one waited in line for Sally Tyler's assistance, so he was able to show the evidence to her directly, rather than having to go through her supervisor.

There was no return address, and neither the recipient's address nor the note itself revealed the identity of its writer.

Bane sighed. If Sally wasn't able to identify the person who'd addressed the envelope or penned the message, he doubted that Chester Reynolds would be able to do so. After all, the postmaster handled far less mail than his clerks.

"Sorry, Marshal," Sally said.

Bane nodded. "Thanks for trying."

It seemed that, although Don Lombardo and Andy Sanders had been identified, tried, convicted, and sentenced for threatening District Attorney Benson and the man who'd been the jury foreman during Spencer Rowelings's trial, the culprit who'd threatened Judge Hawthorne wouldn't be prosecuted for his role in posting his menacing message.

* * *

Back at the courthouse, the judge, awaiting Bane's return to his chambers, had a surprise for him, one that Bane would never have anticipated.

"Are Lombardo and Sanders still languishing in the city jail, Marshal?"

"Yes, sir."

"Bring them to me, here in my chambers."

"Yes, sir."

"Once we've disposed of this matter, we can get back to focusing on arresting, trying, and sentencing the rabble who prey on the law-abiding men and women of this city, this county, this state, and our nation."

"Yes, sir." Bane rose, then paused.

"What is it, Marshal?"

"Lombardo and Sanders might not be the men responsible this time, Your Honor."

Judge Hawthorne smiled. "I doubt very much that they are."

* * *

Ten minutes later, Bane was back, in the company of one of his deputies, Badger Thompson, who held fast to Lombardo's upper arm, just as Bane kept a firm grip on Sanders's biceps.

"Gentlemen," Judge Sanders greeted the convicts.

Lombardo and Sanders exchanged looks expressive of their mutual distrust of the jurist.

The judge handed the threatening note to Bane. "Marshal, would you show this communiqué to Mr. Lombardo?"

Bane passed the note to the designated recipient.

Moving his lips as he read, Lombardo frowned toward the end of the message, then, his eyes widening, he looked at the judge. "I never sent this!"

"Pass the note to Mr. Sanders," Judge Hawthorne directed.

Lombardo handed the folded sheet of stationery to his partner in crime.

"It wasn't me, either."

"Did either of you post the note on behalf of its author," Judge Hawthorne asked, "whoever that person might be?"

"No, sir!" Sanders averred.

"How about you, Mr. Lombardo? Were you the courier of this threat against my person, or did you post it?"

"No, I am not, and no, I did not."

"Very good. In that case, we can move on to another matter. I asked Marshal Messenger and Deputy Thompson to escort you here for the purpose of teaching you a bit about the law."

Their exchange of looks suggested the prisoners' wariness and confusion.

"Specifically, I am referring to the Thirty-fifth Rule of Criminal Procedure. Am I correct in assuming that neither of you are familiar with it?"

The two jailbirds again turned to each other. It was as if they shared one brain between them, Bane thought, each depending on the other for an answer to the judge's question.

"Obviously, not," Judge Hawthorne concluded. "Let me recite the passage that I believe may be of interest to you gentlemen, namely paragraph 'b,' subsection one, to wit":

> Upon the government's motion made within one year of sentencing, the court may reduce a sentence if the defendant, after sentencing, provided substantial assistance in investigating or prosecuting another person.

"Now, then, Mr. Lombardo, can you think of any reason that District Attorney Benson might make such a motion on your part?"

This time, neither prisoner looked at the other. "No, sir."

"How about you, Mr. Sanders? Do you see any application?"

"I'm not a lawyer, Judge."

"Let me tell you why this rule may be of interest to you—or to whichever of you provides 'substantial assistance in investigating or prosecuting another person' by identifying the person who *did* post this note for its author.

"District Attorney Benson has assured me that he will move that whichever of you does identify who posted this message and testifies in court to this individual's having done so should receive a reduction of your sentence by one year. I assure you, further, that I shall grant this reduction when the motion reaches me."

"Your Honor," Bane interjected, "if I may?"

Judge Hawthorne nodded.

"What His Honor is saying is that whichever one of you identifies the person who did post this threat and testifies to that effect gets out of prison a year earlier than he would have otherwise."

"Why should we believe you? You denied the plea bargain we made with Benson," Sanders said.

"The district attorney, not I, made that agreement with you. I'm offering you a reduction in the sentence that *I* set for you. At the moment, my offer stands. It's up to you whether you accept it."

The prisoners exchanged another look, before, turning to the judge, they blurted out, together, "Kyle Evers!"

"And where will I find this Kyle Evers?" Bane demanded.

Again, in unison, Lombardo and Sanders cried, "Dawson!"

"Matches the postmark on the envelope," Judge Hawthorne declared.

"Then I get a year off my sentence?" Sanders asked.

"I'm the one that gets a year's deduction in my sentence!" Lombardo protested.

Judge Hawthorne rapped his knuckles on his desktop.

The prisoners, looking death at one another, nevertheless quieted themselves.

"I am a just judge, gentlemen," he told the convicts. "You'll *both* receive the reduction, as long as your information is verified and you testify to the perpetrator's identity in court."

"I guess I'd better be headed for Dawson," Bane said, "as soon as I return these prisoners to their jail cells."

"That was going to be my recommendation, Marshal," Judge Hawthorne replied.

"You'd best take your deputy with you," Sanders, perhaps feeling expansive, advised. "Kyle Evers is one *tough* hombre."

Chapter 13

Frenchie

"It's not the size of the dog in the fight; it's the size of the fight in the dog."
— Mark Twain (1835-)

State Prison, Carson City

Still watching the gunplay from the security of the guard room, where he and a few other convicts were holed up, Spencer Rowelings frowned at the slender man of small stature who appeared now, in the yard, seemingly out of nowhere.

Where the hell had *he* come from?

The crowd, that's where. The taller men and the thick smoke of the fusillade of gunfire had screened him.

Running among the larger inmates, the bantam of a man struck them savage blows to the backs or sides of their heads with the slung-shot he wielded, dropping them in quick succession, even as a salvo of bullets whizzed past him.

Rowelings laughed, shaking his head at the foolhardiness and bravery of the diminutive prisoner. What he lacked in stature and might, he more than made up for in grit, speed, and accuracy of aim. He must have felled four or five of the prisoners.

"Jennie!" The frantic call of a woman's voice was a wail of agony. Again, she called the girl's name—*her* girl's name, judging by the grievous sound of it.

A small figure's dash into the yard caught Rowelings's gaze. She was the girl after whom the woman had called, he thought.

Again, the cry, full of despair: "*Jennie!*"

The girl, confused and panicked by the gunfire, had run into the yard.

She must have come upon the scene just seconds ago, Rowelings thought. Otherwise, she likely wouldn't have panicked and run into the danger of the guns.

She was young, maybe six years of age—too young to die, some would say, but Rowelings knew that youth was no guarantee against death.

The zigzagging bantam streaked across the yard, heedless of the hail of bullets all around him.

Rowelings chuckled. The little fool had sand; there was no doubt about that!

The girl had stopped, unsure of what course of action she should take. Now, it was as if a spell were breaking and, returning to her senses, she found herself in a desperate situation, the danger of which she was just now coming to perceive.

Her rescuer scooped the child up, into his arms, a feat in itself, since he was but little taller than she, and ran toward the safety—or the relative safety—of the main building.

It was a wonder, Rowelings thought, that he didn't stumble or fall, but he kept his feet and dashed along, ignoring the shots of rifles and six-shooters and the occasional blast of a shotgun.

A door was flung open in the exterior wall of the building, and the girl's valiant rescuer thrust the sobbing youngster inside, where a weeping woman pulled her to her bosom—the girl's mother, most likely, Rowelings thought.

The murderous stagecoach robber had seen, yet again, a display of altruism utterly unfathomable to him. Why would a man risk his life in such a reckless manner? Not only had the little man fought against men taller and stronger than himself, but he'd also risked death to deliver a child from the battle raging all about them when he could just as easily have abandoned the yard altogether and waited out the fight.

Men like Hardesty, the trustee who'd hauled Collins, the captain of the guard, into a cell and saved his life at the beginning of the break; men like the outnumbered guards who'd died, shooting it out with the prisoners in the yard; men like the one who'd rescued the girl at the risk of his own life; men like sheriffs and deputies, bounty hunters and posses, soldiers and marshals—what did they gain that made facing—hell, *courting*—such risk worthwhile to them? Certainly, it wasn't the pittance of pay they received. They might earn the thanks of a town, a write-up in the newspapers, a moment's praise, or even a cash reward, but, next to dying, that was nothing.

Sure, Rowelings had risked his life, too, more than once. But there'd always been a payoff: the cold, hard cash in a bank; a shipment of gold or silver; passengers aboard a train to rob. He had never, and *would* never, stare death in the face for something as intangible and worthless as the life of a child, a mother's gratitude, a column of print buried in the back pages of a newspaper, or, for that matter, a reward that was a tiny fraction of the value of a stolen treasure.

He shook his head, as he saw the small man rush back into the fray. The fool looked like a Frenchman, so Rowelings thought of him as "Frenchie" while he watched him rush into the drifting cloud of dust and smoke. He'd be killed soon enough, but, until then, it amused Rowelings to watch the brave fool's exploits. It was something to do, anyway, until the time was ripe for him to make his own move.

Chapter 14

The Great Escape

"Prisoners seldom ask, or even wonder, what they're escaping *to*."
— Curt Hardesty (1840-)

State Prison, Carson City, Nevada

From the time that the prisoners entered the yard, their one-sided battle with the guards and their supporters was almost continuous. Although those who sought to put down the prison break were few in number, they fought more heroically than the convicts expected. While the criminals fought with nerve, their adversaries displayed such courage and skill that they'd prevented the prisoners' escape, even at the cost of their own lives.

A steady storm of gunfire sounded, six-shooters, rifles, and shotguns firing and blasting away, as a large cloud of smoke and dust befouled the air; the smell of gunpowder was everywhere.

Frenchie, who'd earlier downed several of the convicts and rescued the warden's six-year-old daughter, wasn't finished yet. After saving the life of the young girl, he'd rushed back into the battle.

"Barkeep!" he shouted, "Help me get this man to safety!"

W. C. Burgher, the bartender at the Warm Springs Hotel, who'd earlier joined the fray, shot at a convict who emerged from the smoke and dust. The man staggered and fell, but whether from a bullet or from stumbling, Burgher couldn't say. "Hell, man, no place is safe around here!" he called to Frenchie, but he ran to his aid, just the same.

Bullets shot up the ground before them, as Frenchie and the barkeep ran toward Ives, the valiant, wounded guard who still lay where he'd fallen. Ignoring the bullets whizzing about them, Frenchie took Ives's legs, as Burgher, stooping, hooked his bent arms under the fallen man's armpits, lifting his upper body.

Together, they half-walked, half-ran, carrying the hero to the main building and sitting him against its exterior wall, beneath steep stairs climbing to the second floor. It wasn't much shelter, Burgher thought, but it was better than nothing.

The bartender caught the other man, as he turned. "Where are you going?"

"Back in, of course."

Burgher looked at the diminutive fighter as if he were studying a madman. Maybe he was, the bartender thought. "Fight's over. We did our best, but—"

"It's not finished until *we* are," the other said.

"No doubt, more men will come, but, right now, it's just you and me, and you're one of *them*. They'll kill you, sure as hell, after what they've seen you do."

Frenchie paused, considering. "I have no alternative."

"You do. I'll arrest you, and—"

"Put me back in a cell?"

"—and lock you in one of the rooms at the hotel."

"So I can get more time added to my sentence?"

"More than likely, you'll get paroled, and in short order, too, after what you've done. Hell, you'll probably get that *and* a medal. Most of the people in town will probably think you were a guard instead of a prisoner. I would have myself, if I hadn't known better."

"Lodging come with room service—and free whiskey?"

Burgher laughed. "Guaranteed."

"All right, barkeep; I surrender."

On their way back to the main building, they saw that that the yard was empty.

The convicts had pulled off what the newspapers all over the country would call The Great Escape.

Chapter 15

Naught But Grief and Pain

"Never run a bluff with a six-gun."
— Bat Masterson (1853-)

Excelsior, Nevada

"You're not eating your breakfast," Pamela observed.

"I am," Bane objected, "but, between bites, I'm also organizing writs, subpoenas, and summonses that Badger, Luke, and I need to serve."

"The paperwork can wait," she said.

He consulted his pocket watch.

"Better listen to your wife, Bane," Bradford said.

"Lizzie and I have to listen to Mommy," Ben declared.

"Daddy, it's *rude* to read at the table," Lizzie advised.

Aunt Flossie, who'd taken Bane in after his mother had died giving birth to him and Bradford, crazed with grief, had deserted his newborn son, said nothing, being content to watch and listen to the family dynamics.

"All right," he acquiesced, setting aside the documents.

Bane remembered the judge's plan to set up his would-be assassin. "Why spend your time and energy hunting for Kyle Evers when we could arrange for him to visit me?" Judge Hawthorne had asked, after explaining his ruse of, in effect, advertising his whereabouts in the local newspaper by announcing that he would be in his office today from 10:00 a.m. to noon today.

After considering the judge's proposal, the only criticism that Bane had been able to offer was that there was an element of danger to the judge's scheme. "You'll have given him the time and date of your location, and he wants to kill you."

"That's why you'll be in my chamber's closet, which faces the back of my desk, and burst out when you hear me call out to him."

"He may enter your chambers firing," Bane pointed out.

"I'm fairly certain he means to kill me."

"So am I."

"If that's the case, wouldn't it be more likely that he'd *aim* before shooting than it would that he'd enter my chambers firing?" He paused, before adding, "Wouldn't *you*, if you were Evers?"

"That's the point, Judge: no one knows what another man would or would not do in a particular situation. I've been in some scrapes in which I had no idea myself what I'd do until I'd done it. Your plan's a good one, but it *is* dangerous; you could be killed."

"We'll have some measure of control, however slight, that we wouldn't have if Evers assassinated me on the street or while I was having dinner with Mrs. Hawthorne at a local restaurant or—"

"Point taken, Your Honor."

Returning to the present moment, Bane complimented the chefs, Pamela and Aunt Flossie—and Lizzie, who'd scrambled the eggs. "That was the best breakfast I've had since—well, since the last meal you ladies cooked. Now, though, I have an appointment to see Judge Hawthorne, and—word of advice—never keep a judge, *especially* a federal judge—waiting."

"What time will you be home, Bane?" Pamela asked.

"By lunchtime, I reckon, if lunchtime's around 12:30 o'clock."

"It'll be on the table," Pamela said.

Rising, Bane discarded his napkin, rose, kissed Pamela, Lizzie, and Aunt Flossie, patted Ben's shoulder, and nodded at Bradford before buckling on his gun belt, donning his Stetson, and entering the hallway that connected with the foyer. From there, he called to his father to join him.

When Bradford appeared, Bane told him of the judge's plan and his part in it. "Make sure everyone stays inside until I return," he said, "and keep your six-shooter ready to hand, just in case things go south."

Bradford nodded. As his son turned toward the foyer, Bradford said, "Be careful, Bane."

Over his shoulder, as he strode toward the front door, Bane said, "I will, Dad."

* * *

It was cramped in the closet, which Bane shared with Judge Hawthorne's two spare robes; an extra pair of shoes; a few law books that, apparently, wouldn't fit on the bookcase; a cane; a top hat; a suit; several neckties; and miscellaneous papers.

At least he could stand upright, and, with gun in hand, rather than in his holster, he could, with his other hand, turn the doorknob and be out of the room in a second or two, allowing him, hopefully, time enough to get the drop on Evers.

In theory, the judge's plan was a sound one, but one thing that Bane had learned as a soldier, a bounty hunter, and a lawman, was that, as the Scottish poet Robert Burns had written, "The best-laid schemes of mice and men/ Go oft astray,/ And leave us naught but grief and pain." If anything went wrong, the judge, instead of, or in addition to, Evers, and even Bane himself, might well end up dead.

While these thoughts ran through his mind, he'd maintained focus. Over the years, he'd developed and, indeed, honed the abilities to entertain thoughts while keeping his attention centered on the task at hand. This dual use of his mind had paid off more than a few times.

Now was another of those occasions, for, as he was ruminating about his task and the danger inherent in the judge's plan, he heard Judge Hawthorne declare, in a rather loud voice, "What's the meaning of this intrusion?"

Bane spun the doorknob with his left hand, and hit the door with his shoulder, bursting into the judge's chambers as he aligned the barrel of his Colt with the center of Evers's chest. A single shot would penetrate the man's heart, sending him to the floor as blood burst from the wound. "U. S. marshal! Drop it or die!" he ordered.

Although startled by Bane's unexpected appearance, Evers did not drop his revolver, which was trained on the judge. "No matter what happens to me," he told the man he targeted, "you're going to die, Judge."

The bastard's disregard for his own life was something that neither Judge Hawthorne nor Bane had figured into the equation. They'd both assumed, wrongly, it was plain enough, now, to see, that, like Lombardo and Sanders, Evers would fold under pressure. But Evers was a different breed of outlaw altogether. He'd come to kill the judge, and, regardless of what should happen to him, he plainly intended to do just that.

"Shoot me; I'll still get off a shot," Evers told Bane, while keeping his eye on the judge, "and all I need is one."

"You might," Bane replied, "and you might not. You really want to bet your life on such odds?"

"I've been betting my life on odds like these, and worse, all my life."

Bane had, too. So far, he'd come up a winner, but, sooner or later—well, nobody beat the house forever. If today were the day for him to die, he may as well do it now, rather than later. Besides, he had the drop on Evers. The assassin might murder Judge Hawthorne, but, then, Bane would kill the killer.

"I've come to kill only the judge; you don't have to die, not this day, anyway," Evers said.

"Soon's you squeeze that trigger, you're a dead man," Bane declared. "In case you've forgotten, I have the drop on you."

"Do what he says, Bane!" Judge Hawthorne ordered.

"There's no reason to do that, Judge."

"There's every reason! Didn't I just order you to drop your weapon?"

"Sorry, Judge."

"*Now*, damn it!"

"No, sir. Like I said, if he shoots you, I kill him."

"I'm not bluffing," Evers warned.

"Neither am I," Bane replied.

"Think of your wife," Judge Hawthorne pleaded. "For God's sake, man, think of your children!"

Bane stood silent for a long moment.

"Well, what's it to be, Marshal?" Evers demanded.

"You win," Bane muttered, resignation in his voice. He let his Colt fall to the floor.

"Kick it away!"

Bane slid the revolver away with a sweep of his toe.

"All right, Marshal. Out that door, and you and your family live another day."

"I'm going!" Bane cried, his voice loud with anguish.

He walked to the door of the chambers, opened it, and—

The sound of the shot was loud in the room.

Chapter 16

The Worst Villain

"Quit thinking about what Bobby Lee's going do to us and start thinking about
what we're going to do to him."
— Ulysses S. Grant (1822-)

Excelsior, Nevada

Bane turned back around. Breathing a sigh of relief, he saw Evers lying on his
side, face down in his own blood. He must have struck the edge of the judge's
desk on his way down, the contact pitching him sideways.

Bane checked the body for a pulse. "Dead," he told the judge.

Badger stepped quickly into the chambers, his rifle in hand. As Bane had a
moment before, the deputy marshal breathed a sigh of relief.

Everything had gone as planned. The judge had played his role perfectly, as
had Bane and Badger. It was fortunate, Bane thought, that Judge Hawthorne
was a practical and realistic man, rather than an arrogant and reckless fool, and
had agreed to Bane's addition to his plan, which had added a part for Badger
to play. Had they relied exclusively on Bane's sudden appearance from hiding,
Evers would have killed the judge, it was evident now that they'd seen the
outlaw's grit.

Unlike Don Lombardo and Andy Sanders, Kyle Evers had been a man of courage and fortitude. Bane had no doubt that the assassin would have given his own life for the life of the man he'd come to kill. By appearing to have crumbled under the threat of losing his wife and kids, Bane had put Evers at ease.

Then, from his position, outside a window of the judge's chambers, Badger had taken his cue, Bane's opening of the door into the courtroom beyond the chambers, and had shot Evers just about where Bane himself would have done so. By the time he'd hit the floor, the outlaw was dead.

The third, and worst, villain who'd threatened the life of a participant in the trial and conviction of Spencer Rowelings was no longer a danger to anyone.

Chapter 17

Damned Bad Luck

"Luck or no luck, to win, you have to play the game."
— Bradford Messenger (1837-)

Excelsior, Nevada

"Stepping over to Mother's for a cup of coffee," Bane told his secretary, Angeline Sullivan.

The young woman looked up from the paperwork on her desktop. "Yes, Marshal."

Bane suppressed a smile. She'd worked for him for a while now, and, yet, she still called him "Marshal," instead of Bane, the name by which his deputies and pretty much everyone else referred to him.

She'd become his secretary just before her brother Pete had moved east, enrolling in a seminary, with plans to become a priest after he'd left the murderous gang whose sabotage of the railroads had, in some cases, killed innocent passengers and crew alike.

She'd managed to convince the young man to give himself up. In return for providing evidence against them, Pete had been granted immunity from prosecution. He'd spend the rest of his life, he'd said, doing penance by performing the Lord's work.

Bane hadn't had any sympathy for the young man—at least, not at the time. Since then, he'd given Angeline's brother credit for changing his ways and trading evil for good. It was a start.

Bane mentioned his destination to his deputy, Badger, on the way out.

Walking along the boardwalk that fronted the shops, stores, and saloons, he tipped his hat to the ladies and nodded to the gents he passed, enjoying their smiles and greetings.

He hadn't always been as welcome in Excelsior, Nevada, as he'd become since he'd married Pamela and settled down with their daughter Lizzie and their son Ben. His Aunt Flossie's and his father Bradford's presence in their home was another welcome source of comfort and joy for him.

As a bounty hunter who'd more often than not brought wanted men back dead, rather than alive, Bane hadn't been the most popular man in town. His visits to the brothel owned by Rose O'Sharon hadn't improved his unsavory reputation any, either.

It was a wonder what marriage and children could do to help a man establish a good standing.

Like his presence in the pews at church, his discovery of a gold mine worth millions had also been beneficial to his fellow townspeople's reassessment of him. Ridding Excelsior of a criminal cabal had also aided his quest to become an ex-pariah.

Finally, he'd actually gained friends in town, despite the fact that Rose remained one of them.

He had to admit, it felt good to be a part of the community.

His waitress, Maddie Walker approached, bidding him a good morning, as she offered him a menu.

Declining the bill of fare, he said, "I'll have the usual."

"Paper with that, Bane? There's mighty interesting news this morning, especially for a man in your line of work."

"Oh?" Her comment piqued his interest. "What's that?"

She pretended to frown. "Want me to ruin your surprise?"

He chuckled. "Guess not."

She nodded, turning away.

"Say, Maddie?"

She turned back, toward him. "Change your mind, Bane?"

"Nope, but add a slice of your deep-dish apple pie to that cup of coffee, will you?"

"Will do. Anything else?"

"That ought to do it, I reckon."

She smiled, shaking her head. "Glad we have some *hungry* customers. If we had to rely on you, Mother's would go out of business," she joked.

While he waited, he thought of Pamela and the kids. He ought to bring them here for dinner one evening. It had been a while since they'd had a meal at The Mother Lode. Pamela would appreciate it; so would Aunt Flossie, who did her fair share of housekeeping. Bradford probably wouldn't care one way or the other, but he wouldn't say no.

A few minutes later, Maddie returned, set the cup of coffee and the slice of pie on the table, and presented a copy of *The Excelsior Times* to him with a flourish. "Don't say I didn't warn you, Bane."

He didn't have to search for the story she'd hinted at. It was right there, above the fold, on the front page, despite the fact that the newspaper's first page was, like its last, usually reserved for advertisements.

State Prison Break Results in Escape of 29 Convicts, Some Armed!

Henry S. Phillips, who had been at the prison, in a buggy, when a gun battle began in the prison yard, drove into Carson City to sound the alarm. In response, Sheriff Stanley and twelve to fifteen   other armed men rushed to the scene but arrived too late to prevent the escape.

It was mayhem. The prisoners, some letting out Civil War

battle cries, ran, stepped, pushed, and shoved over and around the fallen guards. Twenty-nine of them made it through the gates and ran off in all directions, hell-bent on freedom.

It was reported that twenty-two of the escapees, marching two abreast, turned east toward the river. Like many exaggerated reports written in the next few days, that was not true. The men simply scattered.

Several who headed toward the Sierras slipped through the outlying regions of Carson City without incident.

One of them followed the Carson River upstream for miles. He was captured without incident two days later, basking in a pool at David Walley's Hot Springs near Genoa in Douglas County. "A warm bath was all I wanted," he explained.

A group of stragglers in prison garb was seen at dusk on a ridge across the Carson River, a few miles southeast of the prison. Lawmen said they would be captured before daylight.

The Excelsior Times will continue to report the consequences of this historic escape as more news becomes available.

Bane's coffee was cold by the time he finished the report and had ruminated over its implications.

He knew some of the lawmen who'd likely play a hand in rounding up the escaped desperadoes. As a U. S. marshal, he'd aided or been aided by one or two of them, despite the distance between Carson City and Excelsior.

The article listed the names of the twenty-nine escapees. Bane was acquainted with several of them, too. They were all hard cases, tough, ruthless, and dangerous as rattlesnakes.

Among them, one name stood out: Spencer Rowelings. He'd been sentenced to hang and was due to be executed next week. Instead, he'd broken out of prison and escaped with the rest of the fugitives.

He didn't envy the lawmen the dangerous work of tracking, capturing or killing, and bringing them back, dead or alive, to face justice.

On the other hand, he mused, chances were, he might be working alongside them—and others—again before long.

"You didn't drink your coffee," Maddie said, when she returned to check on him. "Didn't touch your pie, either."

"Toss the coffee and wrap the pie in a napkin, if you don't mind."

"Can I get you anything else?"

"Just the check."

"Be right back with it," she said, before leaving.

He shook his head. The biggest prison break in the history of the country, for all he knew, had just happened, when he'd begun to enjoy a little of the good life again. He hadn't had to kill anybody since the railroads were sabotaged—and, now, *this*!

It was just his luck, just his damned bad luck!

Chapter 18

A Wolf among the Sheep

"A wolf with an appetite for lamb takes great interest in sheep."
— Flossie Messenger (1840-)

South of State Prison, Carson City, Nevada

Once they were through the gate and outside the walls of the State Prison, with nothing but the wide-open country surrounding them, the convicts separated into groups, most going south or southeast, a few heading west.

For several reasons, Spencer Rowelings accompanied the smallest number of escapees heading south. For one thing, as a lone wolf, he wasn't fond of others. If he *had* to be in the company of other men, especially those who were essentially strangers, he preferred to be with the least number of them.

Another reason that Rowelings had thrown his lot in with the smaller group was that he was a leader. As such, he didn't intend to take orders from anyone else. Should trouble arise, as it almost certainly would, it would be easier to stand against a few other men than it would be to defy many.

It was true, too, that, with many, there was bound to be dissent, which could end in fighting between two sides or among several factions. A single man, if he were a man like Rowelings, could dominate and subjugate the others, if they were few in number.

There was a fourth reason, as well, that Rowelings would join the smaller band. A larger contingent of men was likely to attract attention more quickly and longer than a smaller group was, and one thing fugitives didn't want or need was attention.

Finally, he'd accompany the smaller body of fugitives because the gold and silver he'd robbed from the stagecoach was buried east of the prison. Going south would lead the men he traveled with and others going in that direction away from the cache of treasure, and he knew the territory well. He could double-back when he considered it safe to do so.

As he journeyed south, he watched the far greater groups of escaped desperadoes. Poor dumb bastards! They were making their escape harder, their capture more likely, their eventual sentences much longer. Unless a man were a soldier at war with an enemy who numbered in the thousands, it was always better, Rowelings had found, to lead a small pack of wolves than to be one among them, but it was best to be a lone wolf, whenever situations and circumstances allowed.

For now, and for as long as it benefited him, he would drink with these men, curse with them, rob with them, steal horses with them, kill with them. The moment they became dispensable, he'd dispense with them.

Chapter 19

As Soon As Possible

"Parting is such sweet sorrow."
— William Shakespeare (1564-1616)

Excelsior, Nevada

"Marshal? You have a telegram. Mr. Morton delivered it himself."

Frowning, Bane accepted the sealed envelope from his secretary.

Sure enough, his name was scrawled across the back of it, written in Steve's nearly indecipherable handwriting. Must be important. Usually, Steve Morton would send his boy.

"Thanks," he said, heading into his office.

Once inside, he closed the door so he wouldn't be interrupted. Then, he slit the envelope open and extracted the telegram.

Centered, across the top of the pale-yellow paper, in distinctive, bold, all-capital letters was "**WESTERN UNION TELEGRAPH COMPANY**," and, below this heading, the address of Morton's telegraph office, above the statement of the "Terms and Conditions" of the message's receipt, followed by a box in which the message itself appeared, translated from Morse code into English by Morton, in his damnable script:

To: <u>U. S. Marshal Bane Messenger</u>
From: <u>Nevada Governor Joshua B. Cooper</u>
Received: September 20, 1884

Urgent! The Governor of the State of Nevada requests that you come immediately to Elko with whatever deputies you wish to accompany you to meet with him as soon as possible. Request approved by President Chester Allan Arthur.

As a U. S. marshal, Bane served warrants on men who were suspected to have committed crimes against the U. S. government, sat in on district or circuit courts trials, and appointed deputies as occasions warranted. He didn't enforce state laws. That action was the responsibility of local city police, county sheriffs, and, on rare occasions, a state's National Guard. Why would President Arthur have approved such a request, or, for that matter, *had* he approved it? Was the telegram authentic?

Surely, the operator in the Elko office from which the message had originated would have verified the sender's credentials as well as the sender's authority before dispatching such a message.

Even so, to have received such a telegram wasn't just unusual; it was extraordinary. As far as Bane knew, not even the escape from the State Prison had resulted in any such communiques. Local lawmen, in this case aided by the Nevada National Guard, were handling the situation.

He'd best round up Badger Thompson and Luke Meadows. If whatever the governor wanted to see him about was as important as this message suggested it was, Bane wanted to have deputies who had grit and whom he trusted to be informed of whatever the governor wanted done.

Then, he'd go home, say goodbye to Pamela, Lizzie, Ben, Aunt Flossie, and Bradford.

The message, marked "urgent," asked him to leave for Elko "immediately"';
Governor Cooper wanted him there "as soon as possible," and Bane would
comply with the requests—after he'd bidden his family farewell. That, for him,
was "as soon as possible."

* * *

Don't go, Bane.

Those words were the first that occurred to Pamela; they were the ones she'd
wanted to say.

Those were the words she *always* wanted to say.

But she'd known what Bane was before they'd married. He'd made no secret
of his "calling," as he referred to the way he risked his life, time after time, again
and again, to bring to justice the ruthless men who robbed and raped and killed,
with no remorse. Men without consciences, they ravaged the West. Only men
like Bane dared to stand in their way, at the risk of losing their own lives, at the
risk of losing their own families, at the risk of losing everything.

Bane had saved her life and the lives of many other men, women, and
children. It would be selfish of her to insist, as she had once before, early in their
marriage, that he give up his profession, trading what he did for a living for what
she preferred him to do.

He'd tried to honor his word to her. He'd given ranching a chance, but he
wasn't a rancher, any more than he was, or could be, a farmer, a shopkeeper, a
barber, a blacksmith, or a lawyer. Like most other folks, he was who he was and
what he was, and he could never be anyone or anything else.

Finally, she'd understood that she had no right to expect that he'd change,
that he'd be who and what she wanted him to be instead of who and what he
was: Bane Messenger, a servant of justice and, yes, at times, an angel of death.

So, this time, when he said his goodbyes, she'd smiled and hugged him tightly
to her breast, and kept back the tears somehow, and said, simply, "I'll miss you,
Bane."

"I miss you already," he'd said.

Then he'd kissed the children, tousling Ben's hair; hugged his Aunt Flossie and kissed her cheek; and shaken hands with and hugged his father, Bradford.

And, then, he was gone.

Again.

Riding off, between his deputies.

She prayed for their protection and safe return, wiped away a tear, and, smiling for the sake of her children, took their hands in hers.

"Want to fly a kite, Ben" Bradford asked.

"*Do* I!"

"I'm going to the general store," Aunt Flossie told Lizzie. "Want to come along? Maybe we can find some material for the new dress I'm planning to make for you."

"Really? You're making me a new dress?"

"Soon's we find a bolt of fabric you like."

"Can Mom come?"

"Of course. Afterward, we'll stop at the The Mother Lode for lunch."

Chapter 20

A Man without a Plan

"I never plan, and look where I am today."
— Marcel Gagnon (1848)

South of Carson City, Nevada

Fate, not Spencer Rowelings, had chosen James Baker, Russ Jackson, and Zach Storm as his travel companions. They'd headed south, out of the State Prison, which was the same direction in which Rowelings had decided to flee.

The murderous stagecoach robber had solid reasons for choosing this direction. The others had let their emotions or convenience decide the direction of their flight.

Baker had a woman in El Dorado City who'd written to him while he was a guest of the Silver State. "She was the only thing that kept me from going stir-crazy," he'd told the rest of them. Since he'd regularly received perfumed letters from her, proclaiming her undying love, the prison officials knew where he was likely to turn up. He was as good as caught, Rowelings reckoned. A posse would be able to collect him at his sweetheart's house without much effort.

Jackson had gone south, he said, because he was sure that his parents would stake him. They'd made good money as cattle ranchers, and, among his kin, he said, blood was thicker than water. With a substantial "loan," he could travel a good distance to Chicago or New York, where, he figured, "a man could lose himself and start over." His plan might work, Rowelings thought, if he made his getaway quickly enough and kept his head down, the latter of which actions seemed unlikely, given the man's boisterous and boastful ways.

Storm, who, judging by the man's reminiscences, seemed a devil-may-care, free-spirited vagabond, said he planned to acquire passage aboard a ship "bound for anywhere" and "see the world," despite the fact that he was penniless. He'd earn his passage as a deckhand, he said, as he'd done before, from time to time, between highway robberies and stretches in prison. His was a decent plan, Rowelings thought, if he had enough self-discipline to carry it out without getting diverted by whiskey or a woman before he secured a position aboard a ship.

Although they'd asked what Rowelings's plans for the future were, he'd remained tight-lipped and non-committal, saying he hadn't decided, yet, what he'd do. They'd nodded and grinned, as if his indecision were understandable, when, of course, from his own point of view, such indecisiveness would by no means be comprehensible.

He had a plan, all right, but he sure as *hell* wasn't going to divulge it to these three half-wits, who'd more than likely be captured in a fortnight and would then seek any opportunity to acquire a lighter sentence than they would otherwise receive by sharing any information they could about any of the other members of their group with the lawmen who'd arrested them, including, of course, their comrades' plans.

Of the three with whom he traveled, Rowelings was most interested, at the moment, in Baker. The lovelorn lover-boy was the only one of them to have snagged one of the guards' plain clothes from the prison armory; the rest, like Rowelings himself, wore their prison-issued uniforms.

Chapter 21

A Rectangular Affair

"A rectangle is just a longer or taller square."
— Ben Messenger (1874-)

Elko, Nevada

Bane, Badger, and Luke, traveling north to Huntington Valley, had ridden along the south fork of the Humboldt River, past Dry Valley, Mound Valley, Jiggs, and Coral Hill. Turning east at the Humboldt River, they'd then ridden along it to Elko. Their journey had taken them several days, which was "as soon as possible," as Governor Cooper had requested.

Unlike much of the portion of the Great Basin that made up nearly the whole of Nevada's vast and varied landscape, this part of the region was comprised of relatively flat and open terrain, more or less green, beneath vast blue skies in which, at present, white, wispy clouds drifted. There were trees, although not a forest, here, and mountain ranges in the distance. Without a hotel anywhere along their route, Bane and his deputies had had to sleep under the stars, but they were used to such accommodations.

Still, Bane, and he reckoned, Badger and Luke, were glad to see signs of civilization, such as they were, in Elko, another of the many towns in the West that owed its existence to the building of the railroad. Here, despite the governor's request that Bane meet with him "as soon as possible," they'd at least freshen up before they honored his petition.

Bane rented one of the rooms on the second floor of a saloon. He'd been tempted to linger in the bathtub, but he took mercy on his deputies. After dressing, he returned to the saloon, allowing Luke to trade places with him while the bathwater was still lukewarm, and passed the time watching Badger drink a couple of beers.

Bane himself seldom drank. As a lawman, he preferred, as he had as a bounty hunter, to keep a clear head. When it came to trading bullets with outlaws who were trying to kill him, being sober gave Bane an advantage over those who'd indulged in one shot of whiskey or one beer too many. The way he saw it, such moments made sobriety worthwhile.

He'd never known either Badger or Luke to get drunk, but they *did* drink, and, although they were good with a gun, even a few beers could take any man's edge off.

When Luke concluded his bath, he left the now twice-used bathwater to Badger. It would be cold and about the same color as soil by now, Bane figured.

Fortunately, none of them could be accused of being fastidious. Having lived as long as they had on the frontier, they were glad enough to take what they could in the way of such niceties as baths, and all of them had sequentially shared a tub before now. Even if the second and third to bathe didn't emerge as clean as the first of them, they were still *less* dirty and smelled a whole *lot* better.

Given the circumstances of their travels, they were presentable enough, Bane suspected, to suit the governor, who himself was familiar with the hardships that sometimes attended life in the West.

Bathed, shaved, and his hair combed, Bane hadn't bothered to check how he looked in the hotel room's mirror. He suspected that Pamela would approve of his appearance—well, not "approve," exactly, but she wouldn't *dis-*approve—well, not strenuously, anyway—and her slight disapproval would almost certainly translate to the governor's more-or-less hearty approval. He hoped.

"You boys ready?" he asked his deputies.

Luke pushed his cup of coffee away. "Ready."

Badger scowled. "We're going *now*?"

"The governor did say 'as soon as possible.'"

"Couldn't tomorrow be as soon as possible?" Badger asked. "I—we *all*—could use a good night's sleep."

Bane took one of his arms; Luke, the other. Together, they helped their reluctant friend step away from the bar.

"You've already had more than you should have. You can wait until after we've seen the governor before you belly up to the bar for more," Bane insisted.

* * *

"I can't tell Georgian from Gothic Revival," Bane admitted as he and his deputies gazed at the splendid mansion that was the private home of Governor Joshua B. Cooper. "I can tell you this, though; that's one impressive house."

"Looks like a place that Cornelius Vanderbilt or his son William Henry might have built," Luke said.

"A little too rectangular for my tastes," Badger opined.

"*Your* tastes?" Luke snorted. "When did *you* acquire a taste for anything but raw rattlesnake?"

Badger shot him a contemptuous look. "Spoken by a man who considers horse meat a delicacy."

"It *is* a little on the rectangular side," Bane agreed. He couldn't put a name to most architectural features, but he did recognize the four dormers lined up across the steeply-pitched roof and the twin arched windows above the entrance, which were also rectangular, but at a right angle to the rest of the house, and contained twin doors, also vertical rectangles, of course.

Flanking the arched windows were two upright rectangular windows to match those on either side of the front entrance. A long fence along the front of the edifice and, most likely, around the rest of it, added yet another rectangle to the scene. Bane reckoned that Governor Cooper, or whoever had designed the house, had a passion for the geometric shape.

Despite having only two stories, it was a tall building, which suggested high ceilings for the rooms on both levels. Most likely, an attic ran the length of the dwelling and was, consequently, the size of an entire floor. Although the front of the house looked forty feet wide, it was possible that the domicile extended much deeper.

About thirty feet from the house, a huge fountain, round, rather than rectangular, stood in the center of a circular pool. Spraying water, it might look fine, Bane thought, but standing idle, it looked to him simply out of place. Behind the house, a stand of tall, narrow trees grew straight into the sky, dwarfing the house they shaded, despite the domicile's own considerable height.

"There's not a hitching post in sight," Badger observed.

"Of course not; they're cylindrical, not rectangular," Luke said.

"Maybe we can hitch our horses to one of the trees behind the house," Luke suggested.

The sound of hooves behind them made the marshal and his deputies turn in their saddles.

"That won't be necessary, gentlemen," declared the rider, recognizable by the photographs of him that occasionally appeared in *The Excelsior Times* and other Nevada newspapers.

"Governor!" Bane greeted him.

Joshua B. Cooper raised a whistle to his lips and blew a single, sharp note.

Chapter 22

Budding Entrepreneurs

"No man becomes rich unless he enriches others."
— Andrew Carnegie (1835-)

Near Genoa, Nevada

Sometimes, fate deals a man a good hand. James Baker, Russ Jackson, and Zach Storm, the "cards" it had dealt Spencer Rowelings, weren't aces or, for that matter, even kings or jacks. They were more like jokers, but that suited Rowelings right down to the soles and heels of his boots.

Since they'd begun their flight from the prison, they'd come up with some outlandish schemes as to what they should do. Baker had put forth the idea of squatting in an abandoned miner's cabin. They could acquire seeds—he didn't have any idea as to how to accomplish such acquisitions—and, working together, plant a vegetable garden, despite the short, cold growing season.

"What would we grow?" Jackson asked when Baker had first floated the idea.

"Whatever we want," Baker answered.

"Had a cousin lived hereabouts," Baker replied. "Harvested five tomatoes one season. Lost all the herbs and fruit he'd planted. Chipmunks and squirrels ate most of his other crops. Whole damn 'farm' was overrun with the varmints."

"You got a better idea?" Baker asked.

Jackson didn't seem to have one, but Storm did. "Build us a still and make some moonshine."

"Moonshine?" Jackson's tone suggested that he considered Storm's idea about as loony as he'd found Baker's.

"Liquor," Storm explained.

"I *know* what it is," Jackson said, sounding insulted. "What I can't figure is how you're going to acquire the equipment and tools you'd need to make a still, *if* you know how to make one; how we'd get the equipment and tools here, or wherever you have a mind to build your still; who'd be willing to buy the rot-gut; and how you'd keep the law from destroying your still and capturing us."

"Those are important details, all right," Baker agreed, seeming to be glad to have someone else's plans examined, as his own had been.

"Don't need much in the way of equipment to start with, just two large copper pots, one for the boiler, the other for the condenser; a thermostat; some copper tubing; and some Mason jars for the collection vessels. Heat the mash in the boiler until it vaporizes, cool it in the condenser to turn the vapor back into a liquid, and capture the liquid in the collection vessels. Don't need many tools, either: a drill and a bit. A couple of rolls of tape, a metal file, and some glue—well, and matches.

"Only other cost is a few supplies: a scoop, a couple of long-handled spoons, and a few small bowls. Otherwise, we will need nothing more but sugar, water, coarse ground cornmeal, yeast, and malt—either rye, corn, or barley.

"As for customers, a lot of saloon keepers aren't above cutting their whiskey with anything from water to kerosene. They can buy ours tax-free and cheap enough to cut their stock. We make money, and they make money. Later, if we want, we could approach some restaurants, offering them some fruit-flavored spirits—peach or apple—added to the mash while it's fermenting. All we need's the equipment and tools. We'd hire a wagon to transport them to wherever we build the still."

"Looks like you've given quite a bit of thought to this," Rowelings said, playing along.

Storm grinned, seeming glad to be praised, especially after Baker's idea had been summarily dismissed.

"How much money you got, Baker?" Rowelings asked.

He laughed. "None."

"How about you, Jackson?"

"The same."

"And you, Storm?"

"Well . . . none."

"I have as much as all of you put together: zero." He looked at Storm as if he'd spied a bothersome insect. "How do you reckon we can afford any of the equipment, tools, and supplies we'd need to build and operate your still? Or rent the horse and wagon to transport them?"

Storm smiled. "Got it figured. Along the way to wherever we're going, Baker and I swap clothes, and—"

"I'm *not* swapping clothes," Baker objected.

"—and I hike into a town, pick up an item or two of equipment or supplies and carry them back to camp. By the time we reach our destination, we'll have everything we need in the way of the parts of the still, and we're not likely to arouse suspicion as to the reason I'm buying this or that. After we get set up, we make a few batches of moonshine, as samples, and I hike into town and acquire a customer or two. Before long, we'll be able to rent a wagon. Once we have customers, payment would be due on delivery."

"All that costs money," Rowelings pointed out. "We don't have any."

"I have a plan for that, too."

"Let's hear it."

Storm grinned. "I don't share my sales approach with most, but, since we'd be partners if you agree with my plan, I'll make an exception under the circumstances of our being on the run and all. I wrote a book on it, *Making Money by Moonshining*, complete with recipes. Sent it to a local paper, asking the editor to review it. To my surprise, the bastard did." Storm chuckled again. "He did such a good job that I memorized the damn thing."

"You're not going to recite it for us, are you?" Baker whined.

"I'd like to hear it," Rowelings said.

"Me, too," Jackson agreed.

Puffing out his chest and grinning like a humbug, Storm delivered the review, title and all, without pause, in the rich intonations of an actor soliloquizing upon a stage:

Business Plan Lands Investors

Zach Storm knows the necessity of having a solid business plan in place in order to land potential investors, and he's developed one, which he explains in his book, *Making Money by Moonshining*, which, owing to both its length and focus, ought, really, to be called a pamphlet.

Despite the brevity of his work, he not only explains how to make moonshine, or illegal alcoholic spirits, and includes a number of recipes for various concoctions, such as Apple Pie, Strawberry Lemonade, and Hellfire Jalapeno, but he also lays out a plan, "tried and true," he declares, for interesting investors in fronting the funds needed to commence such an enterprise.

Saloon proprietors and barkeeps have been only too happy to purchase spirits from the author, who is able, in short order, to provide them with a steady supply of whiskey and other alcoholic beverages that his customers can buy cheaply and sell dearly.

The process is so simple and the proceeds potentially so substantial that there seems no impediment to the business, on either the supplier's or the receiver's end, but this reviewer reminds its readers that, despite such encouragements, moonshining is illegal and typically results in fines and imprisonment upon conviction.

"I still haven't heard how we'd finance the start of such an enterprise," Rowelings stated.

"Leave that to me."

"Seems we'd run the risk of bringing the law down on us," Rowelings pointed out.

Storm laughed. "There's that chance, granted, but, it's more likely—*way* more likely—that saloon owners and barkeeps would buy as much as we can supply them. They'd be making six, seven—hell, maybe ten—times what they're making now on their legal whiskey. By and by, we could buy more equipment, and I could train the rest of you. Together, working in shifts, we could keep the still running all day, every day. To keep off suspicion, we'd rotate the shops and stores we buy from."

"You ever build a still yourself, or just seen it done? Rowelings asked.

"Hell, I'm from Tennessee, originally. I've built plenty of them. Damn near everybody thereabouts has."

He'd underestimated Storm, Rowelings thought. Here was a man of some ingenuity and intelligence, although, before now, he'd certainly kept his light under a basket.

After hearing Storm's proposition, Rowelings wasn't sure whether the man had ever planned to work aboard a ship in exchange for passages that would allow him to see the world while he remained at liberty, beyond the reach of the law, or had only said as much to avoid sharing his actual plans for making and selling moonshine.

It could be, of course, that such travel remained his ultimate goal and he'd decided, even long before today, to revert to moonshining as a means of lying low while financing his passages so that he could pay for accommodations as a passenger, instead, which would be far more comfortable than sleeping in the cargo hold or wherever the captains assigned him as a deckhand aboard the ships.

If he'd intended to book passages from the revenue he made by moonshining, he'd earn—well, not "earn," exactly, but acquire—the means to do so much more quickly if he had a crew to help him, and his fellow escapees would provide the muscle he needed to such ends. Then, most likely, he'd then abandon not only the still but the rest of them.

Of course, by then, they'd have learned the trade. Besides, Rowelings didn't mean to make moonshine any longer than it took to finance his own continued flight from the law, and taking a share of the profits from this enterprise would be a good way to accumulate the money he needed.

One thing bothered him, though. Again, it seemed, he'd underestimated someone. Once more, he'd taken the measure of a man before he'd properly observed his behavior. It wouldn't happen again; it *couldn't* happen again. Misjudging somebody could get a man killed, and Rowelings was not ready to die, not yet, anyway.

Chapter 23

Feeling Faint

"There is immeasurably more left inside than comes out in words."
— Fyodor Dostoevsky (1821-1881)

Elko, Nevada

Within a few minutes, in answer to the governor's blast on the whistle, a stableman appeared, accompanied by a couple of youths who were obviously his assistants.

"Take our horses to the barn," Governor Cooper instructed the man, "and tend to them. My guests will collect their mounts when they take their leave."

"Yes, sir."

Along with the governor, Bane and his deputies dismounted and turned their reins over to the groom and his assistants.

"Thank you for coming as soon as you have, Marshal. I see you brought your deputies."

"Yes, sir: Deputy Marshals Badger Thompson and Luke Meadows."

"By my apprising you of the, uh, situation at hand in the presence of your deputies, everyone shall hear the same information and have the opportunity to pose any questions he may have."

The governor shook hands all around.

When he got to Luke, he said, "I thought your name is 'Wayne.'"

"I go by 'Luke' now. My wife prefers it to my given name."

Without asking the reason, Governor Cooper simply nodded. "Nice to make your acquaintance, Luke."

"The same to you, Governor," the deputy replied.

Bane noticed that the governor also had not remarked upon Luke's peg leg. Maybe the chief executive had checked their backgrounds. If so, Cooper knew all about Blood Mountain. Or maybe Cooper just wasn't a man who pried.

"Let's go indoors," their host suggested. "I'd like to discuss the matter not only in private but also in the comfort of my parlor, with a glass of claret by my side, as, I imagine, you gentlemen would as well."

"I'm not usually a drinking man," Bane replied, "but a glass of claret sounds fine to me."

"And me!" Badger announced.

"Much obliged," said Luke.

The house's interior, as Bane had suspected, was much deeper than the mansion was wide. The design, the décor, the furnishings—all were exquisite. Bane felt dismayed. He'd promised Pamela, Aunt Flossie, and Lizzie a complete and detailed description of the lavish home, but he didn't know the types of flooring, carpets, ceilings, moldings, casements, curtains, wallpapers, chairs, sofas, tables, or anything else.

Hell, he didn't even know the names of some of the colors in the corridors he walked through and the rooms he spied along the way. He could recognize only that they were what he would call "stylish" and "ornate" and "colorful" and "plush" and, that they were, undoubtedly expensive. Such adjectives wouldn't do for Pamela, Aunt Flossie, or Lizzie; they'd want to know "details."

The room they finally entered was large and "inviting," as Aunt Flossie might say. A sofa, maybe gold or saffron or some such hue or tone or tint, stood against a wall covered in a sort of yellowish-gray color with sporadic green prints of shapes that seemed now marine, now avian, depending on the point of view and the shift of focus, but were probably neither.

The back of the couch was in three panels, the widest and tallest in the middle, and each was set in an ornate wooden frame with lots of scrolls and such, in the center of which was a sort of seal surrounded by wreaths cut out of the wood. A matching chair stood next to one end of the sofa, at an angle. A high, round table of a different cut of wood, but one that was, Bane assumed, "complementary" to the framed back of the sofa and the back of the matching chair, stood before the sofa, bearing a silver tea set, each piece of which shone in the light of the room, which was cast by wall lamps.

Above the sofa, a painting in a gilded frame depicted a calm lake between high, rugged cliffs, a range of mountains in the distance. A reddish-orange band, two or three inches tall, ran around the top of the ceiling, displaying a series of designs not quite resembling crowns but looking more like them than not. The ceiling was recessed and painted with a mural of a splendid landscape, although why anyone would want a mural on the ceiling was beyond Bane. After going to the expense of purchasing such a huge work of art, wouldn't the buyer want to display it on a wall, where visitors could study and praise it without breaking their necks in the process?

At the other end of the couch, between a reddish-burgundy armchair occupied by a square golden pillow with tassels along its edges, a cabinet stood. Built in tiers and festooned with pitchers, upright plates with flowers and vines painted on their surfaces, a vase of flowers, and other decorations and ornaments, it competed with the other lavish furnishings for attention and, for a moment or two, attained it.

A rug—Pamela would call it "rich"—that was mostly an orange-brown, flecked with spots and flecks of gold and yellow, lay stretched between the sofa and chairs and table, and yet more furniture, including a rocking chair and a cabinet. Everywhere the eye sought to perch there was another piece of furniture or decoration or article that prevented it from resting, so that Bane found his eye constantly traveling, lighting here for a moment, or there, but always moving on. Some might like it. The governor, maybe. Aunt Flossie, Pamela, and Lizzie, undoubtedly. The effect of the dizzying array of furniture, décor, and color simply left Bane feeling faint and dizzy, as did the prospect of his having to describe the madness of the interior of this vast house.

After he'd drunk a glass of claret, he felt a bit better. When he focused on the governor, rather than on the room, he felt even better yet, steadier, somehow, and more balanced. He wondered whether the house had had the same effect on his deputies. They didn't look green about the gills or as if they were struggling not to get sick, so maybe they felt all right or, like Bane, had come to feel better.

"I know you've had a long ride, gentlemen," the governor said, "and I appreciate your traveling from Excelsior to meet with me here, in Elko. I would not have asked you to make the trip if I saw an alternative to my doing so, and, certainly, I would not have disturbed President Arthur.

"Even as I speak, sheriffs from several counties are tracking the fugitives who escaped from the State Prison. Indeed, one, who was tracked from the prison, has already been captured, as he basked in the sun in a pool at David Walley's Hot Springs, not far from Genoa." The governor chuckled. "He told the arresting officer and his posse, rather smugly, I fear, that all he wanted was to enjoy a hot bath.

"A few others, who dawdled after escaping the prison, are being tracked and, according to lawmen, should be in custody shortly. Unfortunately, the vast majority of the twenty-nine escapees remain at large. I have called out the state militia, which is headquartered in Virginia City, to aid in their apprehension, and, in Carson City, where the prison is located, the state armory has been opened, and deputized citizens have been armed and dispatched to the prison to ensure that neither another potential escape attempt nor an attack by insurgents succeeds."

Bane nodded. "Looks like you have all the bases covered."

"Yes and no, Marshal. That's where you and your deputies come in."

Chapter 24

A Change of Clothing

"Clothes make the man."
— classical Greek saying

Near Genoa, Nevada

Actually, two things bothered Spencer Rowelings.

Not only had he once again underestimated a man in supposing Zach Storm to be as lame-brained as James Baker and Russ Jackson, but he'd also neglected to ensure that Storm had even so much as a chance in hell of actually selling a saloon owner or barkeep on the prospect of funding Storm's enterprise. At least he could rectify his oversight. "There's not a town anywhere near here that's big enough to support your moonshining scheme, Zach."

"True," Storm agreed, "not hereabouts, but I know a place that's perfect, and it's only about two-hundred-and-seventy-five miles from here."

Baker laughed. "Two-hundred-and-seventy-five miles!"

"That's only a few days for a horse."

"We don't *have* any horses," Baker observed.

"Not yet," Rowelings said. Yes, he figured, Storm did, in fact, know how to make moonshine and believed that such an undertaking could, in fairly short order, generate enough funds for his plans to travel the world by ship. Rowelings would make sure that, before ceasing their operation, it had also provided the funds that his own plans required.

To the others, Rowelings said, "Zach has presented a proposition, and we've all thought on it. Now, it's time to decide. All in favor, raise your hands."

Storm, of course, signified that he was agreeable to his own proposal.

Jackson also raised his hand.

"James?" Rowelings asked.

"I don't know. I mean, there's a risk, and—"

"Breaking out of prison was a risk," Rowelings reminded him.

"Yeah, but it was worth it. I mean, we're free now, and—."

"We're *not* free," Rowelings corrected him. "We're fugitives."

"Well, yes, but—."

"And to become free—and to *stay* free—we have to move on, not aimlessly, but with a plan, and with money, and Zach has offered us a means to earn that money."

Baker scoffed. "So did I."

Rowelings glared at him. "Farming? How much do you reckon you'd earn farming in a region like this, and how long do you think it would take to earn even that pittance? Now, which is it? You with us—or you against us?"

Baker detected the threat in the last part of Rowelings's question. His hand, a bit shaky, rose.

Rowelings raised his own hand. "It's unanimous, then!" Glancing at Storm, he ordered, "Take off your clothes, James; Zach's going to need them."

"I'm not swapping my plain clothes for a prison uniform!" Baker protested.

Rowelings stepped close to him. Glowering, he thrust his face to within a few inches of Baker's own. When Rowelings bellowed, Baker felt the spray of his spittle in his face: "Do it—*now*!"

Baker looked uncertain. His gaze flitted back and forth between Jackson and Storm. Seeing no support from either of them, he gulped. "All right, all right!" he managed to blurt, as he began unbuttoning his shirt.

In a few minutes, they'd swapped their apparel, except for their boots.

"How do I look?" Storm asked.

Considering his appearance, Rowelings nodded. "You'll pass. Let's get going."

"All of us?" Jackson asked. "We can't pass the way Zach can."

"That's why you and James are staying here," Rowelings declared.

"Hell, you can't pass, either," Storm said.

"Let me worry about that," Rowelings answered. "Let's go, Zach. The nearest town's six or seven miles south of here. I'd like to get there this afternoon, and we have to make a stop along the way."

Chapter 25

A Golden Assignment

"Remember that it is the actions, and not the commission, that makes the officer, and that there is more expected of him than the title."
— George Washington (1732-1799)

Elko, Nevada

Governor Cooper studied Bane for a moment before he said, "Marshal, we have never met before, but I have it on good authority that you are a man of courage, moral convictions, and integrity."

Bane felt a blush warm his cheeks, embarrassed at hearing such praise in the company of Badger and Luke, who flanked him in identical chairs , across the vast desk of their host. Although both men had sense enough not to comment in the presence of the governor, he was fairly certain he'd hear their jibes and wisecracks later.

"No less expert judges of men than the late Allan Pinkerton and President Chester Alan Arthur have told me that you are the man for the task for which I've asked and received President Arthur's consent for you, Deputy Thompson, and Deputy Meadows to complete."

Repressing the urge to ask what task that might be, Bane merely nodded.

"Spencer Rowelings is among the prison's escapees. I believe that you are acquainted with both the name and the man himself."

"Yes, sir."

"And with the crimes of which he was convicted?"

"Yes, sir. I was in court at the time."

The governor nodded. "As you'll recall, the stagecoach that Rowelings robbed was carrying a chest of gold and silver."

"Yes, sir."

"That shipment of gold and silver was, or, rather, is, the property of the United States Treasury, and the president and I want it back. Your task, therefore, is twofold, in this order of priority: recover the gold and silver and capture or kill Rowelings, as the situation dictates. You have the full backing of both the State of Nevada and the United States."

Bane sighed, releasing the stress of the heavy burdens of responsibility and trust that both the governor and the president had heaped upon his shoulders. He was certain that his deputies felt the same way. "Yes, sir."

"We—the president and I, as well as others—believe that Rowelings may have plans for the money that would threaten the security of our nation."

Bane frowned, as he returned the governor's grave expression.

For a moment, Governor Cooper seemed to consider something, as if he were weighing alternatives. Then, he said, "I understand that you are a man of means, Marshal."

Since Bane owned a gold mine worth millions, the governor's declaration was an understatement. "Yes, sir, I reckon that's true."

"You will have, at your disposal, any equipment, materials, transportation, personnel, lodging, or other assets you require. I could establish an expense account for you, but, since you will be traveling, perhaps widely, it would be easier, for both you and me, if you would agree to bear the costs and expenses of your necessities yourself, in exchange for the government's repayment of such expenses, as supported by receipts, bills of sale, or other records of the expenditures that you and your deputies incur in the recovery of the gold and the capture or killing of Rowelings."

"I'd be glad to, sir."

The governor opened a drawer, extracted a sheaf of papers, and extended them to Bane. "Anticipating your willingness to do so, Marshal, I've had the state's lawyers draw up a contract to that effect. My signature's already on it, as you can see. All that's required now is your signature."

Bane chuckled at the thickness of the document. "Lawyers do have a way of saying in a few hundred words what ordinary folks can say in fifty."

The governor laughed. "Or fewer."

Bane autographed the contract and passed it back to the governor.

"Thank you, Marshal." He returned the signed document to his desk drawer. "It's customary for me to show guests around the place," he said, "but I suspect that, given the gravity and importance of your task, you'd prefer to get started at once in completing it."

Bane nodded. "Yes, sir."

He extended his hand to Bane and each of the marshal's deputies. "Gentlemen, you have the gratitude of your state and nation."

"And, soon, Governor—or as soon as possible—you'll have that gold and silver and Spencer Rowelings, dead or alive."

Chapter 26

Bright as a Beacon

"I've never killed anyone, but I frequently get satisfaction reading the obituary notices."
— Clarence Darrow (1857 -)

Near Genoa, Nevada

"Where are we stopping?" Zach Storm asked, after he and Spencer Rowelings had left their campsite. "You said you had to make a stop on the way."

"I'll know it when I see it."

Storm gave him an odd look.

An hour later, spying what he sought, Rowelings bade Storm to wait for him. "Lend me your six-shooter."

"Why?"

"I need it; that's why."

"What for?"

"Shooting."

Eyeing him warily, Storm took a step back. "I'm not lending you my Colt. What's to prevent you from shooting me, right here and now?"

"Your plan to moonshine makes sense; I want in, as a partner. But I've never made hooch, nor has Baker or Jackson. We wouldn't have any idea how to make the stuff, even if I had that book you wrote, *Making Money by Moonshining*."

Storm considered his words. "What are the other reasons?"

"You ever killed anybody?"

"Never had a reason to—not yet, anyway."

"I've killed my share. Some might say I've killed *more* than my share."

Storm studied him as if for the first time. The way Rowelings held himself, tense but focused, as if he were just waiting to spring into action, to pound and bloody, or even kill, gave Storm pause. So did the look in Rowelings's gaze. There'd been a coldness in his words, and there was a hardness in his eyes that Storm hadn't noticed before. Something about Rowelings was chilling.

"It doesn't bother me any, never has, but it bothers most. Killing a man, they tell me, is a terrible thing to live with."

It was clear to Storm that Rowelings spoke from experience.

"A rancher sees an escaped prisoner walk onto his property—well, he's not likely to worry about shooting him. With a gun, I can make sure that doesn't happen." He watched the other man.

Rowelings had given him a way of saving face. If he handed his gun to him now, they could both pretend he'd done so because Rowelings was, in fact, a better gunfighter than Storm and, armed, he could better defend them both.

If Storm didn't accept the ruse, Rowelings might not challenge him, here and now, when Storm was armed and he was not, but Storm had no doubt that Rowelings would look for an opportunity, or create one, to pay him back for defying him. As far as Rowelings was concerned, he, not Storm, was in charge, and he'd demonstrate his dominance sooner or later. After debating the matter for a minute or so, Storm handed Rowelings his Colt.

"Wait here; I'll be back shortly."

Locating a slight rise, Storm sat down, waiting.

* * *

Storm was a smart man, Rowelings thought, as he made his way across the rugged terrain, the ranch house seeming to become larger as he closed the distance.

Not much grew hereabouts, although there were some spindly-looking desert shrubs with long, delicate stems, standing in clumps, that may or may not bear flowers in the fall, and some sage and grass that grew low to the ground. Here and there were some plants that, anywhere else, would be regarded as weeds. Mostly, though, there were rocks and hills and mountains.

The woman he'd spotted from afar was still at work, her red scarf bright as a beacon in the largely desolate landscape. As he drew closer, he could better judge her age. Sixties, most likely. If she were married or there was a hired hand about the place, Rowelings hadn't seen him. Despite the pants and shirts and overalls she was hanging out to dry, she seemed alone. Maybe her man had ridden into town to fetch some items from one of the stores or to have a beer or two.

"Afternoon, ma'am," Rowelings said, smiling, as he closed the short distance that remained between him and the woman at the clothesline.

She started, then turned, answering his smile with one of her own. "Oh! You startled me."

The gunshot was loud as it reverberated across the countryside.

* * *

Fifteen minutes later, Rowelings returned, riding one horse while leading three others. The horse that Rowelings rode was bridled and saddled. The other three were saddled but wore halters, rather than bridles.

One end of the length of rope attached to the halter of the horse farther from Rowelings, on his right side, was looped over the right lead rope and then tied back to the halter. The right lead rope itself was threaded through the end of the length of the inside horse's looped rope, allowing Rowelings to lead both horses on his right at the same time. On his left side, the left lead rope ran directly to the third horse's halter.

The technique was new to Storm, but he understood its advantage. Should the horses break free, colliding against one another as they bolted across the terrain, they could be seriously hurt. The way that Rowelings had tied the two horses on his right, the lead rope could slide free of the looped rope, and the horses would not be bound to one another as they raced away. The horse on his right, of course, would be on its own, should it break away and bolt.

Storm reckoned there was more to Rowelings than he might have supposed—a *lot* more.

Tied across the backs of the horses were a man's pants and shirts. "Help yourself to one of the horses," Rowelings invited.

As Rowelings changed from his prison uniform into the rancher's clothing, Storm freed the mare of the left lead rope tied to her halter, removed the halter, and replaced it with one of the bridles that Rowelings had also stolen from the ranch. As he climbed into the saddle, he thought that it felt good to be on a horse again, even if it was stolen. "Heard a gunshot," he said, keeping his tone casual.

"So did the woman I killed."

"You killed a *woman?*" he demanded, accusation as well as anger in his voice.

"It was quick. One shot to the center of the forehead."

Looking horrified, Storm demanded, "Where's my gun?"

"Relax. I have it."

Storm held out his hand, palm up.

"Think I'll keep it," Rowelings said. He smiled at his fellow fugitive just the way he'd smiled at the rancher's wife.

You're a snake, aren't you, Rowelings? Storm thought it, but he didn't dare say it.

Chapter 27

Traveling by Train

"In the United States 'First' and 'Second' class can't be painted on railroad cars, for all passengers, being Americans, are equal and it would be 'unAmerican.' But paint 'Pullman' on a car and everyone is satisfied."

— Owen Wister (1860-)

Traveling West Aboard the Union Pacific Railroad

"Switch?" Badger asked.

"Haven't finished reading mine yet," Luke replied.

"Helps if you don't move your lips."

"Uh huh."

"How about you, Bane?"

Without looking up, Bane said, "Still reading."

Badger shook his head, as if he pitied his fellow lawmen. Looking out the window, he watched the terrain sweep by.

Hereabouts, the landscape looked as if Mother Nature had tried out as many variations of brown as possible"—coffee, peanut, caramel, gingerbread, and cinnamon, mostly—and had tossed in a few mounds and rocks of the same shades and hues. Even the range of mountains to the north was of the same monochromatic scheme.

A green creek seemingly came out of nowhere, parallel to the tracks, along-side a thickening of sandy clumps of vegetation, a green tree or two, and then a long stretch of nothing but rocks and soil and distant mountains. It wasn't the best view he'd ever seen, Badger thought.

Traveling by train beat riding horses anytime, though, especially when their passage was being paid by the government. Might as well enjoy the trip, Badger thought, as much as a body *could* enjoy being jostled, jiggled, and bounced while cramped up in a sitting position that allowed little room for comfort. Bane would probably have sprung for Silver Palace Car accommodations had they not have had to make their trip at the last minute. As it was, they'd been lucky to snag second-class seats on a mixed train.

Still, the trip from Elko to Reno would be speedier and a whole hell of a lot more comfortable—for them, at least. Their horses, tied in place, on short ropes, to prevent them from moving about within the confines of the closed, modified boxcar in which they traveled, with the sounds of the wheels on the track, wouldn't be the least bit comfortable, physically or otherwise, but they wouldn't have to endure their physical discomfort or their anxiety much longer.

* * *

From Reno, they'd ride south to the State Prison.

From newspaper articles, they'd pieced together quite a bit of information about the prison break besides what they'd learned from Governor Cooper, but Bane hoped to acquire additional particulars from guards and others who'd witnessed the break or had tried to prevent it. In his experience, a man almost always learned more from witnesses than from reporters, the latter of whom were, more often than not, handicapped by the simple fact that they'd not been on the scene at the time of the events on which they reported.

Badger closed his eyes, just to rest them, he told himself.

* * *

By the time he awakened, near Beowawe, the countryside had greened up a little, and a few trees, also green, appeared, signs of a water source somewhere, although Badger didn't see a creek anywhere. Some shacks and houses were scattered, here and there, across the land. A bit more picturesque, the view was still a far cry from lush. A school, a church, a post office, and a general store were signs that the town was edging toward civilization, but the saloon and dance hall indicated that it had a way to go before it equaled San Francisco, or, for that matter, Carson City or Virginia City.

Badger's eyes closed.

"You think you can stay awake long enough to read an article, Badger?" Luke asked, thrusting a newspaper toward him.

Opening one eye, Badger replied, "I've been waiting for you to finish yours." He snatched the newspaper from Luke.

Luke smirked. "Right."

"When you finish his, you can read mine," Bane said.

As Badger read, moving his lips, Luke noticed, his fellow deputy studied the passing landscape. A wide creek parted thick golden, green, and yellow brush. A range of mountains loomed in the distance. Sloping hills, nearer the train, intruded upon a valley in which scattered houses appeared intermittently, among a few trees.

The train followed a curve in the track, appearing to rush toward the base of a towering mountain ahead of them. Spots of greenery along the edge of the creek, which tenaciously followed the railroad track, suggested a breath of life among the otherwise brown and amber vegetation.

When Badger finished the article, Bane handed him the newspaper he'd exchanged with Luke earlier.

Badger scowled but said nothing as he started to peruse the piece.

Outside, the scenery continued to rush past, almost blending together.

When Badger finished the second article, he yawned. "Damn, but reporters have a long-winded way of presenting even the simplest of facts."

"According to the article I read," Bane recalled, "William Boyd, a stagecoach driver down Genoa way, brought in fugitive Ty Carver a day after the break,

Carver having been captured by the local sheriff." He looked at Badger. "What's that tell us?"

Suppressing another yawn, Badger considered the question. "The sheriff had other business to tend to?"

Bane nodded. "That's true, but what's it tell us about the *fugitive*?"

"He was trying to pass himself off as a passenger?"

"I didn't see that in the article," Luke told Badger.

"I was extrapolating."

Luke gave a low whistle. "Where'd you come by *that* jawbreaker?"

"Heard Judge Hawthorne say it one time. I asked the schoolmarm what it meant. Hell, *Lucille* had to look it up in that six-pound dictionary she keeps on her desk."

"That's our Badger," Bane said. "Always trying to improve his mind."

"What did *you* extrapolate from the article, Luke?" Badger asked.

"Simple: Carver headed southwest after the prison break."

"How do you figure?"

"Simple: Genoa's southwest of Carson City."

"Why did the sheriff have the stagecoach driver haul his prisoner in, then, instead of bringing him in himself?"

"If you'd read the article carefully, you wouldn't have to ask; you'd know," Bane said. "The sheriff was with his wife, in a buggy, at the time he arrested Carver. He was going to head after the other two fugitives he'd spotted near the scene of Carver's arrest, but he first had to drive his wife home and get his horse."

"Lots of robberies following the escape," Badger noted, "according to the Carson *Register*, that is."

"Well, he remembered the title of the *newspaper*, anyway," Luke remarked to Bane. "That's a start."

"That it is," Bane agreed.

Grinning at Badger, Luke asked, "Remember any of the article's particulars?"

"I *do* recall something about a fugitive by the name of Pete Mickle. Stopped by the toll house on the Lake Bigler Road, two miles outside Carson City before continuing to Mrs. Kennedy's place. He was wearing a long black overcoat and duck pants, as I recollect, and said he'd been robbed of six horses and all his provisions. Claimed to be on his way to see the Rev. Mr. Howard, but never called on him. Later that evening, some men went to find him, but couldn't. Reporter suspects Mickle went to town, instead." Badger paused, looking at Luke. "That the way *you* remember it?"

Luke looked surprised and a little abashed. "Uh, yes."

"Right."

"I have to admit, Badger," Bane remarked. "You have a good memory when you put it to use."

"All I needed was a little rest, Bane, but that's not all I remember," Badger declared, "not by a long shot." For the next few minutes, he regaled his fellow lawmen with recitations of portions of the report that dealt with several other fugitives who'd been seen and pursued by various lawmen, although, so far, without success.

"We just passed Clark's Camp, which puts us about an hour east of Reno," Bane observed.

After the train's journey parallel to the Humboldt River, through or past Moleen, Carlin, Palisade, Beowawe, Shoshone, Battle Mountain, Winnemucca, and more than a dozen other towns, as well as Humboldt Lake, they couldn't reach their destination quickly enough for Badger.

"Great! I've had about all I can stand of being cramped up inside this rolling torture chamber," Badger said.

"You'll change your mind soon enough once we're back on our horses," Luke predicted.

"I guess you plan to ride out to the prison this afternoon, late as it is?" Badger asked Bane.

"Nope. I've seen, first hand, how a little rest can rejuvenate you. We'll get rooms for the night and head to the State Prison tomorrow morning, when you're bright-eyed and bushy-tailed."

Chapter 28

Shaking Hands with the Devil

"We are our own devils; we drive ourselves out of our Edens."
— Wolfgang Goethe (1749-1832)

Near Genoa, Nevada

"You shouldn't have shot that woman," Zach Storm said.

"I hope I didn't violate one of your ethical principles," Spencer Rowelings replied.

"As a matter of fact, you did."

"I see."

His short reply, coldly and matter-of-factly stated, was more than a little disquieting, Storm thought. He'd heard such a tone before, by hard, unprincipled men like Rowelings. In his own experience, such clipped responses, spoken in such an emotionless manner, indicated barely controlled anger that was capable, with little further provocation, of erupting into a mindless, dangerous rage.

Nevertheless, Storm persisted. "More than that, though, it was the reckless kind of spur-of-the-moment action that could bring the law down on us with the force of an avalanche. Men—*normal* men, I mean—don't cotton to a man's shooting a woman under any circumstance except maybe self-defense."

"You mean that my shooting her was impractical?"

"To say the least."

"I'll need a lieutenant," Rowelings said, as if the idea had just occurred to him.

"I'm not much of a follower."

"Maybe not, but you'll do."

Storm thought about the proposal. Rowelings hadn't meant it as such, of course. Rowelings had meant it as a command; his statement had been an edict, not an invitation.

But Rowelings also had his gun. Storm had handed it to him when Rowelings had demanded it. Storm hadn't wanted to cross him, knowing that to do so would be to risk death, if not then, sooner or later. Men like Rowelings didn't like to be crossed, and they believed in vengeance. Such a refusal on Storm's part wouldn't have been forgiven or forgotten; it would be punished, and punished severely. For men like Rowelings, everything was literally a matter of life and death. If the potential reward was judged to outweigh the risk, they were willing, at any and every moment, to die. Most other men weren't. Storm knew that he sure as hell wasn't. That's what gave Rowelings and men like him them the edge.

"I guess that'll do—for now," Storm said.

Rowelings drew rein. Like his own steed, the horses he was leading stopped as well.

Storm halted his horse beside the other man's mount.

Reaching across the space between them, Rowelings held out his hand.

Storm grasped it, and the men shook. Feeling a chill run through him, Storm thought, It's like shaking hands with the devil himself.

They nudged their horses' flanks, and they and the horses resumed their walk.

"You aren't worried that the discovery of the dead woman will awaken the desire for vengeance in the mind of her kin and their friends? You're not bothered by the thought that her death will provoke the local sheriff to organize a posse against us?"

"Zach, the local sheriff—and, unless I miss my guess, the sheriffs and police chiefs of several towns and counties—are *already* on the lookout for us."

"And that doesn't trouble you?"

"Of course it does, but I'm consoled, in part, by the fact that a good many others also escaped from State Prison with us. Any of them could have shot the woman. Besides, there are many trails to track besides our own and we're not staying put, not here, anyway. You had in mind a better place to sell the moonshine, right?"

"But I thought you wanted to distill and sell moonshine to the local—"

"I do, Zach; I just don't want to make it here or sell it to the *local* locals. Now that you and I have clothes and horses and Jackson and Baker soon will, we don't need to—and shouldn't—stay around here. You said you have the perfect place in mind. Where's that?"

Storm told him.

"Damn! That *is* perfect, Zach! I thought about your idea of buying equipment and supplies along the way, and that's smart thinking. I believe a slight change will make it even better." Rowelings explained what he had in mind.

Storm nodded. "That *is* better," he agreed, "as long as the man can be trusted."

"He can; I've worked with him before."

"What's to prevent the law from following us?"

"I have a plan for that, too, Zach. First, though, I need to ride to Genoa."

"You think that's wise, after killing the rancher's wife?"

"It's likely to be a while before anyone knows she was killed, and there's no reason for anyone to think I did it."

"None except that you're a fugitive who escaped from the State Prison."

"Newspapers have likely printed the story, but I doubt that they've received any photographs of us yet. I have a week's growth of beard, a rancher's clothes, and a pair of spectacles—the rancher's wife was good enough to contribute them, after I killed her. I should be able to slip into town, mail my letter, and return to our camp without being arrested, shot, or killed, and it is a letter of pressing importance. Otherwise, I wouldn't risk it."

"Want to share the contents of your letter?"

"Normally, I would not, but, seeing as how you're my lieutenant now, I will—but don't tell the others anything about it. Subordinates shouldn't know anything more than what they need to know at any moment.

"I'm going to instruct a friend to purchase the supplies and equipment we need, one or two at a time, in different towns along the way, on his trip to our destination, which I'll reveal to him later. I'll need you to jot down the essentials. List them under separate headings of 'supplies' and 'equipment.'"

"Jot them down with what?"

Rowelings took a pencil and a notebook from his pocket. "Always travel with the essentials, Zach," he advised.

After listing the items, Storm handed the notebook and pencil back to Rowelings.

"Wait here for me, back in that hollow, among the trees. It shouldn't take me more than an hour or so ride into town, mail the letter, and return."

"All right. By the way, what should I call you, as your lieutenant, I mean? 'Spencer'? 'Mr. Rowelings'?"

"I like 'Spence.' As my lieutenant, you can call me that. The others can call me 'mister.'"

"Whatever you say, Spence."

Rowelings grinned. "We're going to have a profitable partnership, Zach."

* * *

An hour later, Rowelings returned.

He seemed satisfied, Storm thought. "How'd it go?" he asked.

"Fine, Zach, but, I have to admit, it was stressful, wondering whether I'd be spotted and have to shoot it out with the sheriff or one of his deputies or be captured and sent back to prison. Of course, if I'd been identified as a fugitive, I might also have been killed, which, considering the possibility of being captured and sent back to Carson City, might have been for the best, since the gallows is waiting for me there. But all went well. I sent the letter and lived to tell about it."

Storm nodded. "That's a relief," he said, fairly certain that it was—for Rowelings, at least.

"Let's head back to camp."

Chapter 29

Marked Locations

"It is difficult to free fools from the chains they revere."
— Voltaire (1694-1178)

State Prison, Carson City, Nevada

"How'd you like to call this place your home away from home, Badger?" Luke asked as they followed Bane into the yard of the State Prison.

"I think it would fit you better," Badger declared.

"But you don't deny it would suit you, too?"

"Maybe I'd live here as a guard. That way, I could make sure you didn't get out of line or escape."

Bane was aware of his deputies' repartee, such as it was, but he was focused on the signs of the intense gunfight that had occurred here, only a week ago. The yard was still stamped by the soles of the prisoners and the guards and Carson City's citizens who'd responded to the alarm bell announcing the prison break. The footprints were deep, suggesting the intensity of the men's movements during the skirmish; several marked locations at which men had skidded or fallen. By the look of things, the battle had lasted more than a few minutes and had been violent in the extreme.

There was also a lot of blood; it seemed everywhere—on the main gateway, the inner walkway, the prison's porch, steps and stairways, window and door sills, and walls. The shootout had taken place throughout the confines of the prison's yard and among the buildings within them. Men had been wounded; several had died. More had escaped.

The sight of the struggle strengthened Bane's resolve to return the perpetrators of the prison break to justice, by any and all means necessary.

The sight of the blood and, yes, the gore, of the battle had silenced his deputies, who'd realized, if belatedly, that such a scene as this was no place for frivolity.

A lone figure approached across the yard, raising dust from the ground with every step, just as Bane and his deputies did. He was a tall man, imposing both in height and in bearing. Bearded and mustachioed and wearing a dark suit, a white shirt, and a black bow tie, the authoritative man with unruly curly hair and a scruffy beard and mustache hailed the lawmen. "Welcome to the State Prison, gentlemen."

His salutation seemed to call for a response, so Bane called back, "Thanks."

The men met halfway across the yard, and Bane and the prison official shook hands before their host extended the same courtesy to Badger and Luke, introducing himself as Lieutenant Governor and Warden Franklin Dawes.

Bane identified himself before introducing his deputies.

"Governor Cooper advised me that you'd be visiting. I am at your disposal, gentlemen."

"We'd like to interview the officials, prisoners, and the civilian, if possible, who participated in the attempt to suppress the prison break," Bane said. "We'd like to piece together what each man saw, heard, and thought about what happened."

The warden's face remained impassive, it seemed to Bane, but he stiffened a bit and nodded a mite curtly, as though he wasn't any too sure what to make of the marshal's intentions. "I'll assemble the men here, at the prison. To talk to anyone in town, you'd best set that up with Sheriff Stanley."

Bane nodded. "Will do."

"Where would you like to, uh, interview the men?"

"Right here's fine," Bane said.

"Give me a few minutes to round them up, and I'll send a group of them out to meet with you. When you're done with them, I'll send another group."

"That's fine, sir." As the warden retraced his steps, Bane told his deputies, "You heard the man. We have a few minutes; let's look around."

Chapter 30

Second Thoughts

"It is often said that second thoughts are best. So they are in matters of judgment but not in matters of conscience."
— John Henry Newman (1801-1890)

South of Carson City, Nevada

On horseback, they now traveled an additional mile per hour or more, depending on the terrain. The first day after their escape from the State Prison, Spencer Rowelings, Zach Storm, Russ Jackson, and James Baker had hiked for eleven hours straight, refreshed after having made camp between Glenbrook and Genoa on the night of the prison break. They'd stopped only once, when Rowelings and Storm had visited the house in the hills where Rowelings had murdered the woman just to steal her man's clothes and the four horses in the barn.

It was still hard for Storm to believe that Rowelings had killed a woman. Even in the West, or especially in the West, where women were scarce, such a crime was against everything a man stood for. Even among outlaws, killing a woman was a contemptible act, one that could get the man who did it killed outright. If such a killer escaped a bullet or a lynch mob's noose, he'd almost certainly be sentenced to be hanged.

Despite the taboo, Rowelings had not hesitated to murder the woman. His act put Storm, Jackson, and Baker as much at risk as it put Rowelings himself. The woman's kin, should they catch up with them, would as soon kill anyone associated with Rowelings as they would Rowelings himself. By associating with Rowelings, the others had brought death and destruction down upon themselves the same as if they had shot the woman themselves.

Storm had been sentenced to prison for burglary. He'd fallen asleep while smoking a cigar in bed after coming home, drunk, in the wee hours of the morning, to the Widow Dennison's house, where he'd been renting a room, and burned the house down. Fortunately, Mrs. Dennison and he had escaped before the walls and ceilings collapsed, but, because of his own damn recklessness, both the widow and he were homeless.

The guilt at having destroyed the home of a woman who'd treated him like her own son, rather than a boarder, had nearly driven Storm insane. Fortunately, she had family in San Francisco. Storm himself was an orphan. He'd had to fend for himself, a responsibility he'd never practiced well for long.

He'd shifted about, camping here and there, with nothing to his name but the clothes he on his back, which, bye and bye, had worn thin. As often as not, he'd gone hungry. A few times, he'd considered ending it all. He'd talked a barkeep into buying moonshine, set up a still with money he'd earned cleaning stables, and made enough money to buy some decent clothes and move from the stable's hayloft, where he'd been allowed to sleep, into a hotel room.

When he'd returned, one morning, to his still, he'd found it destroyed. The barkeep had ordered a good amount of hooch, but, with no way to ferment the stuff, he'd have had to refund the barman's money, which he no longer had. Burglarizing his employer, the stable owner, had been his solution to the problem, one that had earned him a five-year stretch in the State Prison.

He'd served three-and-a-half years when the break occurred. Without thought, he'd joined the escapees, and, now, here he was, with a man who'd been scheduled to hang for robbing a stagecoach and killing everybody on board, including a woman, and who had now killed *another* woman as well.

Prison wasn't easy, but he'd only had a year-and-a-half to go before, without thinking the matter through, he'd yielded to impulse, as he had done so many times before, and had acted foolishly, heedless of the consequences of his behavior, and stormed out of prison with the other criminals. He'd be hunted down and returned, to serve a longer term, perhaps another five or ten years, or be killed.

Associating with hardened men like Rowelings had already involved him in a far worse crime than making moonshine, causing a fire that had burned down the house of a woman who'd nurtured and cared for him as though he were one of her own, or burglarizing a man who'd befriended him, given him a place to lay his head, and paid him for the work he performed on his behalf.

No doubt, if he stayed on, as Rowelings's lieutenant, he'd become a participant in acts equally barbarous or worse, if there *was* a crime worse than murdering a woman. Even if he hadn't been the one to shoot her, he'd been with the man who had, which, Rowelings was fairly sure, made him an accessory to the commission of the crime. It was amazing how far he'd fallen in only a few days, amazing but predictable.

Was there any way back?

He wouldn't escape further punishment; he knew that. But would he ever get another chance—a third chance—at turning his life around, at becoming somebody?

Maybe, but, certainly, there were no guarantees.

Now was a helluva time to have second thoughts, Storm told himself. Hell, if he'd think things through *before* he acted, there'd be no need for second thoughts. The problem was he never had and probably never would consider the consequences of his actions until he'd done something stupid.

For now, he had to act as Rowelings's second-in-command or, rather, as the second-in-command to both Rowelings and his partner, whoever that turned out to be.

Meanwhile, he traveled along, side by side, with the killer who'd taken command of him, Jackson, and Baker, confederates he'd use for his own dark purposes, whatever they were.

"When we get back to camp, see to it that the others each get a set of clothes and a horse. Then, we ride."

Chapter 31

Stymied

"I'm telling you that India is *that* way; now, set my course."
— Christopher Columbus (1451-1506)

State Prison, Carson City, Nevada

"Start from the beginning. What did *you* see? What do *you* know?" Bane prompted the prisoner.

"I wasn't there from the beginning," Howard Keel said. "I was in the infirmary.

"Nothing serious, I hope?"

"Nah. Just an upset stomach, the doc said." He grinned. "Probably from eating what, in this place, passes for food."

Bane smiled. In soliciting information from prisoners, he'd learned that it sometimes paid to express concern for their health and welfare, give them a little leeway, laugh at their jokes. Other times, more intimidating methods of interrogation played better. Interviewing a prisoner was, for him, at least, based half on intuition, half on instinct. "Tell me what you *did* see."

"What's in it for me?"

"Maybe I can work something out. Depends on how forthcoming you are and on how much you have to offer pans out."

"When I left the infirmary, shackled to Kent McCay—"

"One of the guards?"

Keel nodded. "One of the better screws. Treats a convict like a man, instead of a devil."

"Go ahead."

"When I left the infirmary, shackled to Kent McCay, whatever had happened inside the prison walls themselves had already taken place. I *did* see a bit of the scuffle on my way back to my cell, though; there were lots of dust and gun smoke in the yard, a few guards, and maybe thirty prisoners throwing down."

"Nothing in particular, then?"

"Didn't see anything particular, but I *heard* something."

Bane waited.

"A stage robber sent here to be hanged said to three men with him, 'north.'"

"In what context?"

The word seemed to stymie Keel.

"The robber mentioned directions, but in relation to what else?"

"I assumed he meant the direction of their intended travel."

"He didn't say 'northeast' or 'north, then east'?"

"Nope. Just said 'north.'"

"Anything further?"

"No—well, the other men, the ones with him—seemed surprised to hear him tell them 'north.'"

"Surprised? How?"

Keel shrugged. "Like maybe they thought he was loco."

"Why would they think that?"

"My guess is that there's nothing much north of Washoe County but hills and mountains. North would be a mighty rugged trip and one mostly without sources of food or water."

"There's Pyramid Lake," Badger pointed out, "and Quinn River, farther north."

"Pyramid Lake's not far from five or six towns, and Quinn River is a far piece from anyplace else but wilderness."

"Anything else?" Bane asked.

"Just one thing."

"What's that?"

"What do *I* get out of this?"

"My mention to the governor of your cooperation."

Keel scoffed. "That's it? That's all?"

"The word of a U. S. marshal to the governor of this state may be worth a whole helluva lot more than you reckon—or deserve," Bane replied.

"What do you think?" Luke asked, after the guard hustled Keel away.

"Seems unlikely anybody would go north," Badger ventured.

"It does," Bane concurred, "but, at this point, I'd say we ought to keep an open mind until we hear what the rest of the prisoners say and, more to the point, what the guards report."

A few minutes, the same guard hauled another prisoner from the group before Bane and his deputies.

"Roland Tidwell, at your service, marshal," the guard introduced the man.

"Start from the beginning. What did *you* see? What do *you* know?" Bane prompted the prisoner.

* * *

By the end of the day, with Bane supervising when he wasn't asking questions himself, he and his deputies had interviewed a dozen more prisoners.

The guard asked Bane whether he wanted to interrogate anyone else.

"I think we're finished for today."

The guard nodded. "I'll return them to their cells."

"Need any help?"

"No, thanks, marshal. The ones still in custody had a chance to escape, just like the ones who ran. They chose to stay. A few are trustees; the rest figure their sentences are short enough to weather and don't want time added for an escape that, more than likely, will fail when, sooner or later, they're recaptured."

Bane nodded. "See you in the morning, then, about eight o'clock?"

"See you then, marshal, deputies."

* * *

One of the guards volunteered to stay at the Warm Springs Hotel in Carson City in order to make his quarters in the State Prison's upper story available to Bane and his deputies. Although not luxurious, the lodgings were better than Bane, Badger, or Luke had anticipated and it gave them the advantage of staying onsite, which would facilitate their questioning of other prisoners and the guards who were on duty during the prison break.

It would also allow them to compare notes concerning what they'd learned so far from the prisoners whom they, or, mostly, Bane, had already interrogated.

As might be expected, the accounts differed in some details. People seldom remember the same event entirely the same way. One witness may see something another misses or may interpret the same situation differently from the way another person who sees it does. Of course, there was always the chance, too, especially among prisoners, that one or more spectator might lie.

"What are your thoughts about Tidwell's comments?" Bane asked.

"He didn't really seem to have any information we haven't already read in the newspapers," Luke replied.

"None of his statements contradicted any of the reports, either," Badger noted.

"Agree. I think we can dispense with his account. It's accurate enough, even though it doesn't shed any additional light on the prison break."

"What about Rogers's statements?" Bane asked.

Darren Rogers, a murderer, had told them that he remembered seeing only two Henry rifles among the prisoners.

"Some newspaper accounts report four," Luke said.

"True, but maybe two's all that Rogers himself actually saw. Two's plenty bad, though," Bane declared. "Colonel Mosby, of the Confederacy, called it 'that damned Yankee rifle that can be loaded on Sunday and fired all week.'"

"Surprised me that the prison armory was stocked with them, though, instead of Winchesters," Badger said.

"Would have surprised me, too," Bane stated, "had the armory not also had three-thousand of the rifle's cartridges on hand. I doubt the guards have had many, if any, occasions to actually use the rifles. They're kept on hand in case there's a prison break like the one that took place a few days ago, but the swift way that the prisoners overpowered the warden and the guards prevented anyone but the prisoners themselves from gaining the opportunity of getting their hands on one."

"You think the way the break went off is suspicious?" Luke asked.

"I think that the warden will have a lot to answer for, but no one, including Governor Cooper, has said that there was any malfeasance. Security wasn't as tight as it should have been. The prisoners were given too much time to mingle. An inadequate number of guards seems to have been on hand. Having civilians, especially the warden's family, living on the prison grounds is probably a mistake. It's debatable whether the lieutenant governor should serve in both that capacity and as the State Prison's warden. The fact is, though, that the break occurred and nearly thirty prisoners escaped, including, among them, some of the worst sort. That's the situation that we have to deal with."

"I'd say that sums up the state of affairs quite well," Luke declared.

"What about Eugene Sykes's statement? Believable?" Bane asked.

"That the majority of the prisoners went south or southeast?" Badger inquired.

Bane nodded.

"Sounds right to me."

"Me, too," Luke agreed.

"I think so, too. Why would anyone travel west or north? West is nothing but tough, rugged terrain and high elevations; north, desert and scarce food and water," Badger stated.

"Why would Keel insist that he heard Rowelings tell the others with him they'd go north?" Bane asked.

Luke shrugged. "He lied."

"Maybe, but why?"

"Hell, Bane: he's a criminal," Badger pointed out. "Criminals lie."

"Usually, they have a reason, though," Bane observed. "What if Keel lied to mislead us? He made it clear to us that he was talking about Rowelings. At the same time, he suggested that he didn't know Rowelings—called him 'a stage robber sent here to be hanged.' Keel also insisted that Rowelings had been very clear in naming north as his intended direction of travel, insisting that Rowelings had said neither 'northeast' nor 'north' and then 'east,' but only 'north.' He insisted, further, that Rowelings's statement had made the men with him look at him as if he were 'loco.' He went well out of his way to sell us on the idea that Rowelings did, in fact, say that he and the men with him should go in no other direction but north."

"You're right, Bane," Luke said. "Keel definitely seemed to have been trying to sell us on the idea—the fact, as it were—that Rowelings headed north."

Badger nodded. "You've convinced me, too, Bane."

"Rowelings wanted *us* to go north, so we'd have been chasing nothing more than a ghost," Bane said.

"But why would Keel want to send us on a wild goose chase? I mean, what would be in it for him?" Luke asked.

"Maybe Rowelings promised him some of the gold or silver he stole from that stagecoach he robbed," Bane suggested.

"Why would he trust Rowelings to honor his word?" Badger inquired.

"Perhaps he didn't, not entirely, but maybe Keel figured, what did he have to lose?" Bane speculated. "However slight the prospect of Rowelings actually cutting him in on the gold or silver might be, if Rowelings *did* come through, Keel would have gained plenty. Unfortunately for Keel, if we're right, and I have little doubt but that we are, Keel's going to find out he has *plenty* to lose, after all: lying to federal lawmen is a felony that's worth up to five years in prison."

Chapter 32

Tension

"Those who voluntarily put power into the hands of a tyrant . . . must not wonder if it be at last turned against themselves."
— Aesop (c. 620–564 BC)

East and South of Carson City, Nevada, to Pine Grove, Nevada

After Russ Jackson and James Baker had helped themselves to the horses that Spencer Rowelings had stolen, along with the clothes he'd taken from the clothesline after killing the woman he'd assumed was the rancher's wife, Rowelings informed them of his plans—or some of them. He'd learned long ago to tell others only as much as they needed to act on his immediate intentions and to fill them in, little by little, as incidents and situations demanded. That way, should any of them be captured, they'd be able to impart only a little information to their captors.

"We're continuing east, then south," he said. "Now that we have horses, we'll make better time, and, now that we have plain clothes, we should escape attention. By now, the law's probably printed and distributed some wanted posters, and newspapers have no doubt published reports on the prison break, maybe even a list of the names of the fugitives, including our own. That shouldn't be a problem, though, as long as we avoid camps, towns, and attention."

"Shooting that woman will most likely draw attention, and plenty of it," Baker observed.

"I believe it will," Rowelings agreed. "By then, though, we should be well on our way."

"Our way to where?" Baker asked.

"You'll know when we get there," Rowelings replied. "Meanwhile, you'll just follow my lead."

"Who put you in charge of us?"

"I did. Want to take issue with that?"

"Where'd you get a holster?" Baker blurted.

"Came with the gun. Now, you plan to put me out of my misery or not?"

Baker looked to the others, but neither Storm nor Jackson indicated they'd back him. Hesitating, he considered the man who'd called him out. He knew nothing about Rowelings, other than the fact that he'd been condemned to hang for robbing a stage and killing six people, one of them a woman.

Baker glanced at the stagecoach robber. Rowelings was tense, but his demeanor—and the look in his eye—showed that the tension wasn't emotional, but physical. It was the same tension in the muscles of a cougar about to spring, the same tension in the stance of a gunfighter who was about to dispatch his opponent to hell.

There was no use dying over his objection that Rowelings should take charge of him and the others, Baker decided. "As far as I'm concerned, you're calling the shots," he said.

"Maybe you're not the complete fool I took you for, James."

* * *

After Genoa, Rowelings had led his gang east, entering the north end of the valley flanked by the Pine Nut Range to their west and the Walker River Range to their east. Jackson was somewhat familiar with the region, Rowelings much less so. As they followed the Big Walker River south, he took note that there were no places worthy of being called towns. The small settlement named for the river was a case in point. There was no way in hell, or even in Nevada, that such a place constituted a town.

Calling some of the others a town was a stretch, too. Wellington, Pine Grove, Cambridge, Washington, and Sweetwater barely merited such a distinction. Although it seemed improbable, one of them might have the only thing that Rowelings was interested in at the moment.

"Any of you know whether any of the towns we're headed toward has a telegraph office?" he asked his men. It was unlikely, he thought. Most of them had been in prison for the past five years or more. Still, it didn't hurt to ask.

"Maybe Pine Grove," Jackson said.

"Why Pine Grove?"

"It boomed a ways back—during the late 1860s, if I'm remembering correctly. Had a newspaper and a post office, a couple of steam-powered stamp mills. Within ten years, the population went from two-hundred to six-hundred and the town had five saloons, three hotels, several blacksmiths shops, a school, a livery stable, two doctors' offices, a dance hall, a barber shop and, I believe, a telegraph office. Pine Grove was also a supply center for the region. The gold mines thereabouts are still in operation."

"That does sound like a likely prospect," Rowelings said. "We'll make camp a few miles outside town, and I'll check it out."

"You think that's safe?" Baker asked.

This time, Rowelings decided not to lambaste the bastard. While he didn't like to be challenged or second-guessed, especially by the likes of James Baker, he couldn't find much fault with a man, even one like him, who was cautious. "I still don't think we have much chance of arousing suspicion. There are a lot of escapees besides us, after all, and we've been careful—more careful than most. We've kept our distance from settlements, except for my trip into Genoa, which is many miles behind us now. With good reason, Russ thinks there may be a telegraph office in Pine Grove, and I need to send a telegram. I think it's worth taking a chance."

* * *

Jackson was right! The telegraph office was still in business, just as he'd thought.

With satisfaction, Rowelings noticed that his presence in town hadn't attracted attention beyond an occasional pedestrian's passing glance. Most of them were women, some with a child or two in tow. Most likely, the ladies were simply being cautious. As adults, they were aware of potential dangers, such as a spirited horse in the street, a drunk stumbling along the walk, or a stray dog; their brood usually wasn't. By staying alert, mothers could prevent a child from stepping into a horse's path, dodge an intoxicated man, or stay the hand of a boy or girl who wanted to pet an unfriendly, possibly diseased dog. None of them had given him a second look.

His beard and the glasses of the woman he'd killed for her husband's clothes, the ranch's horses, and the couple's money comprised a disguise that was perhaps unnecessary in a town like Pine Grove, especially when newspapers or wanted posters may or may not have displayed his likeness, but a man could never be too sure, especially when he was a recent escapee from Nevada's State Prison.

At his destination, Rowelings dismounted and tied his reins to the hitching post.

Entering the telegraph office, he walked to the counter.

"Help you, mister?"

"Want to send a telegram."

"To?"

"Matthew Lewis."

"Town?"

"Luning."

"From?"

"Peter Malcomb."

"Message?"

"Meet me at The Point."

"The Point?"

"That's right."

"The Point *where*?"

"He'll know," Rowelings said. "We grew up not five miles from there."

The operator shrugged. "Just wanted to make sure. That'll be two dollars."

Rowelings paid him the exact amount quoted. Anything more could attract attention.

"Thanks, Mr. Malcomb."

Rowelings nodded.

The telegram to "Matthew Lewis" would arrive almost instantly, even though Matthew Lewis didn't exist—well, not the Matthew Lewis whom Rowelings had invented, leastways. Once its recipient read the message, he'd head for "The Point." Soon after his arrival, Rowelings and the rest of his gang, as he now thought of Storm, Jackson, and Baker—and "Lewis," of course—could start making moonshine.

There were half a dozen things Rowelings would like to do while he was in town: get a shave and a haircut, soak in a tub of hot water, have a decent meal, buy some more fitting clothes, sip a beer or two in a local saloon, bed a beautiful woman. But indulging in any of them could cost him his freedom. A man on the run has to be mindful of everywhere he goes and everything he does.

A man on the run should also have an established network of confederates, experts and otherwise, who, for a considerable price, were willing to assist in enterprises upon which lawmen, judges, and society in general tended to frown. Rowelings employed several such men, "Matthew Lewis" included, whose silence and skills were available to him on demand, without notice, at whatever meeting place he designated in the code that he employed at such times.

"The Point" was a code for one such place, but its location, at present, was known only to Rowelings and Lewis. Once anyone else became privy to its position, Rowelings would discard it in favor of a new site that would be known only to whichever of his confederates he chose to reveal it, always on a necessary basis only, of course.

Such foresight was one of the many qualities that set him apart from common outlaws and one of the many reasons he had always succeeded—until he'd killed the woman in his latest stagecoach robbery. That had been a mistake, and a costly one. It had outraged the few men who had the grit and skill needed to bring a man, especially a man like him, to justice.

By luck, he'd avoided hanging, but good fortune wouldn't spare him from the posses, lawmen, soldiers, and judges who'd taken an interest in recapturing or killing the hardened criminals who'd escaped from the State Prison.

Only his own intelligence, courage, farsightedness, and ability to formulate strategies could save him now.

Leaving Pine Grove, Rowelings smiled. The sheriffs and deputies who hunted him were crafty, valiant men, too, and skilled with guns, but, unlike them, he was a rare breed. As a man without a conscience, he had a tremendous advantage over his enemies, no matter which side of the law they were on.

* * *

Over the next few days, they made good time through the more accommodating terrain. By following the river as it meandered first west, then south, and finally southeast, they would continue to expedite their journey, even as they enjoyed the benefits of having fresh water and a fair supply of food.

Their travel wouldn't be without risk. Probably several posses were hunting the prison's fugitives by now and, most likely, rewards for their capture had been circulated. The break had resulted in the escape of quite a few prisoners; it would attract the attention of Nevada's governor and quite a few lawmen, both in Nevada and in California. It would also get the attention of private citizens bold enough to join the pursuit—or pursuits—of the fugitives.

Fortunately, the number of escapees and the fact that they'd divided into groups and taken two or three directions in their flight favored all of them. It would take several posses to return the fugitives to justice. With luck—and the plan that Storm had cooked up and his own, of course, which he hadn't shared with anyone else, including Storm—he and his men could lay low for quite some time while they took in a small fortune that would serve them well when they disbanded.

Yessir, they weren't out of the woods yet, but they sure as hell were making progress toward that end.

Chapter 33

Men, Not Just Criminals

"If all men were just there would be no need of valor."
— Agesilaus II (c. 444 BC-460 BC)

State Prison, Carson City, Nevada

The warden had the guards who'd attempted to stop the prison break standing by for questioning at eight o'clock the next morning, when Bane, Badger, and Luke entered the prison walls. As Bane suspected, their answers to his and his deputies' questions matched the newspapers' accounts of the prison break. After all, they themselves were one of the sources the reporters had used.

Even so, Bane had found, eyewitnesses and participants in actions, especially those that unfolded in rapid succession and were fraught with violence and confusion, were apt to include differences, if not contradictions. One person's point of view, after all, was just that: one person's point of view. Nobody could see everything, and even the sight of the incidents that one did witness firsthand, either as a participant or an observer, was affected by not only what was actually seen or heard, but also by how it was seen or heard and by the context in which it was witnessed. Observations and accounts were affected by the details to which someone paid attention; distortions, intentional or otherwise; exaggerations; confusions about the chronology of events; faulty memory; misinterpretations;

biases; and other personal matters that could color what was seen or heard—or, in some cases, what a witness *thought* that he or she had seen or heard.

Quinton Collins, the Captain of the Guard, wasn't any help. He'd been knocked out and locked in a cell just a minute or two after he'd ordered the convicts to return to their cells.

G. N. Ives, the guard whom the prisoners had spared due to his valor in the battle that occurred in the prison yard, was a wealth of information, but he didn't shed any new light on the break. The newspapers had been thorough in their reports of his heroism in standing against the nearly thirty escapees.

Likewise, Jesse Norton, having been knocked unconscious after felling one of the prisoners, offered no additional information besides that which the reporters had presented.

Bane thanked the guards for their time and for their courage in fighting against tremendous odds. As Ives started to leave with the rest of them, Bane called his name.

"Yes, Marshal?"

"I'd like to speak to the prisoner who used a chair to defend the warden—"

"Bob Beecham, that would be," Ives said. "He's one who escaped."

Bane frowned. He hadn't expected to hear that. Although serving a life sentence, Beecham had been a trustee who'd served as a trusted factotum to the warden's family. He'd been present all day, every day, in their quarters, with the lieutenant governor's wife, daughter, and occasional guests. He'd never defied or threatened any of them. The fact that he'd joined the escape after working in such a position of trust and had risked his own life to rescue the warden when Dawes was attacked was hard to believe. "I'd also like to speak to Curt Hardesty and the prisoner called 'Frenchie.'"

"Marcel Gagnon," Ives said.

"Yes, thank you. I hadn't known his name."

"Anyone else, Marshal?"

"Not at present."

"Shouldn't be more than a couple minutes."

"This morning's been mostly a waste of time, I'd say," Luke remarked.

"Definitely," Badger agreed.

"Mostly, but not entirely—that is, if I get the second thing I came for."

Badger frowned. "We're here for more than corroborative statements and what we'd hope would be additional information about the break and the men who escaped?"

Bane nodded.

"Such as?"

"You'll see soon enough, Badger."

Ives was escorting two men across the yard, a burly, big fellow with strawberry-blond hair and a short, slender mustachioed dude with a debonair manner. Bane smiled at the latter, who looked as though he should be wearing a top hat, a formal tailcoat with a matching double-breasted evening waistcoat, a white bow tie, and spats. Hell, he ought to be carrying a cane, too.

Ives nodded at the big man. "Hurley." Then, he indicated the smaller man. "Gagnon."

Bane spoke first to Hurley. "Curt, I heard you saved the Captain of the Guard's life by dragging him into a cell when the prison break commenced."

Hurley nodded. "I reckon that's so, Marshal."

"Why'd you do it?"

The question seemed to catch Hurley off guard. He shrugged, "Hell, I don't know, other than that Collins always treated me—all of us—like we were men, not just criminals. He didn't deserve to be killed."

"Why didn't you leave with the rest of the prisoners when they made their break?"

"I robbed a bank. I was sentenced to ten years in the State Prison. I've served four of them. Got what I deserved. It was a fair sentence. I'll do the rest of my time. When I get out, I'll get a job, God willing."

"You a religious man?"

"One of the only books we have on hand is the Good Book, Marshal. I've read it through three times, and, every time, it convicts me of the sin—the *sins*—I've committed and offers me a way to redeem myself, my soul. I'm a different man today than I was four years ago."

Bane thought of Pete Sullivan, his secretary's brother. Indirectly, his actions as a man bent upon vengeance had killed several innocent folks. The guilt he'd felt had turned him to God as well. As a man of faith himself, Bane knew the power of the Lord. As a man of the law, he also knew sincerity when he heard it. "I'll reckon you'll do just fine."

"Do for what, Marshal?"

"Let me speak with Mr. Gagnon first. Then, I'll get back to you."

Hardesty retreated as, in answer to Bane's signal, Gagnon approached.

"Read a lot about you, Marcel," Bane said. "Any of it true?"

"Depends on what you read, Marshal."

"You fought against your fellow prisoners until you'd emptied your pistol. Then, you ran among the mob, delivering blow after blow, heedless of the other prisoners' gunfire, which damn near shredded your clothes. You also rescued the guard G. N. Ives and the warden's six-year-old daughter."

"I'd say the press was accurate in its accounts of my conduct."

"Why'd you risk your life not once or twice, but multiple times, in such a manner?"

"My dear marshal, I may be in prison, but my presence in such an environment by no means defines who I am."

"And just who are you, Marcel?"

"A scoundrel, Marshal, but a scoundrel reformed."

"What led to your reformation?"

"This penitentiary has rendered me penitent."

Bane smiled at the play on words. "How so?"

"The word 'Frenchman' is spelled as one word; it should be spelled as two: while it is true that I am French, it is true, also, that I am a man. In fact, I am a man before I am French. As Diogenes the Cynic observed, centuries before me, 'I am not an Athenian or a Greek, but a citizen of the world,' only, in my case, I am not a Parisian or a Frenchman, but a citizen of the world."

"And a philosopher, like Diogenes, it seems."

"Exactly. I have had plenty of time to reflect upon the course of action that led me here, Marshal, and it is one that I do not care to continue."

Bane nodded. "I'll reckon you'll do, too, Marcel."

"Do? For what?"

Bane asked Ives to escort Hardesty back.

When the other inmate returned, Bane announced, "I'd like you to join my deputies and me, as members of my posse."

Chapter 34

Secrets

"Three may keep a secret, if two of them are dead."
— Benjamin Franklin (1706-1790)

Rowelings's Camp, near Bodie, California

Finally, after their most recent, and most arduous, travel through rugged, steep terrain, Spencer Rowelings, Zach Storm, Russ Jackson, and James Baker paused alongside the narrow trail to look down upon Bodie, California.

Storm, Jackson, and Baker seemed to regard the sight of the town as marking the completion of a monumental task. The ride had been a tough one, involving steep ascents, but the stretches of grass and the clumps of coarse vegetation in the otherwise brown land were welcome surprises.

Rowelings felt no such sentiments. To him, Bodie was just a place to hole up while he made enough money to finance the excursion he'd planned before he'd almost lost his life on the gallows at the State Prison.

Going into town would be a risk, certainly. News of the prison break was likely to have been reported far beyond Carson City or even Nevada. The escape of twenty-nine fugitives from a state prison administered by a warden who was also Nevada's lieutenant governor, following a bloody gunfight with guards and townspeople that had left a number of them and of the prisoners dead, was an event that would likely be reported throughout the country, if not farther.

The escapees' names would be listed. Photographs of some, if not all, of the fugitives might also be printed. If they hadn't been authorized yet, rewards would almost certainly be offered at some point. With money to be made for the desperadoes' capture, sheriffs and police chiefs would be aided by posses of civilians eager to help track and capture the escapees.

But Rowelings was betting that not enough time had yet passed to accommodate all such actions. Only he and his current associates were aware of the facts that he'd stolen not only horses and clothing from the rancher's wife he'd killed, but also the woman's spectacles. Fortunately, neither his gunshot to her forehead nor her fall had broken the lenses or bent the frames.

He'd kept to himself the fact that he'd stolen the two-hundred dollars he'd found under a cushion of the sofa inside the ranch house. He could have used the money to buy the supplies and equipment Storm needed to start their moonshining business, but the man he'd enlisted through the letter he'd sent from Genoa had plenty of ready cash and knew Rowelings would reimburse him for the money he'd spend on the purchases he made on Rowelings's behalf.

"We'll make camp here," he told the other men.

Storm, Jackson, and Baker dismounted.

Chapter 35

Ready to Explode

"Nothing strengthens authority so much as silence."
— Leonardo da Vinci (1452-1519)

State Prison, Carson City, Nevada

"Ives?"

"Yes, sir?"

"I'd like to see Hardesty and Gagnon again."

The guard nodded.

While Ives crossed the yard, toward the prison building, Luke asked, "Why do you want to see them again, Bane?"

"They have sand."

"No doubt about that," Luke agreed.

"Despite their being on the wrong side of the bars, they have grit, all right," Badger concurred, "but I still don't get why you want to see them again."

Bane nodded toward the prisoners walking toward them, in front of Ives. "You will, soon enough."

When the captives and the guard rejoined the lawmen, Bane said, "Each of you are men of valor. You acquitted yourselves gallantly on the field of battle that this prison yard was just days ago. When I asked you why you had done so, your answers suggested that you regret the crimes you've committed and sought to atone for them by risking your lives to prevent an escape of other prisoners who have *not* turned aside from the violence and criminal acts of which they've been found guilty and who would, given a chance, commit additional such offenses and perhaps even worse ones."

The men looked him in the eye, another good sign, Bane thought, since a man who is lauded when he doesn't believe that he should be praised often grins, chuckles, laughs, or, at the very least, puts his head down or shuffles his feet.

"Without regard for your own safety, without heed of your own welfare, without consideration for your own lives, you stood against armed men known for their villainy and violence. Yes, many escaped, but, thanks to you, some did not. Those you prevented from escaping would certainly have perpetuated more of the same crimes as those that landed them here, stealing, robbing, burglarizing, assaulting, and murdering innocent men and women.

"For such men, the sweat and toil, the risk and worry, and the money and long years of hard work that honest folk put into ranching, farming, or running a store, a saloon, or a hotel means nothing. Such men don't care about wives and children, churches and schools, or anything else but themselves. Even the cattle, the horses, or the gold they steal means something only in the sense that such things can enrich them—as *they* count riches. Those who escaped from this prison will return to their crimes, piling up more and more tragedy and loss, without a thought or a care for their victims.

"But you know this, as well as I do. That's another reason that what you did to stop such men is an act of valor. You, who have been predators, became defenders. In doing so, you showed the true colors of the men you are today, rather than those of whom you were yesterday. That's why I want you to ride with my deputies and me, as U. S. deputy marshals, rather than as members of a posse."

That statement left not only Hardesty's and Gagnon's mouths hanging open, but made Ives gape and stare as well.

Bane turned toward the heroic guard. "And that's why I want *you* to join us, too, Ives. You've never broken the law; you've always guarded society against wolves in human form. The gallantry you displayed in resisting the prison break is heroic alongside that of any lawman, any soldier, or any hero, past or present."

"I appreciate that, Marshal, especially coming from you, a man who knows and fights what we're up against, which isn't just crime, but evil itself. Problem is, I don't think the warden will agree to let me join you, and I'm certain he won't allow these prisoners to do so, regardless of their grit."

"Normally, I'd agree with you, Ives."

"But you don't?"

"Let's just say that, in this case, I think I can convince him."

* * *

"No! Never! Not on your life!"

Lieutenant Governor Franklin Dawes, who, by dint of his office, was also the warden of the State Prison, looked ready to explode. His red, contorted face appeared to have inflated, and his mouth gaped, showing his teeth, while his nostrils flared. Even his beard and mustache seemed to bristle. Bane half-expected the man to pounce.

"But, Warden—"

"Absolutely not!"

"I'm up against four desperate, dangerous men—"

"No!"

"—one of whom killed a stagecoach driver, a shotgun messenger, and several passengers, including a woman."

"I've *told* you my decision, Marshal."

Dawes's words were measured, clipped, his voice as cold as his eyes.

"I'm not asking your permission, Warden; I'm telling you my decision."

"How *dare* you!" Dawes demanded, murder in his eye. "*I* am in charge of this prison. Now, I'm ordering you to leave. If you refuse to comply with my order, as both the warden of this prison and the lieutenant governor of this state, I will place you under arrest, and you and your deputies will spend the night in one of my prison cells."

"I was hoping it wouldn't come to this, sir," Bane said, managing, by some miracle, to keep his own voice—and demeanor—calm. Reaching into his inner coat pocket, Bane removed a folded document. "This executive order, signed by your boss, Governor Cooper, authorizes me to have, at my disposal, any equipment, materials, transportation, personnel, lodging, or other assets I require."

The warden skimmed the order. Then, he checked the signature. There was no doubt but that Joshua B. Cooper had, in fact, signed the damned thing, giving Bane *carte blanche* to do whatever the hell he pleased. Thrusting the document back at Bane, Dawes thundered, "Take them, and get out of my sight!"

Returning the order to his pocket, Bane said, "Thank you, sir."

"Wait!" Dawes ordered.

Bane turned to face the warden.

"Leave me Ives, at least. I need the man. As you said, he's an exceptional officer, a man of courage and conviction unmatched by anyone else on my staff."

Bane nodded. "I'll make do with Hardesty and Gagnon."

The warden seemed to release all his anger and frustration in a deep sigh. For the first time, Bane realized how weary the man was. The responsibility of his dual position must have weighed a lot more heavily upon him than usual since the break. Only the man's stoic demeanor had masked his intense fatigue.

"Good luck to you, Marshal."

Having realized the toll that the prison break had had on the man, Bane was reluctant to make another demand, but he wanted—he required—one thing more. "I need a copy of the photograph that was taken of Spencer Rowelings when he arrived at the prison."

The warden looked abashed. "I'm afraid none was taken."

Bane scowled. "You didn't take his photograph?" He's almost shouted the question. "That's been common practice since the 1840s."

"In Rowelings's case, there didn't seem to be any need. The man was scheduled to hang within a week, as soon as the gallows was repaired."

Controlling himself, Bane said, "I see that the repairs to the gallows *still* haven't been finished."

"They will be, soon."

"I hope so, Warden. Before long, they'll be needed to carry out Judge Hawthorne's sentence."

Once Bane reunited with his deputies, he handed Hardesty and Gagnon each a five-hundred-dollar bill.

To say that they looked astonished would have been an understatement.

"What's this for?" Hardesty managed to ask.

"Train tickets from Carson City to Excelsior, Nevada," Bane explained, "and for horses, tack, food, lodging, and any other such incidentals you may require."

Their frowns deepened.

"*Sacre bleu!*" Gagnon cried. "Did you not deputize us as part of your posse to hunt down and arrest the escaped prisoners you seek?"

"I did."

"But why?" asked Hardesty.

"Had to if I wanted to hire you."

"But why *have* you hired us, monsieur?"

"My office, back in Excelsior, is short-staffed. That's where you're needed most, to assist Deputy Stan Trefil, the temporary marshal I swore in to take charge while Badger, Luke, and I are otherwise temporarily disposed."

Hardesty and Gagnon looked stunned.

"We won't let you down, Marshal," Hardesty declared.

"I go by 'Bane,' except when politics makes it better, for the moment, for me to be 'Marshal.' Now, you'd best be going. There's a train to Elko in a couple of hours. Buy a couple of horses there and ride south, through Huntington Valley, to Excelsior. One of the hotels should have rooms. I'll telegraph Stan to let him know you're coming and will need guns and badges."

After they left, Badger said, "I didn't realize we were short-staffed, Bane."

"You just wanted to give them another chance at life, didn't you?" Luke asked.

"Sometimes a man deserves it," Bane said.

Chapter 36

Verisimilitude

"[Gestures and other pretenses are] merely corroborative detail, intended to give artistic verisimilitude to an otherwise bald and unconvincing narrative."
— G. S. Gilbert (1836-)

Rowelings's Camp, near Bodie, California

"Halt!"

The driver, drew rein.

"Identify yourself!"

"Matthew Lewis."

"State your business."

"I'm here to see Spencer."

"Spencer who?"

"Rowelings. He sent for me."

"Come ahead—*slow*—and don't try anything."

The driver slapped the reins lightly against the horses' necks, and, as they pulled the wagon forward, his own mare, her reins tied to the rear of the wagon, followed.

When the driver was within ten yards of his position, James Baker said, "That's far enough, mister. Dismount—and be slow about it."

The other man obliged, tying the team's reins to a low tree branch.

"Don't you know enough to make your presence known when you ride toward a campsite at night?" Baker demanded.

"My apologies."

What the hell kind of answer was that? Baker wondered. "What makes you think this man 'Spencer' is here?"

"He sent for me."

The man's reply matched what Rowelings had told them. Rowelings hadn't told Baker or the other members of the gang *why* he'd invited this man, Matthew Lewis, to their camp. Their leader had a disquieting way of keeping certain details to himself which, as far as Baker was concerned, made him seem to distrust them, which, in turn, made Baker distrust *him*.

It still angered him that Rowelings, a newcomer to the State Prison population and a virtual stranger to them, had appointed himself the leader of their "gang," as Rowelings had come to refer to their group.

Unfortunately, none of them, including Baker himself, had had the nerve to oppose Rowelings's proclamation. There was something about the man—something in his eyes, his demeanor, his voice—that made it clear that he was not someone to cross. And, now, Rowelings had sent for this man, another stranger, for purposes known only to himself.

"Follow me," Baker ordered.

They walked through the area, to a miner's shack among similar structures. At the door, Baker knocked. The buildings, abandoned when the gold had petered out, were now their camp.

A minute later, Rowelings opened the door, six-shooter in hand. He grinned when he saw Lewis. "*Matthew!* Come in, come in!" To Baker, he added, "Don't just stand there; get Russ to unload the wagon's supplies and equipment, and send Zach here—and close the damn door!"

Reaching inside the cabin, Baker grasped the latch and swung the door shut. Clearly, whatever conversation Rowelings intended to have with Lewis and Storm was a private one that didn't include either Jackson or himself.

* * *

Inside the mining shack, Storm said, "Selling moonshine might be harder than you seem to think, Spence."

"I'm confident that Matthew will excel at it."

"Some of it's technical," Storm added. "There could be questions, the answers to which involve knowledge and experience."

"I doubt the kind of people who'd be interested in becoming our customers are likely to give a hoot in hell about *how* the hooch is made," Rowelings argued. "Their sole concern will be the price we charge. Besides, give Matthew some credit, Zach. He's an actor, among other things—"

"I prefer 'thespian,' Spencer; you know that."

Rowelings nodded. "Matthew is a thespian. He's played all the major theaters."

"My last performance was at Ford's Theater in Washington, D. C. The critics loved me, as always."

"I don't mean any—" Storm paused, seeking a term that wouldn't be likely to offend Lewis. "I don't mean any disrespect; I'm sure you're a fine actor. It's just that, to be convincing,—"

"Oh, I'm 'convincing,' all right. I am *known* for my ability to project verisimilitude into my roles."

"I'm sure you are, Mr. Lewis. It's just that—"

"Zach. Matthew is not distilling the spirits; he's merely selling them. Just teach him what he needs to know to sell the hooch," Rowelings said.

"Write it out," Lewis instructed, just the way you'd actually say it to someone. I'll need time to learn and rehearse my lines."

* * *

An hour later, "script" in hand, Storm knocked upon the door of the shack that Rowelings had set aside for the thespian's quarters.

After perusing a couple of pages, the actor, shook his head. "I suppose I can ad-lib some of it."

"You shouldn't—" Storm started to object.

The actor cut him off: "Do not presume to tell me what I should and should not do!"

"Suit yourself."

"Now, get out of my sight! I must have complete and utter quiet if I am to master this—what passes, for you, as dialogue—by tomorrow morning."

Storm hastened out of the mining shack and marched to the one occupied by Rowelings.

So exasperated was he by the thespian's behavior that he almost forgot to knock at Rowelings's door before entering. As it was, he rapped harder that usual.

"Come in," Rowelings called.

"This friend of yours—"

"I have no friends; I have associates, at best."

"This associate of yours, then—he wants to 'ad lib' what I wrote."

"Relax, Zach; he'll do fine. Remember, he's not going to make the hooch; he's just going to sell it," Rowelings said.

"Selling potential customers can be a tough proposition. For one thing, it's illegal. For another, it can be unhealthy, even fatal, if it's not made under close supervision, according to established procedures."

"You'll be supervising the distilling of the product," Rowelings reminded his lieutenant. "If I didn't think that Matthew was up to the task, he wouldn't be here."

"At least let me go into town with him!"

"I invited Matthew to join us expressly to preclude any of us from having to go into town. At the very least, the newspapers have almost certainly listed our names as escapees. They might also have printed pictures of us and announcements of rewards, should the governor have approved them. Matthew's face is apt to be unknown to them, unless they've attended theaters back east, which, I assure you, having knowledge of this town and its residents, is extremely improbable."

Storm shook his head, sighing. "I can see your mind's made up."

"It is."

"I guess there's nothing more to be said, then."

"Just this, Zach. I know Matthew. I've worked with him before. He's as good as he says he is, and that, as you've heard from his own lips, is excellent. Despite his egotism, the bastard is persuasive as hell. His pitch will be believable, I can assure you. He knows people—or, I suppose it would be more accurate to say, he knows *audiences*. He can, and will, deliver.

"But he's going to be valuable to us in more than just this one undertaking. He's going to be our go-between, our intermediary. When we need something—food, supplies, equipment, news, information, whatever—he will be the one we send on our behalf, which will allow us to remain hidden, acting in secret, and, thereby, escaping detection and capture."

"If you say so."

"I do."

Chapter 37
Guilty on Both Counts

"No one truly likes to pose for a photographic portrait; it takes *all* day."
— Lizzie Messenger (1872-)

Carson City, Nevada

"Seems we should be heading south instead of west," Badger remarked.

"The prison is east of Carson City," Bane said.

"I know, but Rowelings headed south, right?"

"Before we start our pursuit, I want to make another call."

"Newspaper editor?" Luke asked.

"Brothel owner would be my bet," Badger said.

"How'd you know there are brothels in Carson City?" Luke asked. "Experience?"

"Hell, Luke, there are brothels in *every* town."

"I wouldn't know, Badger; I'm a married man."

"I think we can skip the brothels," Bane said. "Men just escaped from prison are apt to have more pressing needs than a soiled dove's charms."

By the time they tied the reins of their horses to the hitching post in front of *The Daily State Register*, it was past noon. Badger suggested lunch before business, but Bane preferred "business before pleasure."

"Eating isn't just a pleasure, Bane," Badger protested, "it's a vital function."

"And one that can wait."

Badger grunted, knowing not to press the matter. Bane enjoyed a good meal as well as any. His curt rebuttal of the suggestion to tie on the feedbag before interviewing the newspaper editor indicated just how focused Bane was on capturing Spencer Rowelings and his gang. Of course, Badger wanted to apprehend the fugitives, too, as he was sure Luke did, but, hell, a man had to eat.

Dismounting, they entered the newspaper office.

Inside, a man who appeared to be in his fifties was perusing a newspaper while an older boy instructed a younger one, an apprentice, most likely, how to set type. None of them seemed to have heard Bane and his deputies enter.

"Hello," Bane announced, "U. S. Marshal Bane Messenger and Deputies Badger Thompson and Luke Meadows here to see the owner or editor of *The Carson City Slate.*"

The man set his paper aside, rose, and walked to the counter that separated the front of the building from the rest of it. "That'd be me, Marshal, on both counts. I'm also guilty of being the publisher of this newspaper. Name's Scott Davis. What can I do for you?"

"My deputies and I are in pursuit of the convicts who escaped from the State Prison. I wonder if there's been news in the past two or three days about recapturing any of the fugitives. I thought you'd know the particulars better than anybody else."

"As a matter of fact, Marshal, I was just proofreading the last of the articles for tomorrow's edition of the paper while Tommy shows Jimmy how to set type. There has been some news, but I'd appreciate you and your deputies keeping it to yourselves. Most of a newspaper's appeal is the fact that it prints stories and facts that people *don't* know."

"You have my word, Mr. Davis."

"In fact, I keep a list of the names of the fugitives who've been recaptured, adding to it whenever another one of them is apprehended. That way, I know myself, when I see a captive's name in an article other than my own, whether the capture's already been reported. So far, there have been six.

"Will Bower is one; another is a man who was captured in a pool at David Walley's Hot Springs near Genoa. The article didn't give his name; it just mentions him saying all he wanted was a warm bath. The third is a man by the name of Gates; no first name given—damn, but some reporters are lazy, incompetent, or both, it appears. Then there's J. Bedford Roberts, Connor Buckner, and Will Fielder. That's it, up to now, far's I know."

"You've been most helpful, Mr. Davis."

"I'd like to see the scoundrels back in prison as soon as possible, Marshal."

"We have that in common," Bane agreed. "We're also looking for any leads you might have concerning Spencer Rowelings or his accomplices."

"The stagecoach robber?"

Bane said, "That's the varmint."

Davis thought. "According to one report, he had a visitor while in prison. 'Matt,' he called him."

"Any idea what they talked about?"

He shrugged. "Apparently, Matt didn't stay long; just a few minutes. Mostly, they reminisced about a spot they knew near the place they grew up—somewhere they called 'The Point.' The article stated that Rowelings said something else, too, now that I recall it."

"What's that?"

"He said, 'If my sentence is commuted, once I get out of here, I'll let you know, and we can meet at The Point to celebrate.' I assume the bastard was joking. Then, Matt said, 'Let me know if you are; I'll be there.' That's all there was to their visit, or all the newspaper reported, at least."

Bane nodded. "Thanks for your time, Mr. Davis."

The editor nodded. "Hope you catch him, Marshall."

Bane nodded. "I do, too." As he and his deputies turned to leave, Davis said, "I reckon the lieutenant governor will be glad, too. He's taken a lot of heat in the local paper; people hereabout—and maybe the governor—blame him for the prison break."

"Why's that?" Bane asked.

Davis shrugged, "You know how it is, Marshall. Everybody's an expert after the fact, second-guessing the actions of the man in charge, finding fault, criticizing."

"What were the criticisms?"

"Some say he shouldn't have allowed the prisoners to meet and mix all day in the prison-cell, or hall. Others say there should have been more guards on duty. There's been some statements, too, both in the papers and in the saloons, that the warden's men should have searched the prisoners who worked in the quarry at the ends of their shifts, as if the guards hadn't done so. That way, the inmates wouldn't have had the chance to make slung-shots using chunks of limestone from the quarry they worked in. Things were too lenient all around, some say, such as allowing the prisoners to make plaques and statues and such out of stone. A few, I hear, also contend that Lieutenant Governor Dawes appoints too many trustees, including men who don't deserve such positions."

"You don't think there's any merit to the criticisms?"

"I don't know, Marshal."

"Well, thanks for your help—oh, wait! You wouldn't happen to have a photograph of Rowelings, would you?"

"One just arrived in the mail."

"Could I borrow it?"

"I don't see why not. Give me a minute to find it." He walked across his office to a pair of pie safes, one stacked atop the other, opened the doors of the top cabinet, and rummaged among items stored on the shelves. "Ah! Here's the likeness of the scoundrel."

He closed the doors and returned to the group of his visitors, handing the photograph to Bane.

"That's him, all right," Bane said.

"Anything else, Marshal?"

The editor looked a bit frazzled, Bane thought. Putting out a newspaper every day must be a challenge, especially when it was one of the voices of the state capital.

"I'd like you to run this picture in your newspaper's next edition, along with this notice of a reward." Bane handed him the reward notice he'd written out before visiting Davis.

"The one that's about to go to press?"

"That's right."

"The one the boys and I have been working on for the past ten hours straight?"

"That's the one."

"The one that's been laid out, column by column and page by page, painstakingly and deliberately, written, proofread, edited, and set to type?"

"You'll publish Rowelings's photograph and the reward notice in tomorrow's edition of the paper?" Bane asked.

"Well, I haven't published the two inside pages yet, just the first and last."

"Is that typical?" Badger asked, looking puzzled.

"Yes. Gives the ink time to dry before I post copies in the mail for subscribers." To Bane, he said, "I suppose I can squeeze in the picture on page two, if I cut the Reverend Layton's appeal for funds for the church's roof repairs."

"Page *two*?" Badger protested. "Bane wants the photograph to appear on the *front* page—don't you Bane?"

"Wherever it fits is fine," Bane assured Davis.

"The most current news is *inside* the paper, on pages two and three," Davis explained, sounding impatient. "Stands to reason, doesn't it Deputy Thompson, since the front page and the back page are printed *first*?"

Badger didn't look any too sure. "I reckon," he said.

"I want you to print the reward notice, alongside, above, or below, the photograph, wherever you can fit it in."

Davis shook his head. "Looks like I'll have to shorten Clyde Dennison's death notice, too."

"How much?"

"A paragraph. He was a right mean old cuss, so I doubt his widow will mind much. Besides, I don't charge to print death notices."

"I mean how much to print the photograph and the reward announcement?"

"Normally, I'd do that free of charge, too, Marshal, as a public service, and because it's apt to increase sales of my newspaper, but, considering the time it will take to redo the layout, print the photo—

"All things considered, how much?"

"Well, there's also the chance—indeed, the likelihood, that I'll offend both the Reverend *and* the widow Dennison—"

"How much?"

Davis quoted the amount.

Badger and Luke looked both shocked and offended.

Bane added six more dollars.

"What's the extra for?" the editor asked. "A tip?"

Bane was a generous man, Badger thought, but Davis didn't deserve a tip, as far as he was concerned.

"I want you to mail me a hundred copies of the newspaper with Rowelings's picture and the reward notice in it."

"Where to?"

Bane named the town.

"Happy to oblige, Marshal."

After they left the tuckered-out editor behind, with a smile on his face, Badger asked, "Where to *now*, Bane?"

"Church."

Badger frowned. "It' not Sunday," he pointed out.

* * *

The United Methodist Church, built in 1865, of stone from the prison quarry, was a few blocks away. Bane and his deputies climbed the stretch of steps to the front door beneath an arched window. Bane pressed the handle and gave the door a push. It opened onto the narthex, the back wall of which contained large, closed doors.

The lawmen passed through these doors, into the church's sanctuary.

Soft light, diffused through the stained-glass windows along the parallel walls forming the sides of the sanctuary, bathed the large room in soft colors that somehow lent an aura of holiness to the sacred space. At the east end of the church, where the red carpet leading down the sanctuary's center aisle ended before the altar, the minister, Reverend Layton, stopped in the middle of a sentence of the sermon he was practicing as he stood in the pulpit.

"Sorry for the intrusion," Bane called.

The minister exited the pulpit and met his visitors as they reached the end of the sanctuary. "Not at all, Marshal. The house of God is always open to those who seek the Lord." He shook hands with Bane, Badger, and Luke.

"I'm Bane Messenger, a member of the church in my hometown, Excelsior."

The minister looked a bit discombobulated. "The angel of death?"

Bane frowned, then smiled, as he understood the preacher's reaction. Bane meant "death," just as "messenger" could signify "angel." "There's no religious significance to it, pastor; it's just what my parents named me."

"What can I do for you, Marshal?"

Bane explained how he'd arranged for Davis to include Rowelings's photograph and his own reward notice in place of the minister's appeal for funds for the repair of the church's roof. "I'd like to pay for the repairs," he said.

The clergyman smiled. "The cost is significant, Marshal."

"Would five-hundred dollars cover it?"

The minister gave Bane an odd look, half of suspicion, half of wonder. "That's the exact amount the builder quoted."

"Let's make it an even thousand," Bane said, extracting the bills from his wallet. "I've found that estimates often have a way of increasing, sometimes to double the original quote."

"I don't know what to say, except thank you, of course."

"It's the least I can do for preempting your appeal, which was to be published in tomorrow's newspaper."

As they stepped onto the street in front of the church, Badger asked, "Where now?"

"Wherever you and Luke want to tie on a feedbag. I'd say it's past time we had lunch, wouldn't you?"

"Hell, Bane, I said that well over an hour ago," Badger declared.

Chapter 38

Molasses, Tobacco, Spanish Peppers, and Rattlesnake Heads

"An indignant matron threw her beastly drunken husband out of the house last night, saying, as she did so, that '[I have] worked hard to get money for [you] to buy rot-gut whiskey with long enough.' That was all we heard, as we passed along; sufficient, however, to make the case out in the woman's favor."
—*Pioche Daily Record*, February 9, 1873

Bodie, California

Bodie.

Matthew Lewis had visited the town a few times between 1876 and 1880, after the Standard Company had discovered gold nearby. Overnight, what had been a mining camp in the middle of nowhere had mushroomed into one of the West's biggest, roughest boom towns, attracting men who wanted to strike it rich and soiled doves who wanted to feather their nests by "entertaining" them. If a man wanted something other than liquor to ease his conscience, were he to have such an encumbrance, Bodie's Chinatown offered plenty of opium dens.

Lewis hadn't counted them himself, of course, but *The Standard Pioneer Journal of Mono County* newspaper had boasted that the town had seven to ten thousand residents and two thousand buildings. The newspaper, like the telegraph line linking Bodie with Bridgeport, California, and Genoa, Nevada, was an indication that Bodie had come into its own.

Nine stamp mills operated in the town, and shipments of bullion, between Bodie and Carson City, on their way to the U. S. mint in San Francisco, were fairly frequent. A few times, he and Spencer Rowelings had considered robbing the shipments, despite the fact that most of them were made under heavy guard, but they'd decided that the risk of getting killed outweighed the prospects of getting rich.

Fortunately, although they'd worked a claim together, while engaging, at times, in other, less honest undertakings, always masked, of course, they'd never been seen with one another otherwise, nor had they ever gone into town together. Even back then, Spencer had been a lone wolf with the wisdom not to be seen with others, especially those with whom he occasionally conducted "business" the nature of which a town, a county, a state, or the federal government had deemed illegal.

The only time that Lewis, the actor-turned-outlaw, and Rowelings, the career criminal, were together was in the now-abandoned mining shacks in which Spencer Rowelings, Zach Storm, Russ Jackson, James Baker, and, lately, Lewis himself had made their quarters. The only ones they saw in the otherwise-uninhabited camp were themselves. There was no chance that Lewis's appearance in town, even should he be recognized by one of the former residents who'd remained in Bodie instead of forsaking it for a camp or a town that seemed to offer better prospects, would be connected to Rowelings.

Lewis wouldn't be associated with the horses Rowelings had stolen, either, nor would he be linked to Rowelings's murder of the rancher's wife or his theft of her husband's clothing, horses, and money. He'd picketed the stolen horse that Rowelings had loaned him three miles outside of Bodie and had hiked the rest of the way. When his business here was concluded, he'd hoof it back to the spot and reclaim the animal.

As he looked along the town's mile-long Main Street, Lewis thought, yessir, Bodie had been a wide open town as late as 1880, when miners moved on to Butte, Montana, Tombstone, Arizona, and sites in Utah that promised quick wealth and fast living, and Bodie was still a place where a man could satisfy appetites that weren't considered respectable most other places.

In its heyday, Bodie had been graced—well, maybe "graced" wasn't the right word—but had been home to no fewer than sixty-five saloons. A good many of them remained, despite the exodus of miners over the past few years. It was a likely bet, Spencer thought, that at least a few of the remaining establishments' owners or bartenders would be interested in serving moonshine instead of legitimate distilleries' spirits.

After all, with Spencer's man Zach Storm overseeing the operation, Spencer's gang could make their brand of hooch far cheaper than the saloons' suppliers back east and in the south, and shipping costs would be next to nothing. Hell, Spencer and his boys might even put Atherton Whiskey, Barton Distillery, Brown-Forman, and other legitimate distilleries out of business altogether, in Bodie, at least.

Bodie saloons might no longer serve rotgut whiskey that hadn't aged properly and was cut with such "extra" ingredients as molasses (for "taste"), tobacco (for "color"), Spanish peppers (for "spice"), and rattlesnake heads (for "spirit"), but that didn't necessarily mean that an owner or a barkeep couldn't be persuaded to substitute a little of Zach Storm's elixir for the finer stuff. By buying cut-rate liquor from Spencer, the saloons could charge the same price as they would for the Jack Daniels or Old Tub for which they substituted the moonshine, when a patron was drunk enough not to discern the difference and whenever one of them ordered the house alternative.

He spotted the Silver and Gold Saloon, named for nearby strikes that had occurred only a few years ago, and decided that, if Patrick Morrison still owned the place, he might well strike a deal with the bastard. Even during Bodie's heyday, Morrison had been a miserly old fox who'd skin a flint to save a buck.

Chapter 39

Boyhood Reminiscences

"I once sent a dozen of my friends a telegram saying 'flee at once—all is discovered.' They all left town immediately."
— Mark Twain (1835-)

Carson City, Nevada

"A good night's sleep on a firm mattress in a bed with sheets and blankets in a clean hotel room without scorpions and rattlesnakes among mountain lions and bobcats makes a man feel mighty fine," Badger said, before stuffing his face with a forkful of pancakes smothered in syrup.

"Looks like it's restored your appetite, too," Bane observed.

"Not 'restored' so much as reinvigorated it," I'd say, Luke remarked.

"While there's no doubt that you heat up a mean dish of bacon and beans, Luke," Badger rejoined, "there's nothing like a plate of pancakes served by an actual cook to whet a man's appetite."

"Or even your own, for that matter," Luke said.

"I'm glad you boys feel so refreshed," Bane declared. "We have quite a bit of terrain to travel."

"That did it! Now, I've lost my appetite," Badger said.

"Right, and I reckon hell just froze over, too," Luke suggested.

"First, though, I thought we'd review our notes," Bane said. "Howard Keel, one of the prisoners we interviewed at the prison stated that Rowelings said 'north' with suspicious emphasis, as if he were trying to mislead anyone who pursued him and the inmates he escaped with, which makes me think that he likely went the opposite direction, south."

"Why not east, west, or even northwest, northeast, southwest, or southeast?" Luke asked. "None of those direction is north, either."

"People generally speak in opposites: 'man,' 'woman'; 'up,' 'down'; 'fast,' 'slow'—"

"—or 'north,' 'south,'" Badger concluded.

"Exactly," Bane agreed.

"Makes sense," Luke said, nodding.

"Before he became a guest of the state, Rowelings also enlisted three men: Donald Lombardo, to threaten District Attorney Benson; Andy Sanders, to threaten the jury foreman; and Kyle Evers, to threaten—and kill—Judge Hawthorne."

"Shows foresight and planning," Luke said.

"That it does," Badger concurred.

"It also shows a pattern. Rowelings uses intermediaries to do his work for him, or some of it, as a way of distancing himself from the deeds that others do on his behalf. He pays them, no doubt, but I think he also threatens or intimidates at least some of them so they won't finger him. That way, he can deny having had anything to do with their actions."

"But, under pressure, they did accuse Rowelings," Luke pointed out.

"It's true that there's no honor among thieves," Bane replied, "but Rowelings can always deny that he had any part in threatening the prosecutor, the jury foreman, or the judge. It's his word against theirs. A jury might well decide that Rowelings did, in fact, hire them to threaten the jury foreman and the officers of the court. On the other hand, they might not. Rowelings's denial provides him at least some protection, however slight, and any is better than none.

"In other ways, having a go-between could serve Rowelings, too. He can act through such a person, while concealing his own identity, an ability that could come in handy in his present circumstances."

"You've given these matters some thought," Badger said.

The waitress stopped at their table to ask whether they'd like anything else.

"Just the check, please," Bane said.

"Right away, Marshal."

After she headed off, Bane told his deputies, "Half of capturing a fugitive is thinking things through, especially from his point of view. By doing so, a lawman might even anticipate where a fugitive might light after taking flight."

"You've accomplished that, too?" Badger asked, looking downright astonished.

"Not yet, but I think I may have figured a way to find out."

"How's that?" Luke asked.

"Thank you, Marshal," their server said, smiling, "and, please, hurry back."

Bane handed her a double eagle. "Keep the change."

Her smile widened. "Thanks, Marshal."

"You're welcome, and thank you."

As she left, Bane looked at Luke. "Now, if Badger's finished filling his belly and feels refreshed enough, after a good night's rest, to accompany us, I'll show you just how we might benefit from the boyhood reminiscences that Rowelings and his visitor 'Matt' shared while Rowelings was a guest of Nevada's State Prison."

Badger swiped his napkin across his chops. "Let's go!"

* * *

Except for the large, framed pictures that adorned the walls at haphazard intervals, the Carson City telegraph office was a utilitarian affair as no-nonsense as the transmitter's operator, a portly, gray-haired gentleman with bushy eyebrows and a shaggy mustache more gray than black that complemented the white shirt and dark pants he wore.

"I want to send a telegram," Bane informed him.

"Figured you wanted to send or receive one. Who's it to?"

"Do you have a slip of paper and a pencil?"

"Yep. Lots of them."

"Mind if I borrow one?"

"Sure, Marshal, as long as they don't leave the premises."

"I'm a lawman, not a thief."

"You'd be surprised how many times people forget to return them, lawmen included."

"Maybe you'd like some collateral?"

The operator handed Bane the items he'd requested. "Your word'll do, I reckon,"

"Thanks." Bane jotted down a list of towns. After a few minutes, he handed the paper and the pencil back to the operator. "I want to send the same message to every telegraph operator in those towns."

The man whistled. "That's a lot of towns, Marshal."

"I reckon it is."

"What's the message?"

"Operator, if, in the past week, you sent a message to someone named Matthew Lewis concerning a place or thing called The Point, contact U. S. Marshal Bane Messenger, Cottonwood, Nevada. $1,000 reward for valid response."

"Marshal, that telegram contains thirty-eight words. Each one of them's going to cost you fifty cents, which comes to nineteen dollars."

"That's fine."

"Per transmission. You have twenty towns on your list. That comes to three-hundred-and-eighty dollars!"

"That's fine, too."

"It will be, once those dollar bills are in my hand."

Bane extracted his wallet from his back pocket, opened it, and placed four one-hundred dollar bills in the man's pudgy palm.

"I can't make change for a hundred-dollar bill!"

"That's all right; keep it."

"I can't. Company policy prohibits tips."

"Badger? Luke? Either or both of you have eighty dollars?"

"Hell, Bane, where would we get eighty dollars, even between us?" Badger asked.

"Might I suggest you try the bank?" the operator interjected.

"Think I'll add a few more words."

The operator stared at Bane as if he were loco.

After revising the message, Bane read it out loud, to hear how it sounded:

Operator, if, in the past week, you sent a message to a person named Matthew Lewis concerning a place or thing called The Point, contact U. S. Marshal Bane Messenger, Cottonwood, Nevada. Receive a thousand-dollar reward for a valid response.

He nodded. "That ought to do it."

The operator scanned the altered message that Bane handed to him. "Now, it's forty words! That comes to four-hundred dollars!"

Bane smiled. "Exactly."

Shaking his head at what he clearly viewed as sheer lunacy on Bane's part, the operator said, "It's going to take me a few minutes to send this."

"Before you do, I want to make it clear to you that, should you tell anybody anything—and I mean anything—about this message, anything at all, your next home will be a cell in the State Prison."

Bane's statement made the portly gentleman sit up straight. Eyeing the marshal coldly, he said, in perfectly enunciated words, "I have never in my life divulged the contents of a telegraphic message to anyone but the recipient, and I never will, your threats be damned."

"Glad to hear it, since, when it comes to the commissions of crimes, I don't make threats, just promises."

* * *

"Damn, Bane!" Badger said, as they mounted up outside the telegraph office, "four-hundred dollars for a telegraph message isn't going to look very good on your expense report."

"Who said I'm reporting it?"

"Four-hundred dollars is a lot to pay for a telegraph message, too."

"It's a mite steep, but it's cheap enough to enlist the aid of twenty telegraph operators."

"Both of you need a math lesson," Luke stated. "It's actually fourteen-hundred dollars, if one of them collects the reward Bane offered."

Chapter 40

Untold Riches

"In one dancing saloon I saw the only rational method of art criticism I have ever come across. Over the piano was printed a notice: 'Please do not shoot the pianist. He is doing his best.'"

— Oscar Wilde (1854-)

Bodie, California

Matthew Lewis entered the Gold and Silver Saloon, a vast room in which a long bar stood beyond a sea of small tables. On one side of the vast chamber, games of chance were underway. On the opposite side of the barroom, a piano player performed a sonata, something by Beethoven, from the sound of it.

Over the bar, an eight-by-ten-foot nude painting showed, from the back, a lovely young woman lying on her side and looking over her shoulder. Part of her her left breast could be seen, but the painting's focal point was the model's lovely, if rather expansive, derriere.

Live counterparts of the painted lady roamed, in little more attire, among the tables, sipping drinks—colored water, or tea, most likely, disguised as alcoholic beverages—often, probably, as a prelude to prostitution. Their vocation was dangerous, both to themselves and to their customers, since venereal disease was rampant in the West. Lewis might buy one or more of them a "drink" if the gesture could benefit him, but he drew a line at the likelihood of acquiring syphilis or gonorrhea.

Of course, pregnancy was a potential problem for saloon girls who took men upstairs to one of the rooms set aside for dalliances, but nothing that an injection of mercury, arsenic, and vinegar couldn't cure. The West was hard for unmarried women, who were not offered many respectable means of earning a living besides those of teaching, sewing, selling merchandise, or waiting tables. Once those positions were filled, unwed women mostly had to cavort with men to survive.

As these thoughts streamed through his mind, Lewis made his way to the bar, where owner Patrick Morrison kept an eye on his patrons while helping his barkeep serve customers, as was Morrison's custom whenever the saloon was filled to capacity, as it was at present.

"What'll it be?" the bartender asked as Lewis squeezed between a heavy-set, mustachioed man smoking a cigar between sips of whiskey and a slender younger man hefting a mug of beer.

"I have a proposition for the proprietor of this establishment."

"We don't have one of them," the bartender said.

Lewis studied the man for a moment to decide whether he was joshing.

When the bartender turned away, Lewis clarified his meaning: "The owner, I mean."

"Why didn't you say so?" He set a mug of beer before another thirsty patron before calling down the bar, "Mr. Morrison? Man here to see you."

Morrison, a giant with a thick handlebar mustache, eyed Lewis suspiciously, whether because Lewis was a stranger to him or because not many of his customers requested an audience with him, Lewis wasn't sure. "What is it?"

"I wonder whether I might speak with you privately."

The air of suspicion remained. "About what?"

"A proposition."

"What kind of proposition?"

Leaning toward the proprietor, Lewis said, his voice low, "One that could increase your profits six or seven times over, maybe more."

The giant wiped his hands on the bottom of the black vest he wore over a white silk shirt and a bolo tie before adjusting the waistband of his black slacks. "Something illegal, then?"

"It's best we speak in private," Lewis repeated.

"Twenty dollars."

Lewis frowned. "What's that?"

"My fee for hearing your patter. It buys you fifteen minutes."

Lewis hesitated. It seemed an extravagant amount just to buy a quarter of an hour's time to palaver. On the other hand, if Morrison could be sold, doing business with him could be worth a lot more than that. Taking a bill from the inside breast pocket of his vest, he passed it across the bar to the saloon's owner.

"Upstairs," he said. "Room 3, on your left. I'll be up in five minutes. Clock's running."

What awaited him in Room 3? A bouncer who'd toss him onto a stairway secured to the exterior back wall of the premises? A soiled dove who'd claim he'd stolen something or, worse, had had his way with her before refusing to pay for her services? A henchman who'd rob him? He could go to the room or cut and run, but whichever he chose to do would have to be done now.

Turning from the bar, he faced the crowded room. Half-drunk miners, a few with bar girls on their laps, gamblers staking their savings on a poker bid or a faro game, and one or two drunks passed out and slumped over a table seemed, like the piano music, to suggest a carefree, festive occasion focused on pleasure rather than crime and violence, but Lewis knew the dangers of the Gold and Silver Saloon and other such establishments.

He also knew, though, that, without risk, there could be no gain, just as he was well aware that Rowelings would expect him to land at least a few agreements with saloon owners or barkeeps to purchase his moonshine.

Threading his way across the room to the staircase, he climbed the steps to the second floor.

He hesitated at the door to Room 3, but only for a second. Taking a deep breath, he turned the doorknob, and stepped inside.

Thankfully, the room was unoccupied.

Five minutes later, Morrison joined him.

"My employer has authorized me to approach you—"

"And just who might your employer be?"

"Mr. Mullins."

Morrison's expression didn't change, but he seemed, somehow, to smirk. It was his eyes, Lewis thought—a change in the focus of his gaze, a glint that seemed to come from within, rather than from the small overhead chandelier. "What's 'Mr. Mullins's' first name?"

"James." It was the first name that came to mind, and Lewis repeated it to himself so he wouldn't forget the alias he'd just assigned to Rowelings.

"What is Mr. Mullins's proposition?"

Based on the information he'd learned from Zach Storm, Lewis had rehearsed a presentation over and over until it sounded extemporaneous, natural, and convincing, but, now, as he stood before the gigantic saloon owner who seemed more amused than not, the actor stumbled over his words, looking amateurish, if not foolish, and he realized that Patrick Morrison, who was anything but a chump, had dealt with men far more dangerous than an actor playing the role of a salesman.

The sick feeling in his stomach told Lewis that he should forget the scheme, cut his losses, and get out of here now, before it was too late. But he feared failing Spencer Rowelings more than he did even this gargantuan ruffian. Besides, he could be convincing. He would be convincing. He was an actor, after all, and a damn good one, at that.

"My employer proposes that you buy locally fermented liquor from him. His network of stills can furnish you as much as you want, at a dollar per gallon. While I was downstairs, I observed that your fine establishment sells a shot of the better brands of whiskey for ten cents and a bottle of the same for a dollar fifty. For merely a dollar, you will receive a gallon or one-hundred-and-twenty-eight ounces of our liquor—"

"Whiskey guaranteed to blind those it doesn't kill?"

Expressing indignation, Lewis declared, "Sir, our product is comparable to the very best whiskey. But, since we produce our spirits locally and have no shipping costs to speak of and have lower labor costs than established suppliers, you stand to make a total net profit, per gallon, for shots, of eleven dollars and eighty cents. A gallon of our product equals one-hundred-and twenty-eight ounces. If you sell it in the twenty-five-ounce bottles supplied by conventional distilleries, once they're empty, a gallon of our liquor becomes five bottles of theirs, with three ounces left over, producing a net profit for you of six dollars and eighty cents, total, for both bottles and shots. Of course, you make these profits on each and every gallon you purchase."

"Where is your, uh, distillery located?"

"Nearby."

"And where, exactly, is nearby."

"Close enough to make no-cost deliveries available to you, sir, in whatever quantities you choose to buy."

"Put me down for five gallons."

Taking a ledger and a pencil from his pocket, Lewis made a note as, grinning, he said, "You're on your way to untold riches, Mr. Morrison, all for a mere five dollars."

"When should I expect delivery?"

"Less than a week."

* * *

A stop by The Bonanza was even more profitable. The owner, Porter Hawkins ordered seven gallons.

There were still plenty of other saloons in town, but two were enough for one day, Lewis thought. Twelve dollars in sales in less than an hour's time suggested there'd be plenty more sales to be made, and it seemed best not to sell more until Spencer's crew had distilled a sufficient surplus of spirits.

As Zach had pointed out, the last thing that moonshiners wanted, besides a visit by revenuers, was to prove unreliable to their customers.

Chapter 41

Pay Dirt

"Your own tactic is to train yourself in the art of becoming enigmatic to every-one."
— Søren Kierkegaard (1813-1855)

Near Cottonwood, Nevada

"Although Cottonwood itself, in Mineral County, is shown on the map as a town, it's really a mining district made up of thirty mines or so. The railway starts at the Mound House depot, west of Carson City, and runs south, all the way to Keeler, California. Because of the number of miners who live and work in the area, there's a telegraph office in Cottonwood."

"How do you know all this stuff?" Badger asked.

"Partly from friends in Excelsior, partly from my past experiences as a bounty hunter and a sheriff, and partly from newspapers and other sources. Since I came to Nevada, I've taken an interest in the state's history," Bane explained. "There used to be a lot of settlements, stagecoach stations, camps, and mines in this county and in the adjacent California county: Elbow Jake's, Fletcher Station, Nine Mile House, Del Monte, Antelope Mill, and camp Noble, just on this side of Nevada's border with California. Each one of them has a history, but the settlements themselves are forgotten now, for the most part."

"You're a fount of knowledge, you know that, Bane?" Badger remarked.

"I'm wagering that Rowelings and the men with him went south," Bane resumed, "and I'm betting, further, that I might know where south they're headed. If we're in luck, we'll get a reply to the telegram we sent to operators between here and the suspected location. If so, we'll know the fugitives' location almost to a certainty."

"I'd say that's a gamble worth taking," Luke remarked.

"Riding this train will shave some time off our trip and give our horses some rest, too," Badger suggested.

"As much as a horse can rest tethered inside a moving railroad car on a train like this," Luke agreed.

"I didn't even know there was a Carson and Colorado Railway," Badger said.

"Until a little over four years ago, there wasn't," Bane said. "Most folks, other than railroad workers and miners, don't know it exists."

"How'd you know?"

"Bane has a gold mine, Badger," Luke reminded his fellow deputy.

Badger didn't let Luke's sarcastic tone or the roll of his eyes prevent him from grinning. "Those railroaders sure as hell didn't want us along for the ride, and they especially didn't cotton to us bringing our horses along. I'll never forget the looks on their their faces when Bane told them that we were commandeering space aboard their train for us and our horses!"

* * *

In just over four hours, the train stopped at Cottonwood, Nevada, and Bane, Badger, and Luke disembarked. While his deputies collected their horses, Bane made his way to the telegraph office.

"Howdy," the operator called as the marshal entered the office.

Crossing the room, Bane approached the man. "I'm U. S. Marshal Bane Messenger. I'm expecting a telegram." He'd made this same statement a number of times at telegraph stations along the way from Carson City, always with the same result: there was no telegram for him.

"Been expecting you, Marshal."

Bane could hardly believe his ears!

The operator reached into one of the compartments in the cabinet behind him, removed an envelope, checked the addressee's name, and handed the envelope across the counter between Bane and himself.

Bane opened the envelope and removed the telegram, which read, "'Meet me at The Point' message sent from Pine Grove by Peter Malcomb to Matthew Lewis."

A thrill, like electricity, went through Bane. The fact that the sender's name wasn't Spencer Rowelings didn't bother him. Rowelings would almost certainly have used an alias.

Bane had no idea who the telegraph operator in Pine Grove might be, but, whoever he was, he'd soon be a thousand dollars better off than he'd been before he'd sent this message.

"I'd like to send a telegram." He wrote out the names of the nineteen recipients and their respective towns and handed the list to the operator. "Here's the message: 'Operator, the reward for information concerning a message sent to someone named Matthew Lewis concerning a place or a thing called The Point is no longer in effect.'"

"At fourteen dollars for the message, times nineteen deliveries, that comes to two-hundred-and-sixty dollars, Marshal."

Bane handed him three one-hundred dollar bills. "Keep the change," he said.

The operator grinned. "Thanks, Marshal!"

Bane smiled, thinking of how the Carson City telegraph operator had said that receiving tips was prohibited by the company he worked for, which happened to be the same one that employed this man. "I'd appreciate it if you'd keep all this business between you and me." He tapped his badge. "In fact, I insist on it."

"I won't breathe a word, Marshal."

Just as they concluded their business, Badger and Luke stepped inside. "Horses are ready to go," Badger announced.

"We need to stop by the post office."

* * *

The clerk behind the counter nodded. "Marshal." Looking past him, she added, "Deputies."

Badger and Luke nodded at her.

"I should have—well, a package or a bundle, I suppose—from Scott Davis, the editor of the Carson City Slate."

The clerk chuckled. "So, you're the one! We've been wondering who in his right mind—I mean, who—would order a hundred copies of the same edition of a newspaper."

Bane frowned. "You opened my mail?"

Suddenly, the young woman seemed uneasy. "No, sir! Certainly not!"

"How do you know what I ordered?"

"I'll show you, Marshal." Turning, she called over her shoulder, "Bob? Can you bring those newspapers that we received yesterday to the counter, please?"

"Sure, Betty."

A few seconds later, a tall, lanky young man set two bundles on the counter. Davis hadn't bothered to wrap the newspapers; he'd just stacked them and tied a rope around the stack. The edges of the newspapers were visible from all sides, as was the first page of the one at the top of each stack.

Bane shook his head. "I see," he told Betty.

"But how did you know how many?" Luke asked.

Bob shrugged. "Counted them."

Without Bane's having to ask him, Badger stepped up, the better, Bane thought, to see the clerk, who was quite an attractive young woman, and lifted a bundle from the counter.

Luke collected the other stack.

"Thanks," Bane said. "Good day to you."

"You, too."

As he followed his deputies toward the door, he heard Betty giggle.

When they reached their horses, Bane cut the twine, and he and his deputies rolled each newspaper, each tucking a third of the copies into one of his saddlebags.

"Now, let's ride," Bane said.

* * *

"Why Bodie?" Badger asked.

"It's just a guess, but I suspect that Rowelings is shrewd enough not to have followed the larger groups of fugitives, which would draw attention more quickly than a man traveling alone or with a few others. Besides, he's a loner, by all accounts, who may work with one or two other men when it's necessary to pull off a robbery but who, otherwise, prefers his own company. What we've learned since his escape supports this assumption.

"He made sure to leave the impression that he was heading north after his escape, which makes me think he went in the opposite direction. Under the alias Peter Malcomb, Rowelings sent a telegram from Pine Grove, asking somebody he called Matthew Lewis to meet him someplace Rowelings called 'The Point.' Pine Grove is also south, or southeast, of Carson City, which further suggests that Rowelings and maybe the men he's with are traveling south. Hereabouts, Bodie seems to me to be Rowelings's likeliest destination."

Badger asked, "How far is it to Bodie, Bane?"

"Thirteen miles. If we weren't riding through rough terrain, up steep ascents, we'd be there in three hours or so; as it is, it'll take eight, and, to spare the horses, we'll split it into two days."

"Maybe, the mission that Governor Cooper assigned us will be over in a few more days," Badger said.

"We might capture Rowelings by then," Luke observed, "but our job won't be over until he's back in the State Prison."

"Not quite, Luke," Bane corrected his deputy. "Our task won't be finished until he's hanged."

"Well, we're close, now, anyway, it seems," Badger suggested.

"Or closer," Bane said. "Rowelings is full of surprises. I don't reckon he's run out of them quite yet."

Chapter 42

Gold and Silver

"The vice lies not in entering the bordello but in not coming out."
— Aristippus (c. 435 – c. 356 BC)

Bodie, California

The ride from the shacks of the Bodie Mining District was hell—or as close to hell as Matthew Lewis ever wanted to get.

Sure, his team of mules was more surefooted than horses, but, even so, the narrow, winding trails down steep slopes was harrowing, especially in the driver's seat of a heavy wagon full of casks of moonshine.

Once or twice, rounding a turn in the trail, the wagon had slid sideways a foot or two, toward a precipice, and Lewis had known, certain as death, that his demise was nigh. Fortunately, the mules had pulled the wagon onward, and it had straightened its course again within a few yards. If this was what hauling hooch was going to be like, he ought to be paid extra for the hazard that such transportation posed to his life.

Fortunately—for the mules—the trip into town was mostly downhill. Even unloaded, the wagon was heavy. Pulling it uphill was enough of a strain on the animals without the casks of illegal whiskey. It would have been all the more trying had they had to pull a loaded conveyance in that direction while its bed was occupied by barrels of his customers' new stock.

After what seemed an eternity, the elevation declined from mountainous to hilly, and Lewis breathed a sigh of relief as he spotted the town amid the craggy terrain.

Fortunately, Patrick Morrison was willing to tend bar at his saloon, the Gold and Silver, so his barkeep could help him unload the casks and roll them into the establishment's back room. It was a good thing, too, that the casks were indistinguishable from those in which legitimate spirits were shipped west by lawful distilleries back east and down south. If a patron of Morrison's saloon were drunk enough, he'd never know the difference between the whiskey he'd ordered and the whiskey he was served instead.

"Looks like business is booming," Lewis said, speaking up, to be heard above the din, as he settled up with Morrison.

"Not bad," the proprietor said, appraising the crowded room, where bar girls drifted from table to table, in search of patrons who'd had enough drinks to become willing to splurge by buying a lady a few rounds of sarsaparilla or iced tea disguised as liquor to get them "in the mood." Meanwhile, she'd encourage her admirer to drink up, too, and he'd be supplied with hooch, in lieu of the legitimate whiskey that was now served only to those who had enough sense left in them to distinguish one from the other. That was the plan, at least, and, ever since the first batch of moonshine had been delivered, it was a scheme that had been working, just the way Morrison had hoped. The sales of illegal liquor were so numerous that he placed an order for double the quantity of the original one.

"Thank you, Mr. Morrison," Lewis said, after jotting down the number of casks. "In support of your confidence in our liquor, we will give you an extra cask, free of charge, on your next order."

"Much obliged."

Lewis hoped Spencer wouldn't object. The idea had just occurred to him. Impulsively, he'd acted upon it, as a gesture of good will and appreciation for the increased business. It was a cheap enough gratuity, but he should have broached the idea with Rowelings beforehand. Still, a man, especially a salesman, had to have enough latitude to maneuver. Some situations required a little leeway. "Good day to you, sir."

"Good day."

Making his way across the saloon, through the heavy, low cloud of cigar and cigarette smoke, Lewis dodged a drunk staggering about the room as he tried to dance with a bar girl to the tune that the pianist played. Then, he stepped over a prostrate miner who hadn't yet been collected from the floor and heaved out the door.

Business was, indeed, booming, he thought, smiling.

Chapter 43

Hera's Glory

"The camera is the eye of history."
— Matthew Brady (1822-1824)

Bodie, California

"At last count, there are sixty-five brothels in Bodie. Among us, we've visited twenty-two of them. By each of us visiting three a day, we should be able to make the acquaintance of the rest of them in five more days."

"Sixty-five bordellos in one town sounds crazy, even for Bodie," Badger declared, surveying the shadow-shapes of the buildings at the north end of town, along Maiden Lane, in the light of the full moon.

"It's nighttime now," Bane continued, "and the prostitutes will take advantage of the hours allotted to them between sundown and dawn. The proper ladies of the town won't tolerate the presence of soiled doves on the streets of the town during daylight hours, even here. After the upstanding matrons retire for the evening, though, those whom they disdain by daylight are permitted to take their turns on the streets."

"How do you know these things?" Badger interrupted.

"Bane wasn't always a married man," Luke reminded his fellow deputy.

"Actually, Rose O'Sharon told me. She stays informed about her competition, even when it's located in another town or, for that matter, another state."

"Smart woman, Rose," Luke commented.

"That she is," Bane agreed. "Most of the women encounter their admirers—or the initial ones of the evening, at least—in Bodie's dance halls," Bane resumed, "at which point couples vanish into the cribs or brothels.

"Most of the bawds hope to land a husband, common-law or otherwise, who'll offer them loving homes, although, when it comes right down to it, roofs over their heads will do, loving or otherwise, although a few capture the hearts of prospective beaus only for the attention and the gifts that their swains shower upon them as tokens of their love. Some of the men—mostly miners—who can't dance, or don't want to, settle for a crib."

Bane handed each of his deputies three one-hundred-dollar bills.

"What's this for?" Badger asked.

"If you don't know, there's no sense in your going to any of them," Luke stated.

"Information," Bane said. "Approach the madam—"

"That's the lady who runs the house," Luke told Badger.

"I know what a madam is, Luke."

After a pause, Bane resumed. "As I was saying, first thing, approach the madam. Show her the photograph of Rowelings and tell her if she hangs the wanted notice in a conspicuous location in her brothel, there's a hundred dollars in it for her."

"What if she if agrees but later reneges?" Badger asked.

"Tell her there's a thousand dollars in it for her personally if the person who apprehends the fugitive—don't use Rowelings's name—on my behalf does so after seeing his photograph in her bordello. If she takes the picture down, she'll be losing whatever chance she might have had of collecting the reward, which is an amount a lot larger than a hundred dollars."

"How will we know whether Rowelings's captor actually did see Rowelings's photograph in a particular bawdy house?" Badger asked.

"We won't," Bane admitted, "unless, when we question him or, in passing, Rowelings's captor happens to mention having been in such a place. If he does, I'll pay the thousand dollars. Either way, once Rowelings has been apprehended, it doesn't really matter."

"I reckon not," Badger agreed.

"Let's get started, then. Badger, you take The Red Light, The Soiled Dove, and The Parlor Parade; Luke, you take The Miners' Strike, Golden Bliss, and Nymph's Frolic; I'll take Dawn's Delight, Bodie's Bawdy House, and Hera's Glory."

"How about spending money, Bane?" Badger asked. At the sight of Luke's grin, he added quickly, "I mean, for a drink or something."

"It's the 'something' that concerns me," Luke said.

Bane handed each of them another hundred dollars. "The lady of the house might expect you to buy a drink or a meal, at that," he said, "and the price of either is likely to be high."

* * *

The last place on Bane's itinerary for the night, Hera's Glory, was the most elaborate and ornate. Everything was done up in red velvet—drapes, tablecloths, napkins, and, Madam Elodie whispered, with a wink, bed sheets.

Seated with Bane in a private booth, she ordered champagne for them both. "I don't usually arrange dates between my ladies and my clients, but, when I saw you, I told myself, I just had to make an exception. Most of my patrons aren't as handsome and manly as you."

She was adept at flirtation, all right, Bane thought. "Thanks."

"Do you have a preference for a particular type of lady? Mine hail from Europe, Africa, Asia, South America, and, of course, North America, including Canada. I'm from the United States myself, but I'm not available—well, not usually. I could make an exception in your case."

"I have a different sort of proposition in mind," Bane said.

Her eyes seemed to brighten and her smile widened. "What might that be?"

"I'm seeking the whereabouts of this man." From his pocket, he took a folded clipping of the newspaper reward notice that he'd cut out of one of the hundred copies of the Carson City Slate newspaper that its owner-editor, Scott Davis, had mailed to him and scooted it across the table.

Madam Elodie's countenance didn't change as she read it, but she was surprised, all right, surprised and interested. "A thousand dollars, huh?"

"For his capture and delivery to me or any city, county, state, or federal lawman, on my behalf."

"You must want him badly, Marshal."

"Badly enough to pay you a hundred dollars to post this notice in a conspicuous place here, in your establishment."

"For how long?"

"What do you mean?"

"How long am I to display the notice in my establishment in exchange for the hundred?"

"Until the fugitive is caught, of course."

She shook her head. "I'll pass."

"What amount would persuade you?"

"A hundred dollars."

"That's what I offered."

"Weekly, with the first month in advance, in cash."

"You drive a hard bargain."

"Not if you want this man as badly as you say. My bordello is the most popular in town, and it caters strictly to men of means. Your clothing, like the thousand-dollar reward, suggests that you, too, are a man of means."

"What makes you think I offered the reward?"

"I don't, not for certain. I was willing to bet that you might have done so, given the facts that, judging by your attire, you are obviously a man of means; that you and your deputies are going to houses of pleasure all over town, making the same expensive proposals to my competitors that you just presented to me; that your deputies, and you, have removed your badges for this purpose—a most unusual action on the part of lawmen—"

"Why do you suppose that we're lawmen and that I'm a marshal?"

She snickered. "The ladies of the evening in this town have suspected that you are a lawdog ever since you first paid a visit to one of our establishments, and, considering the authority and confidence with which you act, you are a leader among them, rather than a follower."

"All right. I accept your terms," Bane said.

"Just like that."

He laid four-hundred dollars on the table. "Just like that."

"I think your fugitive will look splendid, framed on the wall behind my bar—as long as he earns his keep. And, now, if you don't mind, I'd like you to leave. Even though you're not wearing a badge, I don't like lawmen in my establishment, regardless of how handsome they might be. Nothing personal."

"One last thing, if you'd be so kind."

She waited.

"The name of your place: Hera's Glory. What's it mean?"

"You ever read any Greek mythology?"

"Can't say that I have."

"Zeus was the chief among the Greek gods of old. He was also quite the scoundrel, cheating on his wife Hera time after time, once in the form of a swan, another time as a shower of gold. He was certainly an imaginative adulterer. One of his trysts, with Alcmene, resulted in the birth of their son Heracles, whose name, it is believed—at least I believe—was an intentional slight, since, as the child of a mortal woman, Heracles, whose name means 'glory of Hera,' was anything but his stepmother's 'glory.'"

Bane nodded. "I see your point."

* * *

It was nearly midnight when Bane rendezvoused with his deputies. They stood on the balcony that ran the length of the front of the Champion Hotel, where the three of them had secured rooms, and watched Main Street as they shared the results of their reconnaissance.

Night or day, the town was busy.

Below, occasionally illuminated by a streetlamp, dim figures,—men, mostly, but also an occasional woman, most of them undoubtedly prostitutes—strolled the mile-long thoroughfare, visiting restaurants, saloons, dance halls, cribs, and bordellos. Others, walking or riding, some on horseback, others in carriages, made their way to more mundane destinations.

"The madams of all the places I went agreed to display the wanted notice in return for a hundred dollars and the chance for a thousand-dollar reward, slim though that chance might be," Luke reported.

"Same with me," Badger stated.

"I met the same results," Bane said. "Nine more brothels down and thirty-four more to go. Learn anything else, either of you, during your visits?"

"I'll say!" Badger exclaimed. "I learned why The Parlor Parade is called The Parlor Parade!"

"One of us better ask him," Luke told Bane. "Otherwise, he's likely to explode."

"All right," Bane acquiesced. "Why is The Parlor Parade called The Parlor Parade, Badger?"

Chapter 44

A Paying Customer

"Man has free choice, or otherwise counsels, exhortations, commands, prohibitions, rewards and punishments would be in vain."
— Thomas Aquinas (1225-1274)

Bodie, California

The next morning, Matthew Lewis was driving along Main Street, wishing the city council would improve the damn thoroughfare. This time of year, the cold that gathered over the mountains surrounding the bowl in which Bowie sat froze the wagon ruts in the mud. Ice, which covered the street, here and there, for at least part of the day, also impeded travel, whether by foot, horse, stagecoach, or wagon.

The town's elevation, which was above the treeline, and the rugged terrain on every side, was plenty rough enough without the severity of the approaching winter's climate. His mules were sure-footed, sure enough, but no animal was footsure enough not to slip and slide on ice and snow, especially when it covered damn near every square inch of the land.

Some winters, there'd been fifteen-foot-tall snowdrifts and buildings had been so encased in snow that they were all but lost in the white stuff. Now, even in early fall, it sure looked like the coming winter would be terrible.

Damn!

It was just his miserable luck.

A week ago, it had been cold in the mountains, where he and the rest of Spencer Rowelings's gang were holed up in the abandoned mining shacks, but, between making batches of 'shine for their customers, whose number seemed to increase every day, they had stoves and moonshine to warm them and food to fill their bellies, and life was good, more or less.

At the same time, money was flowing into their hands as fast as the current in a downhill stream, and each of them was getting closer and closer to fulfilling whatever dreams their shares of the profits would buy. It wouldn't be much longer, Rowelings assured them, with his usual hyperbole, before Baker could buy or build a house somewhere and marry that girl in El Dorado City; Jackson could start over in Chicago or New York or, hell, London or Paris or Rome, if he preferred; and Storm could take to the sea, not as a crew member working for his passage, but as the captain of his own damn ship. It wouldn't be much longer, either, before Lewis and Spencer Rowelings could put their own plan into action.

But, if he froze to death first, he'd never live long enough to partner with Rowelings in the future enterprises that Rowelings had planned and shared with Lewis alone, at least in part.

He turned his team into an alley that led past the western side of The Bonanza saloon. After dismounting from the wagon, he tied ropes to the two mules before fastening their other ends to a nearby post.

Starting back down the alley, toward the front of the saloon, he caught himself. This week, Porter Hawkins would just have to wait another half-hour, maybe even sixty minutes, for his damn hooch.

If he didn't get warmed up, he'd freeze.

Hell, he was *half*-frozen now.

Nobody was likely to find the wagon. Any fool who was outside on a day like this was apt to be intent on completing whatever errand he was tending to as fast as he could so he could return to his home or place of work and get out of the frozen wasteland that Bodie had become over the last week. If somebody *did* happen to see the wagon, though, and investigate, he'd find a load of unattended casks of whiskey just waiting to be driven away.

If somebody stole the moonshine, Rowelings would have his hide—literally.

"Damn!" He wasn't about to risk having a whole wagon full of hooch stolen just to get warm. Muttering curses, he turned back, retraced his steps, and entered Hawkins's saloon.

"Looks like you need a drink," Dean Norton called, as Lewis hastened toward the bar, shivering as he walked.

"He'll have time enough for that after he's unloaded my order," Hawkins said.

"Come on, then, Dean; let's get that wagon unloaded," Lewis urged.

"Can't spare Dean; not with *this* crowd," Hawkins objected. "You'll have to unload the casks and roll them on into my stockroom by yourself this time."

Just my luck! Lewis thought, turning from the bar and the drink that Norton had just about set down for him before Hawkins had denied him both the whiskey and the bartender's assistance.

* * *

It would forever remain a mystery to Lewis just how he had managed to unload the casks and roll them into The Bonanza's storeroom, but somehow, he'd accomplished the task without freezing to death. To reward himself for a job well done, he'd visit one of the town's many brothels.

He deserved a warm, dry, comfortable place.

He deserved a few drinks at an overpriced, elegant bar in a luxurious house of pleasure.

He deserved a beautiful woman to have and to hold, for an hour's time, and he was ready, willing, and able to pay for such warmth and pleasure.

Hera's Glory, he thought, here I come!

It was a short ride to the bawdy house, which both Martin Brennan, the barkeep at The Gold and Silver, and Dean Norton, the bartender at The Bonanza, had recommended as one of the best brothels in town—or in the West, for that matter—with prices to match. A session with one of the ladies, depending on the lady and the time spent with her, would set a customer back anywhere between ten and a hundred dollars, they said.

Fortunately, Spencer shared the moonshining profits—well the half he didn't keep for himself, anyway—equally among Baker, Jackson, Storm, and Lewis himself.

Since muckers received three dollars and seventy-five cents a day; miners, four dollars a day; and skilled laborers and supervisors seven dollars a day, for shifts ranging from ten to twelve hours, the bawdy house charges were extravagant, indeed.

Hell, gold sold for twenty dollars an ounce and silver for a dollar an ounce, so a lady of the evening—at least, the ones at Hera's Glory—were worth between half an ounce to five ounces of gold or ten to a hundred ounces of silver. It put matters into perspective, Lewis thought, to think of prices and costs in terms of the local economy's basis, which, here, was gold and silver.

And the cost of the ladies was just one of the expenses he'd encounter at Hera's Glory, the bartenders had warned him. A lady was expected to be wined and dined.

"The first place you'll go, after being admitted—if you *are* admitted; Elodie's picky about the men she does business with—is the bordello's saloon for a few drinks with the lady of Elodie's choice, after which you'll tie on a feedbag with her in the establishment's restaurant. Then, and only then, will you be allowed to go upstairs," Norton had declared. When Lewis later asked Brennan about Elodie's protocol for guests, Brennan had confirmed Norton's statements.

"You mean, a man—a paying customer—isn't afforded the courtesy of selecting his own woman?" Lewis had asked.

"Not at Hera's," he'd been assured.

Still, they had told him, any of Madame Elodie's ladies was worth every dollar and cent or every ounce of gold or silver.

James Baker, Russ Jackson, and Zach Storm likely dressed shabbily by comparison with Lewis himself, although, before his arrest, Spencer had worn better clothes. Lewis *always* dressed in splendor, both because, as an actor, he was used to wearing fine clothes, which was expected of him, by both the roles he typically played and by his admirers, and because he enjoyed dressing well. For a thespian, clothes did make the man, he believed, just as costumes helped an actor to project a character.

He noticed, too, that the better a man dressed, the better he was treated. Today, his appearance proved acceptable to the butler, who no doubt doubled as a bouncer, and Lewis was admitted.

He followed the manservant to the saloon, Heracles's Labors, where a lady dressed in a fine, full-length white gown, the plunging neckline of which revealed an ample sample of the woman's bosom, led him to a small, red, heart-shaped table bearing a lit candle at its center. "Someone will take your order directly," she said, offering Lewis a twenty-four-carat smile.

He nodded. "Thank you."

Service was prompt, indeed, a woman in similar, but not quite as elaborate, dress as that of the first lady, appearing within minutes to suggest champagne.

"Bourbon," he said.

"Just so. And for the lady, sir?"

What lady? Lewis thought. No women but the hostess and the waitress had approached him since he'd stepped foot in this place. "Champagne."

"Very good, sir."

Before the beverages arrived, Lewis's companion for the evening did.

He rose and, when she presented her hand, kissed the back of it. Rounding the table, he pulled back the chair on the opposite side. "Please," he invited her, "be seated."

As she did so, a framed photograph behind the bar caught his gaze, and Lewis stared, his brow furrowed. To the woman, as gorgeous a redhead as he'd ever seen on any stage, he said, "I'll be back in just a moment."

She frowned, but said nothing.

Crossing the elegant room, he stepped up to the bar.

"May I help you, sir?" the bartender asked.

The question didn't register. Nothing did except the photograph in the frame on the wall.

It couldn't be! he told himself.

Beneath the man depicted in the photograph, there was text: "REWARD $1,000 for the capture and delivery of this fugitive to any city, county, state or federal lawman."

Suddenly, Lewis didn't want bourbon. He didn't want a steak dinner served on a white linen cloth set with china dishes, etched crystal glasses, and silverware, or an ivory figure of a nymph as a centerpiece. He didn't even want the company of the gorgeous redhead, which, a minute ago, he had craved.

He turned, feeling sick. His first thought was to flee the saloon and the brothel, but he checked the impulse.

A sudden, hasty departure would draw attention, and the last thing Lewis wanted and the last thing he, and his cohorts, could afford was attention.

Instead of bolting, as every fiber of his being urged him to do, he returned to the table. "Please accept my apologies, my dear, but I'm afraid I do not feel well. I shall have to forego an evening of pleasure and delight with you, but I shall return another time. Meanwhile, please accept, as a token of my devotion, this gift and my promise to see you again, if I may, when I am able to show you the good time that you deserve." He handed her a twenty-dollar bill.

Although she seemed confused, she smiled, tucking the bill into her décolletage. "Thank you, sir. I would be delighted to see you again, when you have recovered."

Lewis nodded, turned away, and walked toward the set of double doors that provided egress. Although he'd used a sudden onset of sickness as an excuse to take his leave, he did feel sick. The sight of Spencer Rowelings's face on a notice of reward had made him queasy and, he found, as he unfastened the reins of his mules and climbed into the wagon's seat, his hands were shaking badly. He was so discombobulated that he didn't even notice the bitter-cold temperature that had seized him anew, now that he was outdoors again.

Bodie, California

The next morning, Matthew Lewis was driving along Main Street, wishing the city council would improve the damn thoroughfare. This time of year, the cold that gathered over the mountains surrounding the bowl in which Bowie sat froze the wagon ruts in the mud. Ice, which covered the street, here and there, for at least part of the day, also impeded travel, whether by foot, horse, stagecoach, or wagon.

The town's elevation, which was above the treeline, and the rugged terrain on every side, was plenty rough enough without the severity of the approaching winter's climate. His mules were sure-footed, sure enough, but no animal was footsure enough not to slip and slide on ice and snow, especially when it covered damn near every square inch of the land.

Some winters, there'd been fifteen-foot-tall snowdrifts and buildings had been so encased in snow that they were all but lost in the white stuff. Now, even in early fall, it sure looked like the coming winter would be terrible.

Damn!

It was just his miserable luck.

A week ago, it had been cold in the mountains, where he and the rest of Spencer Rowelings's gang were holed up in the abandoned mining shacks, but, between making batches of 'shine for their customers, whose number seemed to increase every day, they had stoves and moonshine to warm them and food to fill their bellies, and life was good, more or less.

At the same time, money was flowing into their hands as fast as the current in a downhill stream, and each of them was getting closer and closer to fulfilling whatever dreams their shares of the profits would buy. It wouldn't be much longer, Rowelings assured them, with his usual hyperbole, before Baker could buy or build a house somewhere and marry that girl in El Dorado City; Jackson could start over in Chicago or New York or, hell, London or Paris or Rome, if he preferred; and Storm could take to the sea, not as a crew member working for his passage, but as the captain of his own damn ship. It wouldn't be much longer, either, before Lewis and Spencer Rowelings could put their own plan into action.

But, if he froze to death first, he'd never live long enough to partner with Rowelings in the future enterprises that Rowelings had planned and shared with Lewis alone, at least in part.

He turned his team into an alley that led past the western side of The Bonanza saloon. After dismounting from the wagon, he tied ropes to the two mules before fastening their other ends to a nearby post.

Starting back down the alley, toward the front of the saloon, he caught himself. This week, Porter Hawkins would just have to wait another half-hour, maybe even sixty minutes, for his damn hooch.

If he didn't get warmed up, he'd freeze.

Hell, he was half-frozen now.

Nobody was likely to find the wagon. Any fool who was outside on a day like this was apt to be intent on completing whatever errand he was tending to as fast as he could so he could return to his home or place of work and get out of the frozen wasteland that Bodie had become over the last week. If somebody did happen to see the wagon, though, and investigate, he'd find a load of unattended casks of whiskey just waiting to be driven away.

If somebody stole the moonshine, Rowelings would have his hide—literally.

"Damn!" He wasn't about to risk having a whole wagon full of hooch stolen just to get warm. Muttering curses, he turned back, retraced his steps, and entered Hawkins's saloon.

"Looks like you need a drink," Dean Norton called, as Lewis hastened toward the bar, shivering as he walked.

"He'll have time enough for that after he's unloaded my order," Hawkins said.

"Come on, then, Dean; let's get that wagon unloaded," Lewis urged.

"Can't spare Dean; not with this crowd," Hawkins objected. "You'll have to unload the casks and roll them on into my stockroom by yourself this time."

Just my luck! Lewis thought, turning from the bar and the drink that Norton had just about set down for him before Hawkins had denied him both the whiskey and the bartender's assistance.

* * *

It would forever remain a mystery to Lewis just how he had managed to unload the casks and roll them into The Bonanza's storeroom, but somehow, he'd accomplished the task without freezing to death. To reward himself for a job well done, he'd visit one of the town's many brothels.

He deserved a warm, dry, comfortable place.

He deserved a few drinks at an overpriced, elegant bar in a luxurious house of pleasure.

He deserved a beautiful woman to have and to hold, for an hour's time, and he was ready, willing, and able to pay for such warmth and pleasure.

Hera's Glory, he thought, here I come!

It was a short ride to the bawdy house, which both Martin Brennan, the barkeep at The Gold and Silver, and Dean Norton, the bartender at The Bonanza, had recommended as one of the best brothels in town—or in the West, for that matter—with prices to match. A session with one of the ladies, depending on the lady and the time spent with her, would set a customer back anywhere between ten and a hundred dollars, they said.

Fortunately, Spencer shared the moonshining profits—well the half he didn't keep for himself, anyway—equally among Baker, Jackson, Storm, and Lewis himself.

Since muckers received three dollars and seventy-five cents a day; miners, four dollars a day; and skilled laborers and supervisors seven dollars a day, for shifts ranging from ten to twelve hours, the bawdy house charges were extravagant, indeed.

Hell, gold sold for twenty dollars an ounce and silver for a dollar an ounce, so a lady of the evening—at least, the ones at Hera's Glory—were worth between half an ounce to five ounces of gold or ten to a hundred ounces of silver. It put matters into perspective, Lewis thought, to think of prices and costs in terms of the local economy's basis, which, here, was gold and silver.

And the cost of the ladies was just one of the expenses he'd encounter at Hera's Glory, the bartenders had warned him. A lady was expected to be wined and dined.

"The first place you'll go, after being admitted—if you are admitted; Elodie's picky about the men she does business with—is the bordello's saloon for a few drinks with the lady of Elodie's choice, after which you'll tie on a feedbag with her in the establishment's restaurant. Then, and only then, will you be allowed to go upstairs," Norton had declared. When Lewis later asked Brennan about Elodie's protocol for guests, Brennan had confirmed Norton's statements.

"You mean, a man—a paying customer—isn't afforded the courtesy of selecting his own woman?" Lewis had asked.

"Not at Hera's," he'd been assured.

Still, they had told him, any of Madame Elodie's ladies was worth every dollar and cent or every ounce of gold or silver.

James Baker, Russ Jackson, and Zach Storm likely dressed shabbily by comparison with Lewis himself, although, before his arrest, Spencer had worn better clothes. Lewis always dressed in splendor, both because, as an actor, he was used to wearing fine clothes, which was expected of him, by both the roles he typically played and by his admirers, and because he enjoyed dressing well. For a thespian, clothes did make the man, he believed, just as costumes helped an actor to project a character.

He noticed, too, that the better a man dressed, the better he was treated. Today, his appearance proved acceptable to the butler, who no doubt doubled as a bouncer, and Lewis was admitted.

He followed the manservant to the saloon, Heracles's Labors, where a lady dressed in a fine, full-length white gown, the plunging neckline of which revealed an ample sample of the woman's bosom, led him to a small, red, heart-shaped table bearing a lit candle at its center. "Someone will take your order directly," she said, offering Lewis a twenty-four-carat smile.

He nodded. "Thank you."

Service was prompt, indeed, a woman in similar, but not quite as elaborate, dress as that of the first lady, appearing within minutes to suggest champagne.

"Bourbon," he said.

"Just so. And for the lady, sir?"

What lady? Lewis thought. No women but the hostess and the waitress had approached him since he'd stepped foot in this place. "Champagne."

"Very good, sir."

Before the beverages arrived, Lewis's companion for the evening did.

He rose and, when she presented her hand, kissed the back of it. Rounding the table, he pulled back the chair on the opposite side. "Please," he invited her, "be seated."

As she did so, a framed photograph behind the bar caught his gaze, and Lewis stared, his brow furrowed. To the woman, as gorgeous a redhead as he'd ever seen on any stage, he said, "I'll be back in just a moment."

She frowned, but said nothing.

Crossing the elegant room, he stepped up to the bar.

"May I help you, sir?" the bartender asked.

The question didn't register. Nothing did except the photograph in the frame on the wall.

It couldn't be! he told himself.

Beneath the man depicted in the photograph, there was text: "REWARD $1,000 for the capture and delivery of this fugitive to any city, county, state or federal lawman."

Suddenly, Lewis didn't want bourbon. He didn't want a steak dinner served on a white linen cloth set with china dishes, etched crystal glasses, and silverware, or an ivory figure of a nymph as a centerpiece. He didn't even want the company of the gorgeous redhead, which, a minute ago, he had craved.

He turned, feeling sick. His first thought was to flee the saloon and the brothel, but he checked the impulse.

A sudden, hasty departure would draw attention, and the last thing Lewis wanted and the last thing he, and his cohorts, could afford was attention.

Instead of bolting, as every fiber of his being urged him to do, he returned to the table. "Please accept my apologies, my dear, but I'm afraid I do not feel well. I shall have to forego an evening of pleasure and delight with you, but I shall return another time. Meanwhile, please accept, as a token of my devotion, this gift and my promise to see you again, if I may, when I am able to show you the good time that you deserve." He handed her a twenty-dollar bill.

Although she seemed confused, she smiled, tucking the bill into her décolletage. "Thank you, sir. I would be delighted to see you again, when you have recovered."

Lewis nodded, turned away, and walked toward the set of double doors that provided egress. Although he'd used a sudden onset of sickness as an excuse to take his leave, he did feel sick. The sight of Spencer Rowelings's face on a notice of reward had made him queasy and, he found, as he unfastened the reins of his mules and climbed into the wagon's seat, his hands were shaking badly. He was so discombobulated that he didn't even notice the bitter-cold temperature that had seized him anew, now that he was outdoors again.

Chapter 45

Red Velvet

"Vice may triumph for a time, crime may flaunt its victories in the face of honest toilers, but in the end the law will follow the wrong-doer to a bitter fate, and dishonor and punishment will be the portion of those who sin."
— Allan Pinkerton (1819-1884)

Bodie, California

At The Red Garter, Bane received quite an eyeful. The furniture, the furnishings, and the décor were in good taste, but they weren't as elegant as those of Hera's Glory and they certainly weren't as fine—or as expensive—as those at Rose's bordellos in and near his own hometown, Excelsior, Nevada, in White Pine County. Bane assumed that the establishment took its name from the red velvet garters that the ladies wore, accompanied by little other attire, high on their thighs. The association of the establishment with the rather risqué item was a clever sales technique, Bane thought, since, for all intents and purposes, it linked Madam Annabelle's bordello with a ladies' undergarment.

"Good morning, sir," she said, as soon as her manservant had ushered him into her presence in her house's front parlor. "I am Annabelle." She extended the back of her hand.

Bane hesitated. Pamela, he was certain, would not approve of his kissing the back of another woman's hand, least of all that of a soiled dove. On the other hand, it would be rude not to do so. In fact, such a slight might cause Madam Annabelle to evict him.

"Is something the matter?" she inquired.

After kissing her hand, he smiled. "Not at all, Miss—"

"Just Annabelle—or Madam Annabelle, if you prefer."

He nodded. "I was just thinking of the proposition I intend to offer you."

She seemed to bristle. "I myself am unavailable, sir," she said icily.

Bane felt his face warm as he blushed. "Oh! I'm sorry! I didn't mean that kind of proposition."

"It seems that you have trouble saying just what you do mean."

"I'm a U. S. marshal."

Her jaw set, and her eyes hardened. "I'm afraid I must ask you to leave my premises. You seem to have come here under false pretenses."

"Hear me out," he urged. "It will be worth your time."

"I have a minute or two to spare, I suppose, but, I must warn you, my prices are much steeper than those of my ladies."

Bane made her the same offer as he had Elodie and the other madams with whom he had spoken.

While her manner didn't exactly soften, she seemed more willing to listen to her guest, despite the fact that he had misrepresented himself, initially, at least, as a customer, rather than a lawman. "A hundred dollars? Just to hang that photograph in my house?"

"In a conspicuous location and accompanied by the announcement of the thousand-dollar reward for the capture and delivery of this fugitive to any city, county, state or federal lawman, yes," Bane agreed.

"That offer of the thousand-dollar reward extends to me or any of my girls, should one of us capture and deliver the prisoner?"

Bane shrugged. "Sure, but doing so would be dangerous work."

"That's why, if one of us were to effect his capture, by means peculiar to women who know how to satisfy certain appetites common among men, we would hire an intermediary to escort the captive to the local sheriff's office." She looked puzzled. "But why would you want him to be delivered there, to another lawman, rather than to you?" Annabelle asked.

"I have my reasons."

As she studied him, a sly look of respect seemed to brighten her features. "I suppose you do, at that. All right, Marshal. It's a deal."

Bane rose from the sofa, extracted a hundred-dollar bill from his wallet, and paid the madam. "Good day." He turned toward the archway that connected with the hallway leading to the front door.

"Wait," Annabelle said.

Bane turned back to her.

"You still owe me for my time." She glanced at a clock on the parlor wall and smiled approvingly. "Five minutes: ten dollars."

Bane frowned. "Two dollars a minute?"

She nodded.

Bane paid her.

"I might have more information," she informed him, "if the price is right."

"What's the right price?"

"Fifty dollars. In advance."

Bane shook his head as, retrieving his wallet, he extracted the fee and paid his informant.

"You seem to have a lot of money for a marshal," Annabelle observed.

"I do all right."

She winked at him. "I bet you do, Marshal."

"What information do you have for me?"

"Brenda—she's one of my ladies; I think you'd like her. Anyway, Brenda told me that, a while back, before Myron printed anything about it in the local newspaper—."

"Myron?"

"Myron Hollis, The Clarion Call's owner, publisher, editor, reporter, janitor—"

"I take your point," Bane said. "What did Brenda hear?"

"One of her customers, a traveling man, mentioned that a rancher's wife was killed near Genoa, Nevada—shot plumb through the center of her forehead—by somebody who knew how to handle a gun, her customer reckoned. Then, the killer stole her husband's clothes off the clothesline. What a man would want with a rancher's clothing, I couldn't say."

He could, Bane thought, but he wouldn't.

"Brenda's customer also said the bastard stole the couple's horses and money."

"He say how much money?" Bane asked.

"Two-hundred dollars!" Annabelle smiled, as if she were enjoying the gossip. "I hope the information was worth it," she said

"Me, too," he replied, knowing full well that it almost certainly was worth it.

As Bane rose, Annabelle said, "I have one more tip for you, Marshal. And this one won't cost you anything."

"Why the sudden impulse toward generosity?"

"You and your deputies should visit a few of Bodie's saloons, if you haven't already."

"Why?"

"To sample the whiskey."

"I'm not a drinking man."

"Make an exception. You'll be glad you did."

"What's in it for you, if not a reward for your tip?"

"After the dens opened in Chinatown, I lost a few of my ladies to opium addiction. I don't want to lose more to the evils of whiskey."

"They're young," Bane pointed out. "It generally takes years for spirits to—"

"If I were a U. S. marshal, God forbid, I'd act on such a tip."

"Thanks, Annabelle. I believe I will."

* * *

"Visiting the town's brothels was worth it, all right," Luke said, after Bane repeated Annabelle's account of the woman's murder and the thefts of her husband's clothing and the couple's horses and savings.

"I'll say," Badger agreed.

"Apparently, the crimes weren't reported in the local newspaper at the time that Annabelle's Brenda heard of them from her customer," Bane said, "which makes Annabelle's statement that two-hundred dollars was stolen credible."

"Maybe not," Luke suggested. "I mean, she could have made up the amount. Two hundred dollars is a good, round figure, after all."

"Yes, she could have," Bane concurred, "but I don't think she did."

"Why's that?" Badger asked.

"For the same reason she probably didn't make up the details about the woman's being shot in the center of her forehead, or the woman's hanging clothes out to dry, or the killer's theft of the widower's clothing from the clothesline, or his theft of the couple's horses," Bane explained. "She could simply have said that she'd heard that a rancher's wife was killed a while back, near Genoa.

"In any event, we learned something. The madam of The Red Garter was telling the truth when she said the killing of the rancher's wife was never reported in the local newspaper."

Chapter 46

Fool's Errands

"... Every discovery of what is false leads us to seek earnestly after what is true."
— John Keats (1795-1821)

Rowelings's Camp, near Bodie, California

"What do you imagine he wants this time?" James Baker asked as he, Russ Jackson, and Zach Storm walked across the compound among the shacks built by the miners of a previous decade.

None of his companions replied or needed to do so. Like Baker, they knew not to question Rowelings, who had a short fuse and a deadly fury.

The shacks had been abandoned when the supply of gold in the mountainous terrain began to peter out. Knowing this, Spencer Rowelings had led them here to hole up.

It was a remote area, in a rugged and inhospitable region of the country that was difficult to reach. As such, it was seldom visited. Chances were good, that, if a posse did risk the ride up the dangerous, narrow trails that cut back and forth along the steep inclines, searching for escapees of Nevada's State Prison, the gang would be able to hold them off a long while. With a little luck, they'd even be able to kill the lawman and his band of deputized citizens.

Meanwhile, they'd already made a fair amount of money selling moonshine to the greedy bastards who owned the saloons in Bodie. It wouldn't be too long before each of them would have made enough money to facilitate his freedom and to pursue his dreams. They'd make a lot more money, too, in a fairly short period of time. Unfortunately, until then, they, like Matthew Lewis, or whatever his name really was, had to answer to Rowelings.

None of them had known him during the short time he'd been imprisoned with them in Carson City after he'd been sentenced to death. Now that they had gotten to know him, they understood that Rowelings wasn't somebody to cross. He was as hard a man as any they'd ever encountered, and they'd each met their share of such men.

There was a wilderness inside Rowelings, too, part madness and part genius, which, coupled with a willingness to commit any outrage, without a moment's hesitation, guilt, sorrow, or remorse, made him as dangerous a menace as John Wesley Hardin, Clay Allison, Jesse James, or Billy the Kid was or had been.

Sure, in their own ways, Baker, Jackson, and Storm were, or could be, dangerous men, but none of them was a Hardin, Allison, James, or Billy the Kid.

They weren't cut out to stare down death any time prosperity seemed possible—provided that a man risked his life to attain it. That was one of the differences between them and Rowelings and his ilk. Men who made a name for themselves, whether enforcing or defying the law, were a rare breed, a breed apart, and men like Rowelings knew it, just as Baker, like Jackson, and Storm—and Matthew Lewis, Baker suspected—knew it. One or more of the lawmen who hunted them might have the grit to stand against a man like Rowelings, but no member of Rowelings's gang did.

Oh, they might gripe and piss and moan, among themselves, but they knew better than to challenge or to defy Rowelings. To do so, they understood, was tantamount to courting death.

At the door to the shack that their leader had appropriated for himself, Storm knocked.

"Come in!" Rowelings called from within.

Rowelings's second-in-command—a spot that Storm had once owned—was already inside, with Rowelings.

Their underlings stepped inside, out of the cold.

"Have a seat," Rowelings invited them.

They claimed a chair, sat, and waited.

Rowelings let the moment stretch, before speaking. "While he was in town, Matthew stopped by one of the local whorehouses," Rowelings informed them, "to sell our hooch to the madam, he says, right, Matthew?"

"That's right, yes," Lewis said, a bit hastily it seemed to Baker.

Bodie's brothels hadn't been on their list of potential customers as far as any of the rest of them knew. Had it been business or pleasure that had directed Lewis there? Storm wondered. If the latter, Lewis might have had hell to pay in advising Rowelings of his visit, which raised the question as to why he would have done so.

"Tell them what you told me," Rowelings directed.

Lewis informed his audience of the reward notice he'd seen framed on the wall behind the bar in Hera's Glory's saloon—the notice with Rowelings's photograph printed on it.

A sense of panic surged through Storm. "You mean to say that our presence in the area is known?"

"No," Lewis said. "I doubt that it is. The notice read 'REWARD $1,000 for the capture and delivery of this fugitive to any city, county, state or federal lawman," which suggests that our presence remains unknown. Otherwise, the notice would probably require our delivery to a specific lawman at a specific location."

Storm breathed a bit easier. "Yes, that makes sense."

"Matthew and I have discussed the matter, and we have decided that it introduces an excellent means by which we may obfuscate the matter of our whereabouts."

"I don't see how," Baker said.

"No, you wouldn't, would you?"

Baker gritted his teeth, but looked away from Rowelings's baleful gaze. The bastard had said the same thing or something similar about him a while back. It had grated on him then, and it grated on him now. He also chafed under the fact that, angered though he might be, he didn't have the sand to stand up to the man who'd insulted him, openly and contemptuously, before Jackson and Storm as well as before Lewis.

"Here's how," Rowelings said. "Over a series of days, we mail first one, then another, tip as to the location of Spencer Rowelings."

"Are you plumb loco?" The words had spewed forth from Baker's mouth of their own accord, as involuntarily as a heartbeat or a sneeze. Now spoken, they were impossible to recall. Looking aghast, he said, "I mean, uh, what I meant to say was, uh—"

Rowelings's smile resembled a death's-head grin as he assured Baker, "No harm done, James."

Neither Rowelings's smile nor his tone of voice, which had seemed calm and understanding, reassured Baker. Instead, they horrified him, since Baker was certain they meant exactly the opposite of what they seemed to mean. "I'm sorry, Mr. Rowelings!" Baker nearly screamed. "I meant no disrespect; I was just shocked when you said—"

Again, the grin of death. "No offense taken, I assure you, James."

That was another clue that Rowelings meant the opposite of what he'd said. Rowelings seldom called him 'James.' He nearly always referred to him by his last name. Sometimes, he called the others by their given names, 'Russ' and 'Zach' and 'Matthew,' but he almost always called him 'Baker.'

"Now, if I may continue?"

Baker nodded vigorously. "Please!"

Rowelings scoffed. "As I said, on separate days, we mail a number of tips as to my location to Madam Elodie of Hera's Glory and to her counterparts at Bodie's other bordellos, apprising them of my location. They apprise our adversary, whoever he may be, and, as a result, we send our foe off on one wild goose chase after another."

"Didn't the notice require your capture and delivery to a city, county, state, or federal lawman?" Storm reminded Rowelings.

"It does, indeed, Zach, but, of course, the ladies will not themselves seek to arrest me any more than they will try to deliver me to a lawman, whether of a city, county, state, or the federal government itself. I trust that the ladies, however, will have other means to persuade my nemesis to act upon their tips. For instance, might they not suggest a lesser, but still substantial, amount of money if their tip leads to my enemy's own capture of me, even if he is compelled to undertake the capture himself?"

Storm nodded. "I believe so."

"As do I," Rowelings said, "and Matthew. We shall have amused ourselves while sending our foe on as many fool's errands as he cares to pursue while we remain safe and secure in our present abodes, building our fortunes as we distill whiskey that our customers can sell at huge profits to miners and others who have an unquenchable appetite for our product. Eventually, my foe will no doubt tire of his fruitless sallies hither and yon, but, by then, he will also have become quite skeptical of any tips by anyone, offered by any means. Until then, we have moonshine and fortunes to make."

As Baker, Jackson, and Storm rose, Rowelings said, "Zach? Have you a moment?"

"Of course."

As Baker and Jackson headed for the stills, Rowelings asked, "Could you get by without Baker for a few days?"

"Sure."

"Longer than that?"

Detecting the menace in Rowelings's words, Jackson hesitated. "A while longer, I suppose.

Rowelings grinned. "Excellent!"

Chapter 47

Cocking the Hammer

"Whenever you get into a row be sure and not shoot too quick. Take time. I've known many a feller slip up for shootin' in a hurry."
— Wild Bill Hickok (1837-1876)

Bodie, California

"I could use a drink," Badger said, as he pushed his empty plate away.

"It's barely past noon," Luke noted.

Badger looked puzzled. "What's the time of day have to do with having a drink?"

"Just make sure you don't have one too many," Bane cautioned his deputy.

"Have I ever?"

"Not so far," Bane admitted, "as far as I know."

Signaling the waitress, Bane paid the check and left a tip.

They crossed the crowded hotel restaurant. At the door, Bane told Badger, "The point is not to make this the occasion when you do have one too many drinks. We all have to keep our wits about us. Needless to say, this is an occasion on which we can forego wearing our badges." He slipped his own into his interior vest pocket.

His deputies also unpinned their badges from their shirts and pocketed them.

"Hell, Bane; plenty of folks have seen us on the street, in stores, in saloons, and in bordellos, and those who haven't seen us themselves have probably heard about the presence of a U. S. marshal and two deputy U. S. marshals in their town."

"That's true, Badger," Bane admitted, "but it's also true that we don't need to make our identities as lawmen known to those who haven't seen us sporting badges or remind folks who have seen our badges that we're in their midst."

"Just act casually," Luke advised his fellow deputy. "If anybody tries to provoke you, leave."

"We don't need to call further attention to our presence by engaging in a knock-down, drag-out brawl in a saloon," Bane agreed. "Act intoxicated, have a sip, then leave. If anybody objects, stay a minute longer; take a second sip; spill the rest; and stagger outside."

* * *

An hour later, they regrouped on one of the town's side streets to compare notes.

"I see why Annabelle thought visiting saloons might be a good idea," Bane said.

"There are a lot of watering holes in Bodie," Badger observed. "There's no way that the three of us can cover all of them in one day."

"There's always tomorrow," Luke reminded him.

"I don't think we'll have to visit all of them," Bane said. "A few more, here on Main Street, will probably tell us all we need to know. You two take two apiece one side of the street; I'll take one or two on the other side. When you've each checked two, cross the street and give me a hand. Then, we'll move down a block or two and repeat the process."

Badger grinned. "Sounds like a plan, Bane."

"Here's some spending money," Bane said, handing his deputies each a twenty-dollar bill.

* * *

"Howdy, Marshal!" The barkeep waved to Bane as he staggered into the Sagebrush Saloon.

Most of the men turned to stare, their hostile gazes making it clear to Bane that his presence was an unwelcome one.

"You see a badge on me?" he demanded, as he lurched to the bar.

"Not at the moment," the man admitted, "but I saw one on you earlier today and on other days as well."

Some of the Sagebrush's clientele continued to stare, but others had looked away, returning to whatever business, cards, whiskey, or women, they were pursuing inside the raucous barroom.

"I'm off-duty now, and I'd like to keep it that way." He weaved a little as he spoke, slightly slurring his words.

"Whatever you say, Marshal."

"Name's Bane!"

"Whatever you, say, Mar—" Looking up from the bar he'd been wiping with a rag, he saw Bane's penetrating gaze. The lawman's eyes, cold and intense, looked as deadly as those of a rattlesnake about to strike. A chill ran up, along the bartender's spine. "—uh, Bane."

Bane nodded, letting his head bounce a bit. "That's better."

"What can I get for you?"

"Whiskey."

The bartender started to turn away.

"The cheap stuff's good enough," Bane added.

A man stepped up to the bar, beside Bane, crowding him on the right.

Swaying slightly, Bane said, slurring his words, "There's plenty of room, mister; no need to stand in my boots."

The man was tall, about the same height as Bane himself, and muscular, with thick arms and big hands. A miner, most likely, or a mucker.

"Any law against it?"

Another man, shorter and heavier than the one on Bane's right, bellied up to the bar on Bane's left.

The bartender turned back, a bottle in one hand, a shot glass in the other. Setting the glass on the bar, he poured a jigger full of amber liquid into it. "That'll cost you a dollar," he said.

Bane paid for the shot and dumped the whiskey into his mouth.

Damn, if it wasn't the vilest booze he'd ever tasted! It was so bad he had to force himself not to spew it out of his mouth. Instead, he swallowed the liquor and raised the back of his hand to his mouth. From the corner of his eye, he'd seen the tall galoot lean away from him and draw back his fist.

Bane wiped the back of his hand across his lips, using it as a makeshift napkin, before jerking his elbow hard into the tall man's jaw.

Knocked back a foot by the force of the unanticipated blow, the bastard cursed.

The man on the left tried his luck next, but Bane was ready for him, too. Turning quickly, he threw a punch with the same arm he'd used to strike the man on his right. His fist's impact snapped the squat man's head back sharply, and the would-be attacker's knees gave way, as he fell to the floor.

The tall man shoved Bane, and the marshal spun around, staggered a few feet, and pointed the barrel of his six-shooter, which seemed to appear, as if by magic, in Bane's hand, at the other assailant's midriff.

That stopped him in his tracks.

Cocking the hammer, Bane said, "Mister, I don't want trouble. I just came in for a drink, and I've had that, so I'll be leaving now."

The shorter, thicker man had picked himself up, off the floor, and he didn't look a bit happy about having been there.

As he stepped toward Bane from the left, the taller man approached from the right. "You'll be leaving, right enough," the latter said, grinning.

"Pete!" A voice called above the murmurs and shouts of the drunken audience that the saloon's regular crowd had become. "Henry! We have company!"

Both Pete, the taller man, and Henry, the shorter, looked toward the saloon's
entrance.

"What's all the ruckus, Bane?" Luke's voice called above the din.

"Looks like he could use a hand," Badger said, equally loudly.

Unchallenged, they made their way to the back of the large room, their own
Colts drawn.

"Come on, Bane," Luke suggested. "Let's find a bar where our company's
wanted."

"Or at least tolerated," Badger said.

Although most of the men in the saloon were armed and, no doubt, in
certain circumstances, dangerous enough, none of the rest of them seemed
interested in bringing the law down on themselves by getting into a fracas with
a U. S. marshal and his deputies. Maybe they were wiser, or maybe they just
weren't as drunk, yet, as the two men at the bar.

Outside, Badger chuckled. "I thought you agreed that we should just act
casually," Luke told Bane.

"'If anybody tries to provoke you, leave'—that's what I told Badger," Luke
declared. "I didn't think I'd need to tell you that, too, Bane."

"You agreed that we shouldn't call attention to ourselves by engaging in 'a
knock-down, drag-out brawl' in a saloon, Bane," Badger reminded him.

"All right, all right!" Bane groused. "You boys sure like to pile it on, don't
you?"

"Do we, Badger?" Luke asked, playing the innocent.

"I know I don't, and I'm right sure you don't, either, Luke."

"If you've had enough fun at my expense, maybe we can get back to business,
just for a moment," Bane ordered.

His deputies affected a serious demeanor.

"The whiskey I tasted was horrible," Bane said. "How about yours?"

"Rotgut," Luke declared.

"So bad I had to force myself to swallow it," Badger agreed.

"We've had a sample in, what, now? Eighteen saloons?"

Badger and Luke nodded.

"All with the same results?"

"I'd say the drink I had at The Lonesome Dove was all right," Badger said.

"How about the dove? Was she all right, too?" Luke asked.

When he saw that Badger meant to ignore his question, Luke said, "I think the liquor at The Drifters was likely from a distillery in Tennessee or Louisiana."

"So, of the saloons' stock we sampled, maybe sixteen served whiskey of a questionable source?"

Badger nodded.

"Sounds right to me," Luke said.

"Then we agree? Somebody hereabouts is making moonshine and selling it to the saloon owners?"

The others nodded.

"Well, then, I think our afternoon on the town's been a success."

"Bane? If I may make a suggestion?"

"Shoot."

"If we ever have to do something like this again, let's pick a day that's not the miners' day off."

Bane grinned. "I'll certainly take that recommendation under advisement, Luke."

Chapter 48

A Flock of Vultures

"A vulture feeds upon [a man's] heart for ever; that vulture the very creature he creates."

— Herman Melville (1819-)

Rowelings's Camp, near Bodie, California

"You killed him!" Russ Jackson cried, looking aghast at Spencer Rowelings.

Like Zach Storm, Jackson had grabbed his own weapon, abandoning the stills, and come running after hearing a gunshot, thinking that maybe a posse had found their campsite.

Instead, they found James Baker, lying blood-soaked and dead on the ground, between his shack and Rowelings, who stood in the doorway of his own shanty. Although he'd holstered his six-shooter, it was plain that he'd shot Baker.

"That's right," Roweling admitted.

"Why?" Storm demanded.

"You said you could get by without him," Rowelings reminded his some-time-lieutenant.

"That's no reason to have killed the man," Storm contended.

"I decided I could get by without him, too. In fact, he was a danger to the rest of us. He was stupid, impulsive, and reckless, and he shot off his mouth far too often."

Storm shook his head. "So, you decided to kill him, just like that, in cold blood?"

Rowelings shrugged. "Hell, we all die, sooner or later. Today just happened to be his time."

Jackson frowned. "Where's Lewis? You kill him, too?"

"Never mind about Matthew. Get yourselves a pick and shovel, and bury Baker, before he draws a flock of vultures."

Chapter 49

"If you can't afford the passage to China, Chinatown will do."
— Bradford Messenger (1837 -)

Chinatown, Bodie, California

"We agree, then, it appears," Bane said.

"Those saloons are selling rotgut whiskey, all right, and in greater quantities than the legitimate stock they're buying," Luke asserted.

"They're making a fortune," Badger declared.

"Which makes me wonder," Bane continued, "where they're buying their equipment and supplies."

"General store, most likely," Luke suggested.

Bane nodded. "Probably, but I want to find out."

"Where else could they be buying it?" Badger asked.

"That's what we need to discover."

The three of them started across town.

* * *

The sign read, "Gerald B. Hess, General Store."

"What might I interest you in purchasing today, gentlemen? New boots, perhaps? Vests? I'm running a sale on shirts this week."

"You have any idea what a man would need, in the way of supplies and equipment, to make moonshine?" Bane asked.

"Nope, and, even if I did, I wouldn't sell it. Making whiskey's illegal, unless it's made by a licensed distillery."

"Yes, I know."

"I reckon you would, Marshal. What I'm confused about is why you'd think I would sell such merchandise. I'm a law-abiding man, and I run a legitimate business."

"I have no doubt of that, but, being the owner of a general store, and quite a large one, at that, I thought that maybe you might have seen some equipment, maybe in a catalog, such as moonshiners might use."

"I've seen all kinds of equipment for cooking, which may or may not be useful to moonshiners. Whether it actually is, I couldn't say."

"Well, thanks, anyway, Mr. Hess." Bane and his deputies headed for the door.

"Wait!" Hess called.

They turned back to the merchant.

"There's another emporium in town. It doesn't offer the variety or quality that mine does, of course. It's located in the northern part of Bodie, between Chinatown and the seedier bordellos. It's run by Liu Wei. He deals in some unusual items. Keeps a stock of fireworks on hand year round. Independence Day celebrations are huge in Bodie, lasting five or six days.

"But, supposedly, he also caters to the tastes and inclinations, criminal and otherwise, of locals. Mind you, I'm not saying Liu Wei sells the items you're interested in, but it might pay you to see for yourselves; on the other hand, it might not."

Bane nodded. "Thanks for the tip."

* * *

"It's hard to believe that a town the size of Bodie just sprang up, out in the middle of nowhere," Badger commented as they walked north on Main Street.

"The discovery of gold and silver often has that effect on real estate," Luke said. "So did cattle trails, railroads, and military outposts."

"I know, but it still seems incredible."

Bane agreed with Badger to the extent that the almost-overnight eruption of tents and shacks, followed by houses, stores, hotels, schools, churches, post offices, and newspapers, seemed an unlikely occurrence, despite the incentives to expansion and settlement that Luke had mentioned.

Only a few decades ago, Nevada had been carved out of Utah Territory, to become, itself a territory, not being granted statehood until the end of the Civil War. Even now, in 1884, eleven territories remained: the Dakotas, Oklahoma, Montana, Wyoming, New Mexico, Utah, Arizona, Idaho, Washington, and Alaska. Hell, Seward's Folly hadn't even been purchased from Russia until 1867!

Their walk eventually led them into the north end of Bodie, where the buildings looked much like those in the rest of the town, except that most of them were festooned with banners, signs, and bunting of bright colors that gave them a festive look, and the streets were occupied by a passel of food vendors whose offerings filled the air with succulent aromas. A bevy of vegetable stands added to the colorful atmosphere.

Storefronts were dedicated to laundries, restaurants, and stores selling wood, metal, fish, poultry, and, yes, despite the fact that the Fourth of July wouldn't arrive for several months yet, fireworks. According to Madame Annabelle, Chinatown was also home to a number of opium dens, which, despite fines of five-hundred dollars for users of the illegal drug and a thousand dollars for its sellers, remained open, just as their product continued to be widely available.

The Chinese Cooperative Emporium was located on King Street, two blocks north of Chinatown's northernmost extremity. The two-story mercantile, a block long by a block deep, was packed with every item a body could want and then some. Shelves, racks, and counters were so crowded with clothing, fabrics, hardware items, groceries, medicines, toys, candy, dinnerware, cosmetics, toiletries, and other wares that Bane felt lost in the vast sea of merchandise.

A young Chinese man appeared, smiling and bowing at the waist, before asking, "May I help you?" His English was better than that of a lot of outlaws Bane had interrogated, and his demeanor and language was a whole lot more refined.

"I'm Marshal Bane Messenger, and these are my deputies. We'd like to speak to Mr. Liu Wei, please."

"Ah, so. I will let him know."

"Thank you."

Badger picked up an item from a nearby shelf; turned it this way and that; set it down; examined another article; and stepped a few feet down the table on which an assortment of other goods were laid out or, in some cases, jumbled about in heaps, probably from customers having handled them, just as Badger was doing, and then setting them down wherever it was handy.

"Don't go too far, Badger," Luke warned. "If you get lost in a store this big and well-stocked, we might never find you."

"You wish to speak to me, Marshal?"

Bane turned to face the man who'd spoken to him from behind.

"You're Liu Wei?"

"Yes."

Bane was surprised, again. First, the clerk or salesman to whom he'd spoken, and now the store's proprietor himself, had spoken perfect English, tinged with a Southern accent. Speaking a second language fluently was a rare skill anywhere, but it was exceptional here in the West. "You were born here?"

"At age seventeen, my younger brother Zhi Peng, whom you met a few minutes ago, and I immigrated from Cuba to work on plantations in the American South. When work began on the Transcontinental Railroad, we came west, where we helped to build part of the Central Pacific Railroad. While others spent their money, in their free time, on alcohol and ladies of easy virtue, Zhi

Peng and I saved ours. When the Central Pacific and the Union Pacific were joined in Utah, in 1869, we were discharged."

"You and Zhi Peng earned enough money working on the railroad to start this business?" To Bane's own ears, his question sounded as incredulous as the likelihood that such a feat were possible.

Liu Wei chuckled softly. "This establishment, although it is not located in San Francisco or New York, cost many times what both Zhi Peng and I earned in the plantation's fields and working for the railroad, Marshal, but we made many friends among the Chinese railroad workers who, like my brother and I, saved, rather than spent, as much money as we could over the years.

"Together, and with the financial support also of many of our families, we were able to lease this property and stock it with merchandise, the amount and variety of which has increased, year after year, as profits have allowed. Zhi Peng and I, as well as our staff, receive little pay, but all of us have equal shares of stock, in our company."

"I see," Bane said, impressed by the ingenuity of Liu Wei's and Zhi Peng's business plan.

"You did not come to ask me about The Chinese Cooperative Emporium, though, I suspect, Marshal."

"No," Bane admitted. "I came to ask you whether you see such supplies and equipment as are used to distill liquor."

Liu Wei frowned. "Illegal liquor, you mean?"

Bane nodded.

The thought seemed to amuse the merchant. "No, Marshal, I assure you that such items are unavailable at The Chinese Cooperative Emporium."

"Do you have any idea where such items might be bought?"

"You and your deputies are on the trail of moonshiners? Here, in the West?"

Although the way in which Liu Wei asked the question made the very idea sound ludicrous, Bane nodded.

"You are surprised that I know the word 'moonshiner,' perhaps?"

"It's not one that's commonly used here, in the West."

"Ah, so, but it is frequently used in the American South—and in Cuba, where it is el destilador ilegal de licor—and in China, too for that matter, where it is □□□□□□."

Bane chuckled. "I'll take your word for it, Liu Wei. Thank you for your time."

"I do have a suggestion, though, as to who might help you in your quest to find the□□□□□□you seek. Teamsters contract with stores and individuals, such as ranchers, to bring supplies and equipment into Bodie on a regular basis. If you've tried both me and my chief competitor, Gerald B. Hess, you've already spoken to the biggest merchants in Bodie. That still leaves a few individuals. If you know, or suspect, who's buying the moonshining supplies and equipment, you could check with the local teamsters. Maybe one of them has a contract with the party you're looking for."

"That would be a good idea, Liu Wei, if I had any idea of the type of supplies and equipment moonshiners use."

"Now, there, I can help you, Marshal. Browse my store for a few minutes, and I'll jot down the items commonly used in such enterprises."

Bane, Badger, and Luke had each selected a few items to buy before Liu Wei returned. "There you go, Marshal." He handed him the list. "Now, if you and your deputies will step over to the nearest counter, I will have one of our associates tally your purchases."

Chapter 50

Bookkeeping

"Doubt can be removed only by action."
— Johann Wolfgang von Goethe (1749-1832)

Rowelings's Campsite, near Bodie, California

Spencer Rowelings sipped his coffee.

He yawned.

He took another sip of the hot, bitter beverage. He'd forgotten to add sugar to it, but he was too tired to tend to the matter. And his damn head ached.

He was concerned.

Opening the ledger on the small table occupying the corner of his shack, he perused the entries that Zach Storm had made. Since they'd begun their moonshining operation, they'd made considerable money—more than any of them, except Storm, had anticipated. There was a hefty stash of cash in the locked crate beside the desk. It belonged to all of them equally. At least, that's what Rowelings had told them.

In spite of the persistent pain in his head, he smiled. For outlaws, all of them were more or less gullible, even Matthew Lewis, who'd worked with him long enough to know better.

He winced, as another shaft of pain lanced through his brain.

Lewis!

He'd nailed the reason for his concern!

The actor might not be as gullible as he seemed.

Hell, after having worked with him for years, how could the bastard be green enough to believe that Rowelings would split the moonshining money four ways when he could keep it all for himself?

The answer, of course, was that Lewis didn't believe it. He hadn't believed it from the beginning.

Lewis was an actor, a "thespian," as he sometimes called himself. His belief that Rowelings would deal with him—with all of them—fairly was nothing more than an act.

Oh, the bastard was good; Rowelings had to give him that.

But not good enough.

Another pain shot through Rowelings's head. He grasped the Mason jar of hooch on the table, opened its top, and poured a couple of ounces of the rotgut into his coffee.

That should help.

If Bodie's sheriff caught on to the fact that the supplies were the makings for illegal whiskey, he could arrest Lewis. Faced with serious prison time, the actor might agree to incriminate Rowelings and the rest of them. He didn't care about Jackson, Storm, or Lewis, but he did care about himself.

Wincing, he sipped the coffee laced with hooch.

The pain in his head seemed to decrease.

The trouble with his plan, Rowelings had realized, was that Lewis was a good actor, a great one, according not only to Lewis but to critics in New York City. Lewis had shown him the reviews he'd snipped from newspapers and magazines to save in a scrapbook. But, like many of his kind, Lewis was also vain.

Worse yet, the bastard was an actor all the time, not just when he was on stage. He was always acting, every moment of every day. For him, all the world really was a stage, and he, at least, if not all men and women, was a player having his exits and his entrances, as he played his many parts.

The pain became a throbbing at his temples, matching the cadence of his pulse.

Rowelings had known that Lewis was always on stage. The actor's ability to project himself, believably, into any role, had been the chief reason, in fact, that Rowelings had maintained contact with him over the years, during which the actor had rendered invaluable services again and again.

Although Rowelings trusted no man, woman, or child, he had come to let his guard down around Lewis. He had come to imagine, if not to believe, that Lewis was a loyal subordinate, a rare man who might be trusted, although not fully, never fully.

Rowelings cursed himself for having been such a fool.

If Lewis were discovered to be smuggling moonshine to Bodie's saloons and he were arrested, how quickly the actor would be willing to deal with his captors! The weasel would do anything to escape incarceration. Lewis would have no qualms about turning upon Rowelings, Jackson, and Storm if, by doing so, he could minimize or escape punishment for his own part in their doings.

Rowelings drained his cup.

The warmth of the coffee, modified somewhat by his addition of the moonshine, had warmed him slightly, just as the hooch had eased his pain and anxiety.

He returned to the ledger, tallying the amounts of their net profits.

Yes, they had made good money by making and selling illegal whiskey.

Plenty for all.

But, when it came to divvying the spoils, it would not be one for all, as he had promised the others. It would be all for one, and Spencer Rowelings would be the one.

The pain subsided further, and Rowelings grinned.

Maybe it was about time to break camp. Chances were, aided by the rugged terrain of the high country, they could escape down the mountainside before the marshal and his men gained the high ground.

Then, it would be time to settle up with the others.

On the other hand, he could probably put off leaving the area for another few days, since they weren't scheduled to make another delivery of hooch for a week.

The pain was gone now, along with the worry.

He considered another cup of coffee, but decided there was no need.

Chapter 51

West of Bodie

"A fact merely marks the point where we have agreed to let investigation cease."
— Bliss Carman (1861-)

Bodie, California

After introducing himself and his deputies, Bane produced the list of supplies and equipment that Liu Wei had written out, passing it to Bill Pomeroy:

"Anybody claimed such articles from you?" Bane asked.

"Couldn't say, Marshal."

"Why's that?"

"Shipments are arranged between the buyer and the seller; I just transport the orders to their destinations. I don't have any idea what's in the crates themselves."

"Do you have a list of the buyers and sellers?"

"I reckon the office, back in Bridgeport, would."

"Bridgeport, California?"

"Yep."

"You say you transport the purchases to their destinations. What constitutes such destinations?"

"Ordinarily, the address that the customer provides."

"Otherwise?"

"A merchant, livery stable owner, or other agent with whom the customer's arranged to accept the delivery on his behalf, or hers, as the case may be."

"Who might that be, here, in Bodie?"

"Most likely, the livery stable."

"You have any competitors out this way?"

"Just Ralph Bell."

"Does he handle freight the same way you do, transporting it to whoever ordered the merchandise or whoever they've designated to receive it in their place?"

"That's usually how it's done."

"Have you delivered any freight west of here, in a settlement or a camp in the mountains?"

"As a matter of fact, I did! A while back, I drove a wagon up Bodie Road, to a camp of mining shacks. I was surprised, because, hell, there are no settlements in the mountains west of Bodie, and the only camps are those of miners who worked there during the early days of Bodie's boom. They're all abandoned now. Have been for several years—or so I thought, until I made that delivery."

"No idea what you delivered, though?" Luke asked.

Pomeroy shook his head. "Nope."

"Could have been the items on the list the marshal showed you?"

Pomeroy nodded. "Could have been. Could have been 'most anything."

"Anybody travel west with a load after the one that you delivered?" Badger asked.

"Not that I know of."

"Do you know if Bell did?" Bane asked.

"No idea, Marshal. We seldom see each other. When we do, it's just to say hello."

Bane nodded. "Thanks, Mr. Pomeroy."

* * *

After the lawmen conferred with Bell, who verified that he had not driven any freight into the mountains west of Bodie, Bane told his deputies, "We've learned what supplies and equipment are needed to make bootleg whiskey, and we know that a shipment of freight was made to a supposedly abandoned shack in the mountains west of Bodie."

Chapter 52

High Time

"Dying is a wild night and a new road."
— Emily Dickinson (1830-)

Rowelings's Camp, near Bodie, California

The morning's frost made the steep ascent of the mountainside road more difficult and dangerous than usual, and, two-thirds of the way up the long, seemingly endless slope, Matthew Lewis was scared stiff.

If he made it back to the campsite, this would be the last time he made the trip to Bodie. From now on, one of the others would risk his life transporting their hooch into town. If Spencer didn't like it, he could go to hell, as far as Lewis was concerned.

More than once, one of the mules pulling the heavy wagon had slipped, and the wagon had slid toward the precipice.

So far, Lewis had been lucky.

But nobody's luck lasted forever, whether at keno, craps, poker, or profiteering from sales of illegal whiskey.

It might be time, in fact, to get shut of Spencer. Winter was coming, and, when it arrived, this "road" would be impassible even if a hundred-mule team were pulling the wagon. They could all be stranded in the camp, miles from

Bodie, without anybody's knowledge that they were there, on the side of this mountain. Even if their location were known, what man in his right mind would risk his life to save those of strangers?

Maybe he should cut ties with Spencer not just for now, but forever.

While he had made a lot of money, over the years, working with Spencer, he had also risked arrest, injury, and death more times than was healthy for anyone but Grigori Rasputin, the Russian mystic who ultimately came to his end as a guest of Prince Yusupov.

Finally, the campsite came into view. Lewis wanted to lash the mules, but he dared not. Were he to do so and they were to break into a run, the wagon could easily be thrown off course, into the abyss at either side of the trail.

* * *

Spencer Rowelings stood in the doorway of his shack, in the cold morning air, one hand clasped by the other, behind his back, looking at the distant hills.

He had plans for Matthew Lewis.

The actor's skills could be invaluable at times.

Although Rowelings trusted no one, regarding the very word itself as expressive, at best, of a naive notion that was apt to get a man killed, he had found, over the years, that Lewis was, at least, a man who could be useful. But the task upon which he had sent the thespian should have taken Lewis no more than a day or two at the most, and this morning was the beginning of the third day.

Lewis had been polite, as always, around him, but Rowelings had seen a flash of temper on Lewis's part around Jackson and Storm that was uncharacteristic of the man. Judging by the circles under the actor's eyes and his sluggishness the past few weeks, Rowelings had suspected that Lewis's outburst had been brought about by his lack of sleep of late or maybe due to his feeling under the weather. He'd been sick to his stomach for a day or two around the time he'd snapped at the moonshiners. That was the cause of his haggard look, Rowelings had supposed. Now, he wasn't so sure. Maybe Lewis was worried.

Whatever the cause in the changes in Lewis's mood and demeanor, whether peevishness, insomnia, or nausea, his condition could endanger both Rowelings himself and his plans for the future. A man in Lewis's condition could get Rowelings captured and returned to prison to be hanged.

He had been wrong, Rowelings decided, to have waited for Lewis's return to camp.

He should have left this location the day after Lewis had failed to return.

Lewis might have been captured, he might have confessed, he might have provided lawdogs with evidence against Rowelings, in exchange for a more lenient punishment for himself.

Their sales of illegal whiskey to the saloons in Bodie had netted them—or, rather, himself— considerable profit, enough to move forward with his plans.

Yes, it was time to act, all right.

High time, in fact.

* * *

Returning to the relative warmth of his shack, Rowelings retrieved a stick of dynamite from the cache he'd found shortly after they'd taken possession of the abandoned miners' shacks. He examined it closely. The cardboard cylinder was dry, without rips or tears, the attached blasting cap in good condition. Examining the fuse wrapped around the spool, he found it, too, to be in good repair. He placed both items in a small drawstring gunnysack and tucked it inside the left pouch of his saddlebags, along with a box of matches.

He also stuffed, in the saddlebag's other pouch, the profits he and the others had earned by selling their illegal whiskey.

Now, he was ready.

He went back outside and walked across the space between his own shack and the larger one in which the biggest still was located.

Inside, Russ Jackson was monitoring the cooking of their latest batch.

"Where's Zach?" he asked.

Without turning from the still, Jackson replied, "Tending the still in the hollow."

Rowelings's shot struck Jackson in the back of the head, sending a gushing stream of blood and brains against the still.

Rowelings stepped outside.

Storm was rushing toward the shack, gun in hand. "What happened?" he shouted.

When he'd run several yards closer, Rowelings said, "This." His bullet brought the moonshiner down.

Rowelings smiled.

It had been easy.

The sound of the wagon and the mules arrested Rowelings's attention.

Lewis! The bastard had returned, after all.

Rowelings's mind raced, as he debated with himself whether to follow through on his plan to kill the actor. No, he decided, despite the thespian's faults, chief among which was his questionable trustworthiness when the chips were down, Lewis had been a boon in times past and, Rowelings believed, he could be again in the future. The man's uncanny ability not only to pretend to be somebody else, on or off the stage, but, for all intents and purposes, to become another person, made Lewis a valuable commodity, and it was wise to part with such an asset only if absolutely necessary.

Besides, he could just as well get shut of Lewis later, if need be.

Lewis watched Rowelings closely, alert to any clue that the miscreant harbored ill will toward him.

With him, a man could never tell.

"I was beginning to think you weren't coming back," Rowelings called, as Lewis halted the wagon.

"Of course I was coming back," Lewis declared, as if there had been no doubt about it. "Where's Storm and the others?"

"Dead."

Behind Rowelings, Lewis caught sight of Storm's body, lying face down on the ground. "Dead? What the hell do you mean' dead'?"

"I killed them, same as I killed Baker."

"Why the hell—"

"We're finished making moonshine," Rowelings decreed, "so we're finished with them." He grinned. "With them dead, we split our profits two ways instead of five."

"That wasn't the deal."

"Not originally." He stared defiantly at the sole remaining member of his gang. "Things change."

"If we're not making moonshine anymore, what are we doing?"

"It's time to put the next phase of my plan into action. We're riding to Bridgeport."

"What about the wagon? The mules?" He looked at the body of Storm. "Their horses?"

"Hitch their horses, and Baker's, to the wagon. Follow me."

For a moment, Rowelings thought that Lewis might say something, but he didn't. He climbed down from the wagon, led the dead men's horses to the vehicle, tied them to the wagon, and climbed back into the vehicle's seat.

Rowelings rode up to him, having taken some of the cash from his saddlebags, and handed Lewis a portion of their take. It wasn't half, but it was enough, he thought, that Lewis might believe that it was his fair share of their moonshining profits.

"What about the stills' fires?"

"Most likely, they'll burn out."

"But, Spencer, they could explode; they could catch the sagebrush on fire for miles around."

"Let them."

"They'd draw attention."

"By the time they do, we'll be long gone."

"It would only take a few minutes to douse the fires."

"If somebody got curious about your driving that wagon up into these hills, a few minutes could make all the difference. We've wasted too much time talking about it, as it is."

Rowelings turned his horse west, and Lewis followed.

Chapter 53

Rugged Terrain

"... For all of us, our particular creature waits in ambush."
— Horace Walpole (1717-)

On the Bodie Road, west of Bodie

The elevation ascended continuously, slowing their travel.

Their horses weren't used to such a long climb, especially up terrain that offered few breaks in the steep ascent.

Bane and his deputies were obliged to stop along the way to let their mares rest.

They weren't making good time, but Bane reckoned that wasn't likely to matter. The fugitives they sought probably supposed that he, Badger, and Luke were on the wild goose chase Rowelings had sent them upon with the false lead that he and his gang had traveled south out of Bodie, past Mono Lake. It was obvious that the murderous stage robber who'd stolen a shipment of gold and silver had a few contacts in Bodie and maybe an intermediary who communicated with them, since, it seemed, nobody had seen Rowelings himself in town or anywhere else, for that matter.

He was a wily one; Bane had to give him that.

He was also a fugitive whom Bane intended to capture or kill.

According to the U. S. Army topographical map in his possession, there was nothing north of them but Bridgeport, California, and, further north of it, Silver Creek and Markleeville. To the south, there were only Mono Lake and Benton. A stretch of the Sierra Nevada Mountains to the west cut off travel in that direction, other than by the Bodie Road.

If, as Bane suspected, based on the information he'd received from the teamster Bill Pomeroy, Rowelings had gone west out of Bodie, it would have been along the same route that Bane and his deputies now followed, the Bodie Road, a circuitous route, full of twists and turns, that eventually meandered north to Bridgeport.

The railroad was Rowelings's immediate or eventual destination, Bane thought. From there, Rowelings, still cut off to the west by the Sierra Nevada Mountains, could travel but north or east. North would lead him past a cluster of towns in Alpine County and to the Central Pacific Railroad, which led from San Francisco to Omaha, Nebraska, the Midwestern terminus providing connections with other railroads, giving him access, essentially, to the whole country. It was a long, difficult ride to Bridgeport, but access to the railroad would be invaluable to Rowelings's escape.

That was his immediate destination, Bane thought—well, his immediate destination after he'd dug up the gold and silver he'd stolen, wherever it might lie.

"Let's give the horses another breather," Bane said.

He and his deputies drew rein and climbed down from their saddles. Using ropes, they tethered their horses to sagebrush. The plants wouldn't prevent the animals from running off if they were spooked. Otherwise, though, the restraint, slight, though it was, would encourage them to stay within the confines of the lengths of their ropes while they grazed on the plants' tender stems.

"Well, we haven't been ambushed," Badger observed. Having finished fastening his rope to a trunk of sage, he joined his fellow lawmen, who'd hunkered down among the silver-green brush.

"Not yet," Luke said.

Bane nodded toward a steep, rocky incline topped by a sharply pitched mound. "There's Potato Peak. It's about four miles from Bodie, which leaves us about twenty more miles to go before we reach Bridgeport. There's still ample time for an ambush. The lay of the land offers multiple chances for such an attack as well. We'd better continue to keep a sharp eye out and be prepared to react."

"Not much room to react in these hills," Badger observed.

"All the more reason to be aware of our surroundings," Bane said. "That way, we can get down, among the sage, and crawl off from our original location."

"They could shoot our horses," Badger pointed out.

"Maybe one, but the others are likely to run off."

"Leaving us stranded."

"At most, we'd have to walk less than twenty-four miles."

"That's a long way in terrain like this, Bane."

"That's why you get such good pay. Let's mount up."

The men freed their horses, climbed back into their saddles, and resumed their ride along the road wandering up the sloping hillside.

The ruts in the rough road showed Bane that somebody had fairly recently driven a load over the same route that he and his deputies were now following. The supplies and equipment needed to distill illegal whiskey weren't tremendously heavy. In fact, they'd make a fairly light load, which suggested that the wagon used to transport the freight was itself a heavy vehicle, probably one such as a teamster like Bill Pomeroy or his rival, Ralph Bell, used. The number of mule tracks, between the lines cut into the soil by the wagon's wheels, suggested as much as well.

Apparently, the same idea had occurred to Luke, who asked, "You think Pomeroy or Bell is hauling moonshining equipment and supplies to Rowelings and his men?"

"It's possible," Bane said, "but most of these tracks are fairly old, although awfully deep, and the Bodie Road is mostly used to haul supplies from Bridgeport to Bodie. Some of the mule tracks point west, but plenty more point east. Most likely, these are the tracks of teamsters hauling legitimate loads."

"Sounds right to me, Bane."

"Of course, that doesn't mean that one of Rowelings's men isn't also hauling moonshine equipment and supplies along this road, from Bodie to wherever their camp is located," Badger added.

"True," Bane agreed.

"Wouldn't one of the teamsters traveling on the road have spotted the smoke from the cabins Rowelings and his men are using?" Luke asked.

"Or the smoke from the stills?" Badger added.

"This road's not much used, even by teamsters, this time of year, but, yes, most likely," Bane agreed, "but they'd probably attribute it to some hermit or dreamers looking for an untapped mine that miners during Bodie's boom had overlooked."

"Wouldn't they have investigated?" Badger asked.

"You, Luke, or I would, but we're lawmen. A teamster would probably be more interested in delivering his load and going home again."

Badger considered his words. "I reckon you're right. If I weren't wearing this badge, I know I would."

The trail took a series of other sharp bends and curves, and Bane expected to hear shots fired at any moment.

There were none, despite the fact that they'd passed several spots perfect for an ambush.

Why not?

A few hours later, his question was answered.

Chapter 54

Fame, Fortune, and Glory

"Sometimes, nightmares are disguised as beautiful dreams."
— Pamela Messenger (1844 -)

North on the Bodie Road

Reaching the north fork of the Bodie Road, Spencer Rowelings felt revitalized.

He was glad not to have lost Matthew Lewis. As an actor, Lewis had his uses.

Still, he didn't need Matthew Lewis. Spencer Rowelings needed no one. Like James Baker, Russ Jackson, and Zach Storm, Lewis was nothing more than a means to an end. As an intermediary between him and Bodie's saloon owners, store owners, and brothel madams, Lewis had been useful, allowing Rowelings to act without being seen or heard in person. Baker, Jackson, and especially Storm, had enabled him to make the money he carried now, upon his person and in his saddlebags, by supplying Bodie's watering holes with cheap, if illegal, whiskey in large quantities, with much less risk and expense than the saloons otherwise might incur in making rotgut themselves, using tobacco, molasses, red Spanish peppers, river water, and the like to doctor liquor they bought from legitimate distilleries back east and down south.

Now, he had the money he needed to travel, and, soon, he would have a fortune with which to buy guns and ammunition and horses, to dispatch telegrams, to bribe officials, to pay lawyers, and to accomplish the multitude of other tasks that he'd need to complete before he could accomplish his master plan.

Then, the whole damn country would know who Spencer Rowelings was, and people would tremble with fear at the mere sight of him.

He spurred his horse, turned it into the fork of the road, and headed north.

Some distance behind him, Lewis followed Rowelings's lead, turning the mules pulling his wagon—or the one he'd rented this morning, at any rate, which was now his, more or less, since he hadn't returned it and didn't plan to do so.

Rowelings couldn't ride much farther before giving his horse a break, not if he hoped to reach his destination on horseback, rather than on foot, but he wanted, at least, to be on the final leg of this particular journey before he drew rein for an hour or so prior to resuming his ride to what would be eventual fame, fortune, and glory.

He wished he had a winged horse like the Pegasus of Greek mythology, but he'd have to get by with an earthbound mount.

By this evening, though, his horse would be in a livery stable, with Jackson's, Storm's, Lewis's, and Baker's horses and Lewis's mules, and he and Lewis would have rooms in one of the finest hotels, such as they were, in Bridgeport, California.

Chapter 55

Guns at the Ready

"Let us live so that when we come to die even the undertaker will be sad."
— Mark Twain (1835-)

Rowelings's Camp, near Bodie, California

From the crest of a hill, Bane and his deputies surveilled the camp below.

With autumn coming on, smoke should be discernible above the chimneys of some of the rough shacks scattered among the sagebrush covering the surrounding hills.

Horses and, likely, mules would occupy a corral or be picketed near the campsite.

Since it was late morning, activity would probably be underway in the camp.

If Rowelings's gang were making moonshine, there'd be smoke from the burner fires, kegs standing by, men at work. There were none of these signs, nor any others.

In fact, there was no movement in the camp, not that Bane, Badger, or Luke could see.

His deputies' puzzled expressions suggested that they, like Bane himself, were baffled.

A few years back, gold mining had been ubiquitous in these parts. Likely, other such camps were hidden among the surrounding hills, perhaps many. If so, that would explain the stillness of this camp; it was, indeed, abandoned.

Bane lifted his binoculars to his eyes.

He turned his head, shifting his field of vision to the right.

Something caught his eye.

Wheel ruts.

Mule tracks.

Not only on the road, but also in the camp.

Recent tracks, too, from the look of them.

He told Badger and Luke what he'd observed.

They hadn't been ambushed because, although the camp before them showed signs that it had been recently occupied, it was now uninhabited.

"Mount up," Bane ordered.

Once they were back in their saddles, Bane led the way down the road and into the camp.

Guns in hand, Bane, Badger, and Luke scanned the compound, their eyes darting among the shacks.

They saw nothing out of the ordinary.

They heard no sounds but those of nature.

Although they saw neither smoke nor fire, they did smell the odor of ashes, which suggested that the camp had been recently inhabited.

Their senses were on high alert.

"There!" Bane said, "On the ground, in front of the largest shack."

Badger and Luke looked.

The body of a man lay face down, near the door of the shack.

"And there!" Badger cried, pointing.

A second man, lying on his back.

Bane and his deputies dismounted.

Guns at the ready, Bane and Badger approached the supine body, while Luke, his gun pointed ahead of him, walked warily toward the other man.

Kneeling, Badger checked the man's pulse while Bane kept his revolver aimed at the victim.

"Dead," Badger said.

From their left, they heard Luke call, "This one's alive!"

Bane and Badger hastened to Luke's side.

"Mister? Can you hear me?" Bane asked.

No response.

"I'm U. S. Marshal Bane Messenger. These men are my deputies."

"Marshal," the man croaked, "is Russ all right?"

"He's dead. What happened?"

"Rowelings. He shot us. From behind. Killed James, too; earlier. Made Russ and me bury him. So he could keep all the moonshine money for himself." He burbled blood as he chuckled. "Wanted our shares as well as his own."

Bane tensed. "Spencer Rowelings?"

"Yes."

The man sounded weak. The red stain that had spread under his upper body suggested that he'd lost a lot of blood. Probably too much blood, Bane reckoned. Likely, he'd be dead in minutes. It was a wonder he'd lived this long. He was beyond hope, but he might have information vital to their pursuit of Rowelings. "Where is he?"

"Gone. Headed west . . . . " He made a gurgling sound as his voice caught in his throat. He swallowed. ". . . with Lewis."

"Who's Lewis?"

"Matthew Lewis. Actor. Accomplice. Inter—" His voice failed again.

Blood welling up in his throat, Bane thought.

"—mediary." The fugitive winced. "Rowelings had—had a cache—of gold—and silver—stolen—hidden north of—here."

The man's breath came in raspy gasps. He wasn't long for this world. Bane wanted to ask more questions than there was time for the man to answer. Maybe it was best just to let him talk.

"Was going to use the gold to—to do—'something really—big,' he said."

"What was he planning to do?"

There was no reply.

There was nothing.

Nothing, now, but a corpse staring heedlessly into the sky.

"Mount up," Bane ordered.

"Shouldn't we bury them?" Badger asked.

"We'll notify the sheriff in Bridgeport."

"Bridgeport? That's north, Bane," Luke declared. "Man said Rowelings was going west."

"Have to go west from here to go north to there."

Chapter 56

The Promise of Gold

"Never use dynamite, except as a last resort."
— Bradford Messenger (1837 -)

West of Mason, Nevada

The tall, lean man was the last to arrive, and now, counting Matthew Lewis and Spencer Rowelings himself, they were seven.

Five had come at once to Sweetwater, lured by Rowelings's promise of gold.

He hadn't mentioned the precious metal in the cryptic telegram itself, of course. He'd sent the same message to Bob Loon, Ken Wheeler, Ray Tyler, Clark Grant, and John Camden: "Help wanted. Apply to Share and Share Alike, Sweetwater."

The phrase "Share and Share Alike" had been made known to the men months ago, as it had been made known to others besides these five men, well before Rowelings had robbed the stagecoach of its cargo of gold and silver, killing the driver, the shotgun messenger, and four passengers, one of whom was a woman.

The recipients of the telegrams he'd sent to each of them while Lewis and he had stopped over in Bridgeport, California, would understand that Rowelings wanted them to join him in an exploit he'd planned, also well ahead of time, for which they'd be paid in equal shares of the stolen gold.

Tough, capable men, adept with fists, knives, and guns, they were among the other thirty-odd men whom Rowelings had had in mind when he'd planned the criminal acts that would make him a powerful emperor of crime, feared and loathed throughout the southwest and beyond.

These five were the first to be called for the simple reason that they were also the most expendable.

Fortunately, his visit to the telegraph office in Bridgeport hadn't resulted in his being identified as a fugitive and arrested on the spot. He'd been able to send the telegrams, and his recruits were waiting for him when he'd arrived, this morning, in Sweetwater, Nevada.

Now that the last of the chosen had joined the rest of them and had had a couple of beers, Rowelings saw no reason to spend any more money on them. "The sooner we get where we're going, the sooner you boys get paid," he announced, "so drink up."

Almost in unison, the five tossed back their mugs.

When the Sidewinder Saloon girl sashayed up to their table to ask whether one of them would buy her a drink, none of them volunteered.

"We have to get about our business," Rowelings said.

Damn, but she looked pretty when she pouted, he thought. Too bad, for both of them, he was in a hurry.

The other men shoved away from the table, and the group made their way out of the saloon.

Unhitching their horses from the post out front, they mounted up.

"Where we headed, anyway?" Loon asked.

"North," Rowelings said, "along the Big Walker River." As he answered the man, Rowelings smiled. Ironically, the State Prison was only about sixty-five miles east of their destination. In a way, the wheel of fate was coming full circle.

* * *

Despite the slow, grueling journey up steep elevations, through difficult, rugged terrain, Rowelings and his men made it to Cleaver, Nevada, on the morning of the sixth day after he and Lewis had left Bridgeport, California.

Lewis had bought lanterns and matches in Sweetwater and a wheelbarrow in Cambridge. To spell the actor from driving the wagon he'd stolen in Bodie, Rowelings assigned that task to Ray, who'd been a teamster before embracing the life of crime. Now that the land had leveled off considerably, Ray made fairly good time trailing the other men's horses, his own steed tied to the rear of the heavy vehicle.

"We have only a few more miles to go now, before we reach the spot," Rowelings called. There was enough of the precious metal to make all of them wealthy beyond their dreams. "We'll be rich," he reminded them, again, now, as they approached the northern tip of the Walker River Range.

Three miles west of Mason, he ordered the procession to halt. "Unload the lanterns and the wheelbarrow."

The other men gave Loon a hand.

"Follow me," Rowelings said.

They walked across the rugged lay of the land to a site near the base of the mountain.

"A cave!" Grant cried.

The site of the underground chamber here, in the middle of nowhere, seemed to astonish the man, Rowelings thought. He could understand Grant's feeling. Rowelings seldom felt anything but animosity toward life and humanity in general, but, when he'd discovered the cave a few years back, he'd felt the same way as Grant did now.

In fact, the find had given him the idea of robbing the coach, which ran, as the line still did today, east, out of Carson City, then south and west, to Bridgeport, California. They'd followed the same road, in reverse, as they'd ridden from Bridgeport to Cleaver.

"Lewis will stay with me, at the wagon, to guard against anyone who might come this way. "Wheeler, you take the wheelbarrow," Rowelings instructed. "Follow Camden, Loon, Tyler, and Grant. A few yards into the mountain, the passageway turns left. The gold's buried a few feet beyond the turn, in an alcove on the right. Load as much as Wheeler can push into the wheelbarrow. Follow him back here, and transfer the gold to the wagon."

The men lifted the picks and lanterns, setting out as Wheeler pushed the empty wheelbarrow over the rough, rutted ground.

"There's a lot of gold in there," Rowelings said, as if he were making casual conversation.

"I doubt any of the men you summoned would be here now, if they didn't think there was," Lewis remarked.

"There'd be more for both of us if we split it two ways instead of seven."

"You mean—?"

"Let me show you what I mean." Rowelings walked to the side of his horse. Unlatching the saddlebag on his horse's left side, he drew forth the stick of dynamite he'd taken from the shack back at their campsite in the hills west of Bodie. "When they go inside the cave to get the last load of gold, I plant this near the mouth of the cave and set it off."

"We'll lose whatever gold's still inside the mountain!"

"The last of the gold won't exist; I'll just tell them there's more."

Lewis grinned. "I like the way you think, Spencer."

As Camden, Loon, Wheeler, Tyler, and Grant brought the second wheelbarrow full of gold bullion to the wagon," panting and wiping sweat from their brow, they started to return the lanterns to the wagon, staring at the gold they'd retrieved. Heaped in the wagon bed, it looked like even more than they'd brought out of the cave.

Rowelings frowned. "What are you doing? Get the rest of it!"

The men looked puzzled.

"The rest of it?" Tyler asked. "That's all of it."

"Did you follow the passageway any deeper after it turned left?" Rowelings's tone suggested that he was speaking to a bunch of cretins. "It curves again, to the right. That's where the rest of the gold is. Get it!" He snapped the last two words as though they were the lashes of a whip.

Looking both taken aback and uneasy, Camden, Loon, Tyler, and Grant picked up the lanterns and followed Wheeler back toward the entrance to the cave.

Once they were inside, while Lewis spread and secured the canvas tarpaulin over the wagon's freight, Rowelings hastened to his horse and grabbed the dynamite and a spool of rolled fuse.

Running to the side of the mountain, he set the stick of explosive on the ground, by the entrance to the cave; attached the fuse to the dynamite's blasting cap; and hastened away, backward, unspooling the fuse as he went.

When he reached the wagon, he stopped, snatched a box of matches from his pocket, lit one, and held the flame to the end of the fuse lying on the ground, where he'd dropped it.

The sparking flame followed the line forward, toward the cave's entrance.

A few seconds later, a resounding BOOM! occurred as the explosion of nitroglycerin brought down tons of rock in a cascade of bouncing, rolling fragments.

"Just a two-way split now, for sure!" Lewis grinned, smiling at the heap of gold in the wagon.

Setting Loon's horse free, to roam with the others, Lewis hitched his own mount to the back of the wagon, climbed aboard, turned the team toward the road leading south through Mason Valley, and followed Rowelings.

Chapter 57

Coolness Under Fire

"Fast is fine, but accuracy is everything. In a gun fight. . . . You need to take your time in a hurry."
— Wyatt Earp (1848-)

North, to Mason, Nevada

Two days ago, Bane, Badger, and Luke had studied the U. S. Army map that Bane had obtained at the outset of their campaign to arrest Spencer Rowelings and recover the gold and silver that the killer had stolen from the stagecoach he'd robbed.

According to the map, he and his deputies had two routes of travel from which to choose. The shorter route led northwest before continuing northeast, in a diagonal path, from Washington, Nevada, to a point just east of Mason, Nevada. After cutting across Big Walker River, it struggled up the steep elevations of Mount Siegel. On the other side of this ascent, just west of Mason, the road joined the route to Carson City and beyond.

The longer road swept southeast, through a narrow gap between Mount Brawley and a ridge of the Excelsior Mountains, before snaking northwest, through the Soda Springs Valley, past Walker Lake, to Mason.

"Which way do you think Rowelings went? Bane asked his deputies.

Badger was in favor of Spencer's selecting the shorter route, despite the obstacle of Mount Siegel.

Luke favored the longer route, through Soda Springs Valley.

"Why do you think Rowelings took the shorter route?" Bane asked Badger.

"It's shorter; it has a good water source along most of the route; and there are plenty of towns along the way, if he needs supplies."

"Solid reasons," Bane said. "Why do you think he took the longer route, Luke?"

"Despite its being roughly three times as long as the other route, it has its advantages. It may not run parallel to a river, but it does have a water source: Walker Lake.

"There are lots of places, among the foothills of the mountain ranges to make camp or hide if Rowelings thinks he's being followed. There's also plenty of towns along the way, if he needs supplies.

"The mountain ranges along both sides of the valley give him natural cover, cutting off travel from the east and the west, although a posse could get at him traveling east, through gaps in the mountains. If a posse of, say, a U. S. marshal and two deputies were following him, there'd be a number of spots from which he could ambush them, especially if Rowelings isn't traveling alone."

"You both make convincing arguments," Bane said. "I think the best thing to do would be to split up. I'll take the Soda Springs Valley Route; you and Badger take the shorter one. We'll meet up again at the hotel in Mason."

"You sure trailing Rowelings alone is a good idea, Bane?" Luke asked.

"Especially since, according to that girl in the Sidewinder Saloon, back in Sweetwater, he's not traveling alone," Badger added.

"Three against seven are a whole lot better odds than one against seven," Luke declared.

"My Colt's a six-shooter," Bane replied, "should it come to that."

"What about the seventh?" Luke asked.

"He'll probably have run by then. If not, I'll scoop up one of the dead men's guns."

"If you have time," Badger said.

"Personally, I think you're loco," Luke declared, "but you're the marshal."

"See you in Mason," Bane said.

* * *

Storm, Bane's horse, was a big, strong, well-conditioned mare. She had made her way through some of the most difficult terrain in the West. Although the slopes of the long, narrow valley through which the animal now traveled were taxing, they slowed her progress by only a fourth of her normal gait over level ground.

Bane reckoned that, over the past couple of days, he had made good time since splitting up with his deputies. Although they had the shorter route, Bane was betting that Storm was equal to the challenge of arriving at Mason at nearly the same time as his deputies' horses.

Two against seven were poor odds, but they would be worse yet for a pair of men who lacked his deputies' coolness under fire, deadly accurate aim, and grit.

One against seven were preposterous odds, even for a man who was as good with a gun as Bane. Most likely, he'd get wounded in the fray, if he came up against Rowelings and his gang. There was a good chance he'd be killed.

The gold mine on Lightning Hill would continue to provide a life of luxury for Pamela and their children, Lizzie and Ben, but Bane didn't want Pamela to become a widow, nor did he want Lizzie and Ben to grow up without a father.

He also didn't want to lose the father he'd only come to know a few years ago, after he had reconciled with Bradford for having abandoned him, his newborn son, after Bane's mother had died in childbirth.

Imagining his Aunt Flossie, who'd raised and loved him as a mother, grieving over his death was agonizing.

Bane Messenger, the angel of death, had a lot to live for.

But he also owed his deputies a great deal.

Both Badger and Luke had been there for him, always. Without hesitation, they'd put their lives on the line more times than Bane could remember, just as he'd risked death for them. He, Badger, and Luke were more than a marshal and his deputies. Like many men who'd fought together, they were like brothers.

Not many men were willing to die for one another. Bane, Badger, and Luke were willing.

They'd proved as much time after time, against odds as great, and greater, than the ones they faced now. Bane owed Badger and Luke every advantage, no matter how small or inconsequential, and, even if two against seven were bad odds, they were better than one against seven, especially when their foes were ruthless and pitiless. Putting himself at slightly greater risk than his deputies didn't improve Badger and Luke's chances of survival much, but it was all that Bane could do.

* * *

The sun would set in half an hour or so.

Bane had been riding for four days, and Storm was tired.

Bane was, too.

Travel had been arduous.

He should stop, make camp, give Storm the rest she needed and deserved.

But having almost passed Walker Lake, he was approaching Agency. He was nearly at the border between Esmeralda County and Churchill County. Mason would be only a few miles farther now.

He squinted. A dark shape moved slowly toward him in the twilight.

He raised the binoculars hanging around his neck.

As Storm stepped along the steep trail, Bane peered through the high-powered lenses.

A wagon drawn by mules.

Two horses tethered to the wagon's rear.

Bane trained the field glasses on the driver's face.

At first, he saw nothing distinct, but, slowly, the man's features became clearer.

Although Bane judged that he must be at least a mile away from the driver, he could now see the man's features.

They were the eyes, nose, mouth, facial shape, and hair color of a stranger.

So was the man's tall, medium build.

Bane turned his binoculars on the passenger.

He knew that face, sure enough!

Like Bane himself, the wagon's passenger, Spencer Rowelings, was traveling during twilight.

But where were the other five men the saloon girl had said were traveling with him?

Had they parted company since they'd left Sweetwater?

Why, of all the men who'd joined Rowelings, was this one man still with him?

And why were Rowelings and his companion traveling south again, after just having ridden north?

These were questions to which answers could wait.

The fugitive hadn't seen him, Bane thought, nor, at this distance, could Rowelings have heard Storm's hooves against the ground.

The chance to ambush the killer was excellent.

All Bane had to do was to locate a hiding place. Then, as Rowelings passed by, Bane would dash out, six-shooter in hand, and arrest the bastard and the stranger with him. If his guess proved correct, the gold and silver that the robber had stolen from the stagecoach would be in the back of the wagon.

Concealing himself behind a hill that connected to the Walker River Range, west of Walker Lake, Bane waited, watching Rowelings's approach. The outlaw's progress was slow, which suggested that the weight of the wagon couldn't be due solely to the heavy planks and iron wheels of its construction. The weight of the stolen gold and silver might account for part of the heaviness. Had this been the reason for Rowelings's trip north? Had he reclaimed the gold and silver he'd hidden after his heist? The possibility seemed too good to be true.

Slowly, the mule team pulled the wagon closer.

Bane released his binoculars, letting them rest against his chest, and drew his revolver.

The wagon was approximately fifty yards away.

Rowelings seemed unaware of anything amiss, as the driver drove steadily onward. Rowelings and the other man had passed Agency. The next town was Hawthorne, which was miles away. Apparently, with good reason, the fugitives trusted in the surefootedness of the mules and their ability to see in the faint light of dusk.

Thirty yards.

Twenty.

Ten.

Five.

Bane nudged Storm's flanks, and the horse sprinted forward.

"U. S. Marshal! Halt!" Bane commanded.

Instead, with a swift sweep of his hand, Rowelings grabbed his six-shooter from the seat beside him and turned it toward the marshal.

But Bane's Colt was already in his hand, and he fired as soon as Rowelings made his move.

The sharp sound of another gunshot seemed to sprout yellow flame surrounded by a fiery orange nimbus.

The driver had gotten off a shot, but it had gone wide.

Bane returned fire, aiming for the spot at which the driver's six-shooter had spouted fire.

The sights and sounds of the gunfire were gone in an instant, silence again engulfing them.

The driver grunted, falling sideways, across Rowelings's lap.

The mules shifted their weight, but, well-trained, didn't break into a run.

Rowelings yelled curses.

Running to the vehicle, Bane reached up, grabbed a fistful of the fugitive's shirt, and yanked Rowelings out of the seat, onto the ground.

"Bastard!" Rowelings yelled. "You broke my damn arm!"

"Get up!"

"Go to hell!"

Bane seized the culprit by his other arm. "Get up, or I'll break this one, too."

Rowelings twisted, trying to break free. "You're an officer of the law, in case you've forgotten."

With considerable effort, Bane hoisted the fugitive to his feet.

Rowelings swung, connecting solidly with the side of the marshal's head.

Bane staggered, and Rowelings ran.

But he didn't get far before Bane seized him by the back of the shirt.

Rowelings lunged forward, as the garment ripped. Freed from Bane's grip, he stumbled onward, got his feet under him, and ran.

Despite the near-darkness, Rowelings's silhouette gave him away.

Bane fired his Colt into the sky. "If I have to fire again, you won't survive," Bane warned.

Rowelings stopped. "Marshal, you appear to be a reasonable man," Rowelings said. "There's a million dollars of gold in that wagon. Send me on my way with half of it, and the rest is all yours. What do you say?"

"I'd say that's a mighty tempting offer."

Rowelings grinned.

"It's also another crime to add to your resisting arrest, attempting to bribe a U. S. marshal, being in possession of stolen property, murder, and Lord knows what all else."

"I didn't resist arrest. I thought you were a highway man. I was defending myself!"

"Jury might believe that. Somehow, I doubt it."

"I never bribed you, either, Marshal, and I haven't stolen anything."

"Except that stagecoach shipment of gold on the wagon there, with which you tried to bribe me, not to mention the silver you stole along with it."

"And I haven't killed anybody."

"Except the men and woman on that stagecoach and a couple of men involved with you, in moonshining, which, by the way are other crimes to add to the list of charges against you. I'm fairly certain you've committed a number of other offenses, too, including additional murders, most likely."

Seizing Rowelings around the left bicep, Bane forced him toward the wagon. "Get that tarp off!" he ordered.

"Go to hell!"

"If I have to do it, I'll have to buffalo you first, and getting hit over the head with a six-shooter's not an experience you'll enjoy."

"All right, all right, damn you!"

Alerted by the scramble of hooves, Bane caught sight of Rowelings's confederate as the wounded driver hightailed it northward along the rough road. While Bane's attention had been focused on Rowelings, Lewis, who, apparently, hadn't been as badly wounded as he'd seemed to have been, had freed one of the horses tied to the rear of the wagon and escaped!

Well, there was nothing he could do about that at the moment, and it was Rowelings he'd been after, anyway.

"Pull back that tarp!" Bane ordered.

"I can't! You broke my arm!"

Bane pointed his Colt at his prisoner. "The next time I shoot will be the last time."

When Rowelings pulled back the tarpaulin, Bane shoved him into the wagon.

After dragging him into the back of the wagon, Bane hogtied him.

Then, he tied Storm to the back of the wagon with his prisoners' horses and climbed into the driver's seat.

Lightly slapping the mules' backs with the reins, he turned the wagon around.

It was getting late, and Bane was tired.

He was glad that Mason was only a few miles north.

On the way into town, he met his deputies, who surprised him by having taken Rowelings's escaped companion into their custody.

"Met him along the way. No doubt, Mt. Siegel slowed him down quite a bit, but he was sure riding as though he were trying to outrace the fires of perdition when we encountered him on our side of the mountain," Luke explained.

"We might never have suspected him of anything if he'd just kept up his gallop, but when he shot at us, we reckoned he'd been up to no good," Badger added.

"See you got your man," Luke said.

"He was with yours," Bane explained, "driving the wagon. Yours took off while I was subduing Rowelings."

"Looks like he was in a shootout," Luke remarked. "Have anything to do with you, Bane?"

"We exchanged shots. I made the mistake of thinking I'd wounded him badly or maybe killed him, judging by the way he keeled over, into Rowelings's lap, on the wagon's seat. He's quite an actor."

Chapter 58

Full Circle

"The moving finger writes; and having writ, moves on: nor all your piety nor wit shall lure it back to cancel half a line, nor all your tears wash out a single word of it."
— Omar Khayyam (1048-1131)

Mason, Nevada

The next morning, as Spencer Rowelings cooled his heels in the local hoosegow, alongside Matthew Lewis, Bane gave Rowelings the bad news. "Dr. Hirsh, the local physician, confirmed that you're fit to travel."

Bane didn't mention that the doc had also stipulated that twenty-minute rests every fifteen miles along the way would be required. Bane calculated the travel time, straight through, as about twelve hours. With the twenty-minute rests, they could make the trip in about fifteen hours."

With his captives in the custody of the town's sheriff, Bane and his deputies took the sheriff's advice and visited The Express, a local restaurant.

"The Express sounds more like a newspaper than a restaurant," Badger said.

"According to the sheriff, Thelma, the woman who runs it, is the wife of TheExpress's owner."

"TheExpress being the chronicler of local events?" Luke inquired.

"Local, regional, national, and international," according to the sheriff.

When the waitress arrived, they ordered steaks, potatoes, coffee, and apple pie.

"Although there have been a number of forts in Nevada, some of which date back to the state's days as a territory, most have been abandoned or converted to uses that no longer involve the Army," Bane said. "Today, only two continue to operate: Fort McDermit and Fort Halleck. Governor Cooper authorized us to return the recovered gold to either one of them.

"Fort McDermit, which was established in 1865, is located near Quinn River Station on the East Fork of the Quinn River. It protects the stagecoach route and the wagon road between Virginia City and Star City and fielded troops during the Snake War, the Modoc War, and the Bannock War.

"Built a year later, near Elko, Fort Halleck supported explorations through central and southern Nevada, and protects the Central Pacific Railroad and the California Trail."

"So, we're headed for Fort Halleck, once we get shut of Rowelings?" Badger asked.

Bane nodded. "Fort Halleck is a distance from Excelsior, but it's closer by far than Fort McDermit, and Fort Halleck's proximity to Governor Cooper's mansion in Elko will allow us to kill two birds with one stone: deliver the recovered gold and then brief the governor on its recovery, on Rowelings's arrest and imprisonment, and Lewis's arrest as an accomplice in Rowelings's more recent crimes. Afterward, we can take a train to Elko and another from Palisade to Eureka, which will shorten our trip home."

The thought that, soon, they'd be traveling back to Excelsior heartened Bane. If Badger's smile and Luke's nod were any indications, they were just as glad that their mission was nearing completion.

In a few days, they'd be back in Excelsior, Bane with Pamela and the rest of his family, Luke with Penelope, and Badger with Lorraine, the young woman he'd finally told them about, whom he had begun to date a month ago.

Then, life could return to normal.

For a while, at least, until the next miscreant thought he was above the law.

* * *

State Prison, Carson City, Nevada

"Here you are, Rowelings: home sweet home!" Badger declared, as they waited at the gates of the State Prison in Carson City.

Four guards stood ready inside the yard to receive their prisoner.

Bane cut the lengths of rope that tied his prisoner to the wagon's seat and pulled the fugitive off the conveyance.

"Much obliged, Marshal," one of guards said.

Bane nodded in reply.

As two of the officials hustled Rowelings across the yard and the other two stationed themselves at the gates, Lieutenant Governor-Warden Frank Dawes marched toward them, passing Rowelings without so much as a glance at the captive.

"He'll be confined to his cell until he's hanged," Dawes assured Bane. "Only one guard, Conrad Senseney, will have access to him."

Bane nodded.

"The only visitors he'll get to see are the preacher, the hangman, and me."

"You're attending the execution?"

"Governor Cooper insists upon it."

"I see."

"You're invited, too, if you want to see him swing."

"Thanks, but I'd prefer to spend time with my family."

Dawes laughed, which was an action that Bane, never having seen him do, hadn't been sure the warden was capable of performing. "So would I, Marshal; so would I."

He stuck out his paw, and Bane clasped it.

As he shook hands with Bane, the warden glanced at Badger and Luke. "My compliments to you, too, Deputies, for a job well done."

He even went so far as to shake their hands, a gesture that almost bowled them over, judging by their expressions.

"I have to go," Dawes said. "I want to make sure that Rowelings is photographed, the way he should have been when he arrived here the first time."

As the warden strode off, the guards began to close the gates.

"Is that the same man we saw a few weeks back?" Luke asked.

"Yes," Bane answered, "and no."

"We'd best get going," Luke suggested, "if we're going to transfer this gold to a box car and catch the train to Elko."

"I've never had the pleasure of riding in a boxcar before," Badger said.

"Look on the bright side: we only have to sit on the floor in the dark for a few hours," Bane declared, "before the Army takes the gold off our hands."

Luke nodded. "Yeah. Then, we get a seat in one of the passenger cars, if any are still available."

"True, but we get to see the governor again," Badger pointed out.

"Sometimes I think I should get extra pay just because I have to listen to you two whine."

"Who's whining?" Badger asked.

"I'm not whining," Luke declared. "Are you whining, Badger?"

* * *

Elko, Nevada

After the train deposited them and their horses in Elko, Bane, Badger, and Luke rode to the governor's mansion, where they were received with congratulations and the hearty thanks of the state's chief executive for their capture of Spencer Rowelings and the government's stolen shipment of gold.

"I can't tell you how much your service has aided our country—or, perhaps, in this instance, I shall—in part, at least. What I impart must remain in strictest confidence, however, as I'm sure you'll understand once you hear from what you have likely saved this nation."

Badger and Luke exchanged glances as they straightened their postures.

"You have our word," Bane said, looking at his deputies.

Luke nodded. "My word on it," he told their host.

"And mine," Badger agreed.

Governor Cooper nodded. "Spencer Rowelings stole a hundred-and-fifty-thousand dollars in gold bullion, all of which you gentlemen have recovered."

Bane repressed a smile, thinking of Rowelings's claim to have stolen a million dollars' worth of the precious metal.

"With part of that gold, he planned to hire as many of the best guns he could find among those with low morals, including former soldiers and lawmen gone astray and as many convicted criminals who'd served their time as were willing to fight and die, if necessary, in helping him to achieve his ends."

"That kind of money could hire a lot of hands, Your Excellency," Badger said.

"Please, call me 'Josh'; you've earned the privilege, all of you. As for your observation, Deputy Thompson—"

"'Badger,' if you please, Your Ex—uh, Josh."

The governor nodded. "Indeed, it could, but not nearly as many as Rowelings had in mind to recruit. With those initial hundred or so, he planned to attack the Utah Territorial Prison near Salt Lake City, which is, as I'm sure you know, operated by the U. S. Marshals; the Yuma Territorial Prison; and, of course, our own State Prison. If Rowelings were to have been successful in his campaign, he might well have added as many as another hundred men to his 'army.'"

"It's an ambitious plan," Luke said, "but it seems unlikely to have succeeded."

"Does it?" Governor Cooper asked. "Prior to the attack, the prisoners would riot, which would occupy the guards as they restored order. Meanwhile, Rowelings's men would attack from without, so the prison officials would have to battle the prisoners inside the prison while defending themselves against their attackers from outside."

Bane shook his head. "An audacious plan that just might succeed, at that, if Rowelings, his men, and the prisoners could carry it off before help arrived, which certainly seems possible, I'd say. Of course, after the first prison was attacked, others would be on alert, possibly with reinforcements, including militia, standing by."

"Possibly," the governor agreed, "but, Rowelings might have doubled his original hundred or so, as the result of his initial attack. That's a sizable force, even for a reinforced group of prison guards. Even if Rowelings didn't succeed, a good number of guards, posse members, and militia would likely be killed."

"What did he plan to do with his 'army' after he'd formed it?" Badger asked.

"Pretty much the same thing that the Vikings did throughout Europe during their day."

Badger looked lost.

Interpreting the governor's statement for his deputy, Bane said, "Rape, pillage, and burn."

"Throughout the territories of Utah and Arizona and our own state," Governor Cooper added. "And that was only the beginning of Rowelings's plan. I'm afraid that I can't tell you anything about the rest of it, except to say that it might have posed a threat to national security.

"Now, with Rowelings in prison, scheduled to be hanged, we don't have to worry about that. There are only two other matters we haven't attended to. The first is the silver that Rowelings stole. Was it also recovered?"

"I'm afraid not." Bane said. "If there was silver in that cave, it's most likely still there. He didn't have any on the wagon when I caught up to him. After he—or his stooges—retrieved the gold, Rowelings blew up the entrance."

"I see."

"But why wouldn't he have retrieved the silver as well?" Luke asked.

"I would say that he had uses for it that had nothing to do with his plans to aid and abet the escape of additional prisoners," Governor Cooper replied. "In any event, you accomplished the mission that I set before you. The gold has been recovered and the threat to our national security has been thwarted. The silver is safe where it is until it can be removed. Each of you will receive a commendation from me for your valor in successfully completing the mission I assigned to you."

"We didn't do anything more than earn our paychecks, Josh."

The governor laughed. "You know you did a whole hell of a lot more than that, Bane, which brings us to the second unresolved matter: how much money does the state of Nevada owe you?"

"Nothing."

"You've had considerable expenses, no doubt. If you'll just hand over or send me the receipts—"

"There aren't any receipts."

"But you've had travel expenses. You've had to rent hotel rooms, pay for meals, purchase supplies—"

"They've all been paid for in full."

"And you don't want to be reimbursed?"

"If I had, I'd have kept the receipts, Josh. I'm a rich man; I don't need the money."

Governor Cooper laughed. "You're one of a kind, Bane, one of a kind!"

"I do have one thing for you, though." Bane handed him the signed receipt from the Army major who'd been in charge of the platoon of soldiers to whom Bane had delivered the gold bullion that Rowelings had stolen and that he, Badger, and Luke had recovered.

Chapter 59

A Sleepless Chameleon

"If all men were just, there would be no need of valor."
— Agesilaus II (c. 445 – 360 BC)

Carson City, Nevada

Conrad Senseney couldn't sleep.

It wasn't the responsibility with which Warden Dawes had saddled him in assigning him exclusively to the duty of guarding Spencer Rowelings that disturbed him. He'd guarded a lot of men as ruthless and cunning as Rowelings. In fact, his record of reliability had almost certainly recommended his present assignment to Dawes.

Nor was it his conscience. Although it troubled him, it didn't bother him enough to prevent him from sleeping.

A man, he believed, didn't have any essential personality, no self unto which to be true. A man was a chameleon, changeable and changing to suit his various environments. He was a husband to Nancy, a guard to Dawes, a crony to the boys with whom he drank at the saloon, a son to the woman who'd conceived him and to her late husband, the man who'd fathered him. Yes, Conrad Senseney was all these things and more, without being any of them.

A man of the moment, he changed with the moment. If he were required to have a conscience, he had one or, at least, pretended to have one. At work, he was a trustworthy and dutiful guard; at home, a loving husband; in a saloon, one of the boys. He was what was required at the moment in whatever particular environment he must inhabit for the nonce.

Alone, he was no one; he was nothing.

Well, that wasn't true, not entirely.

He was a schemer, at times, at least.

Like now.

At present, he was thinking of Rowelings's offer of silver.

The stage robber and killer had stolen more than Army gold, he'd confided. He'd also stolen silver.

Or so the prisoner had claimed.

It was Senseney's, all of it, Rowelings had promised, payable in advance, if the guard would merely help him to escape.

Leave the door to his cell unlocked.

That's all Senseney had to do, Rowelings had assured him.

Just leave the door to his cell unlocked.

And, oh yes, place a ladder against the wall surrounding the prison and leave a rope beside it.

Once Nancy confirmed her receipt of the silver, sending to him the note that "the package arrived," Senseney would do these things for Rowelings.

If he tried to double-cross Rowelings, refusing to follow through with the plan after receiving the silver, Rowelings would reveal Senseney's part in his escape plan and tell Dawes that his trusted guard had backed out at the last moment. Senseney's wife, charged as an accomplice in the crime, would likely turn against her husband to save her own neck, and Senseney himself would take up residence in one of the prison's cells, if he wasn't hanged instead.

The risk wasn't high, if he did what he was paid to do, Senseney thought.

After Rowelings escaped, Senseney could hit himself over the head and claim that Rowelings had struck him when he'd opened the prisoner's cell door to check on the prisoner's welfare after Rowelings had refused to answer him.

Senseney could either remove the ladder from the wall and discard the rope or claim that Rowelings had obviously planned his escape beforehand. There was evidence that Rowelings had planned several of his crimes in advance, long before he was incarcerated in Nevada, just as it was known, now, that Rowelings often used intermediaries to assist him."

There was some risk, but, next to the silver that Rowelings would pay him, through Nancy, the risk seemed worth taking.

Rowelings was scheduled to be hanged in three days, which would give the good folks who'd been invited to the criminal's execution time to arrive, should they decide to attend.

If Nancy confirmed the receipt of the silver in time for him to put Rowelings's plan into effect, Senseney would do it.

There were better places to live than Carson City, Nevada, after all—provided a man had the money to afford them.

Darkness claimed him as, smiling, Senseney drifted off to sleep.

Chapter 60

A Near-Death Experience

"Joy is not in things; it is in us."
— Richard Wagner (1813-1883)

Excelsior, Nevada

Her arms open, Pamela rushed across the front lawn, past the banks of flowers and the shrubs and trees that stood, like sentinels, along the walk.

As Bane entered the gate, she seized him and held him tightly to her breast, tears streaming down her beautiful face. "Bane!" she cried. "How I've missed you!"

He held her close, delighting in the passion of her embrace, the scent of her perfume, the softness of her curves, and the delicacy of her body, which, he knew, belied her strength. It was good, he thought, that he'd telegraphed her of his expected arrival date.

"Be careful!" Aunt Flossie called to Lizzie and Ben as they raced across the yard to embrace their father, hugging him around the waist when their mother stepped back to make room for them.

Stooping, Bane wrapped an arm around each of them.

"Did you bring us anything?" Ben asked.

Bane smiled. "Just me this time, Ben."

"That's all we wanted, isn't it, Ben?" Lizzie asked.

Ben considered her question. "Yes," he decided.

"Let me say hello to Grandpa and Aunt Flossie," Bane said.

Reluctantly, they released their father, and Bane strode quickly up the walk to the porch, where Aunt Flossie awaited him, tears in her eyes. "Bane!" she said, clutching him to her bosom.

That was all she said, but it was plenty. Bane knew and loved the heart of the woman who'd raised him as her own son after his father Bradford, her brother, crazed with grief after his wife had died giving birth to Bane, had abandoned his newborn son to Aunt Flossie's care. That was all water under the bridge now, although Bane had held a grudge against his father for over twenty years, a grievance he might still have let separate his father from him, even now, if not for the intercession of both Aunt Flossie and Pamela and Bane's own faith in God, which rightly required the forgiveness of true penitents.

Bradford, still a bit awkward, despite his reconciliation with his son, stuck out his hand.

Bane ignored it, clasping his father to his breast.

"I've missed you, son."

"I've missed you, too, Dad."

Bane released him, and Bradford stepped back. He'd never been one to express his feelings, although there was no doubt that he had a heart large enough to encompass his family and the rest of the good things in life.

"Come inside," Aunt Flossie invited her nephew. "You're home now, Bane."

Bane smiled. "I reckon I am, at that."

He led the rest of his family into the luxurious mansion he'd had built to Pamela's and Aunt Flossie's specifications after the "war" at his ranch had destroyed their previous house, Mountain Crest, north of Excelsior.

"Surprise!" a chorus of friends cried as he entered the foyer.

A troop of men and women stepped out of the parlor.

"Welcome home, Bane!"

Badger and Luke stood before him, as did Badger's girlfriend Lorraine and Luke's wife Penelope. His secretary Angeline was also there, as were his other two deputies, pardoned former State Prison inmates Curt Hardesty and Marcel Gagnon.

In an aside to Pamela, Bane quipped, "This is some surprise; it damn near killed me!"

Chapter 61

A Rude Awakening

"Cunning and treachery are the offspring of incapacity."
— Francois de La Rochefoucauld (1613-1680)

State Prison, Carson City, Nevada

"Conrad?"

Senseney's dream ended with him seated atop a mountain of silver.

He didn't like being awakened. He slept little enough as it was, playing nursemaid to Rowelings and listening to the din that went on constantly in the cells. Among the prisoners, several were loco, and they bellowed and howled all night, possessed by what demons Senseney didn't know or care.

"What is it?" he demanded.

"Note," Kyle Brock said, "from your wife. Thought you might want to read it."

He sounded surly. Probably he hadn't appreciated Senseney's tone, since, in delivering the message, Brock was doing his colleague a favor of sorts.

Senseney sat up. Across from him, in an isolation cell, Rowelings awaited execution. That cold-hearted bastard slept well enough, despite both the noise and his imminent fate. "Sorry, Kyle. Haven't gotten much sleep lately."

Brock handed the sealed envelope through the bars to Senseney. "Hope it's not bad news."

Senseney nodded. "Me, too. Oh, and thanks for bringing Nancy's note."

Brock nodded. Looking at Rowelings asleep in his cell, he said, "It'll be over soon, Conrad." He turned, retracing his steps.

It's good, Senseney thought, that he wasn't a prisoner. If he were, his note would have been opened and read by a guard. If it contained any forbidden information, it would have been destroyed without its intended recipient ever being any the wiser. Of course, as a prison official, the regulation didn't apply to him.

Besides, he was above suspicion. The fifteen years of his life he'd spent as a prison guard paid dividends. Unlike some of his colleagues, he'd performed his tasks conscientiously, responsibly, and, until now, honestly. He'd refrained from beating prisoners who'd disrespected him. He hadn't harassed them simply because he could have done so. He hadn't shaken any of them down. He'd treated them with dignity and respect, despite their crimes.

He'd never shirked his duties, either. In fact, he'd always been available for extra duty and overtime. He'd discharged his duties faithfully and thoroughly, earning his superiors' respect. As far as Warden Dawes was concerned, Conrad Senseney was as much above suspicion as he was beyond reproach. Dawes's confidence and trust in him is what had prompted the warden to assign Senseney as Rowelings's only guard. He would remember Senseney's commitment to his job, Dawes had vowed, as if such a promise meant anything. The warden was good at spouting empty words. This assignment would pay, though; Senseney had made sure of it.

The same day that he and Rowelings had agreed to exchange the prisoner's stash of silver for Rowelings's escape, Senseney had sent for Nancy. When she'd arrived, he'd told her that he'd arranged to have "a package" sent to their house and that, when it arrived, she was to send him a note to the prison to confirm its arrival. He'd refused to answer any of her questions about the arrangement, had ignored her objections, and had assuaged her misgivings to the best of his ability, promising that, although he wasn't at liberty to divulge any details, he was doing nothing illegal; in fact, he was ensuring that the prison's security system was sound.

She might not have entirely believed him, but she'd agreed to play her part.

To ensure the package's delivery, Senseney had also had Nancy deliver a handwritten note from Rowelings to a man named John Smith who was staying at The Carson City Hotel. Senseney had been tempted to open the envelope and read the note, but he'd decided that doing so would be taking too big a chance. His tampering might be noticed, in which case the whole deal with Rowelings might be jeopardized.

The risk of discovery, compounded by the loss of the silver he would otherwise have received, was too great, Senseney had decided, especially when he held the keys, both literally and figuratively, to Rowelings's escape.

Now, it seemed that he'd made the right decision.

He opened the sealed envelope, removed the note, and read:

The package arrived.

* * *

Carson City, Nevada

Nancy Senseney felt woozy.

When she lifted the teacup, it rattled.

It had been two days now, and her hand was still shaking.

She felt tense, frightened, the way she had since she'd gone to the post office with that frightful stranger, the tall, lean man in the dark clothes who'd worn a holstered six-shooter on his hip, the stranger she'd passed off as a cousin visiting from Reno.

Her husband had sent him, the man had claimed, to escort her to the post office. To "protect" her.

From what, he wouldn't say.

What in the world had Conrad become involved in?

It had been creepy walking arm-in-arm with a grim stranger whose cold eyes and impassive features made her skin crawl. It was as if she were being escorted by a killer. Maybe she had been, she told herself, shuddering at the thought.

It had been frightening when he'd insisted upon seeing the note she had written before she'd sealed it inside the envelope she'd addressed, under the man's unwavering gaze, to her husband at the State Prison. It had been terrifying as he'd walked beside her to the post office and mailed the note.

It bothered her that she'd lied to her husband, telling him, in the note, that a package had arrived when none had. But what else could she have done? The armed man who'd arrived out of nowhere had been intimidating. When he'd told her what to write in the note, his tone, like his demeanor, had made it clear that she'd had no choice but to pen the lie about a package's arrival.

"You won't see me again," he'd told Nancy afterward.

She'd felt relieved—for a while.

But would the stranger be true to his word?

Oh, how she wished that Conrad were home!

He should never have taken such a dangerous job as that of a prison guard, risking his life every day.

She herself had refused to live on the site, despite the prison's provision of quarters for guards and their families. Instead, she'd insisted that Conrad pay for the small cabin she called a cottage on the outskirts of town.

It was dangerous to be on her own, especially in the West, and lonely, too, but it was safer than living inside the walls of a prison.

At least, that's what she had thought until two days ago.

She lifted her teacup.

Her hand shook.

The tea quivered in the cup.

She set it down again.

It was cold now, anyway.

She felt empty.

And frightened.
And alone.
She wept.
And trembled.

Chapter 62

Fine Fare

"He made up his mind to kill the other man before the other man had finished thinking."
— Buffalo Bill Cody (1846-), speaking of Wild Bill Hickok (1837-1876)

Excelsior, Nevada

Ben spilled his milk.

Lizzie scolded him for it.

Pamela chastised Lizzie for scolding Ben, gently, as was her way.

Badger seemed both proud and awkward in Lorraine's presence.

He wasn't a bad-looking fellow, but Lorraine was a true beauty, almost as striking as Pamela herself.

Luke and Penelope seemed to be even more comfortable together now than the last time they'd shared a table with Bane and his family.

Curt Hardesty didn't seem at ease in the opulent surroundings of Bane's mansion, but the other former prisoner whom Bane had drafted as one of his new deputies, Marcel Gagnon, seemed as much at home as if the house were his own and Bane, his family, and their other invitees were his guests. Marcel was as fearless and adept a fighter as any man Bane had ever seen, but he also conveyed a diplomat's suave, debonair demeanor.

Bane's secretary, Angeline, as charming as she was attractive, was the only
other member of their dinner party, Bane reckoned, besides Pamela and Aunt
Flossie, who could match Marcel's smooth, polished bearing.

Bradford seemed to be holding his own, and, of course, Aunt Flossie was
completely at ease. She was, after all, in her element.

"The foie gras, oysters, truffles, and, of course, the Châteaubriand are excellent!" Marcel exclaimed. "And the wine—I would have thought such a vintage
impossible to come by as far west as Nevada; even the wineries of California
cannot have produced such an exquisite beverage as this."

"Thank you, Marcel," Pamela said. "Aunt Flossie is a marvelous chef, and
Bane and I have a few bottles of various wines sent to us from France each year
for just such occasions as this one."

"The fare, Flossie, is beyond compare, except, perhaps, in the very finest
restaurants in Paris."

Aunt Flossie blushed at the compliments. "Je suis heureux que vous ap-
préciiez le menu, monsieur."

"You speak French, also!"

Her blush deepened. "I had to learn the language to cook the food."

Marcel chuckled. "Beauty, intelligence, wit, culture, and excellence in the
fine art of cooking—what more could a woman offer a man but the pleasures of
romance?"

Bane started to say something, but Bradford beat him to it.

"That's my sister you're talking to, mister!"

"Ah, yes, monsieur, but, if she were a stranger to you, she would be as fair
and intelligent and witty and cultured and excellent in preparing feasts fit for a
king."

"We don't have kings in this country," Bradford noted.

"More's the pity."

"Bradford!" Aunt Flossie spoke up. "I am perfectly capable of speaking on
my own behalf, and, I must say, I find Monsieur Gagnon's compliments most
pleasant." Her gaze softened as she directed it from her brother to their guest.
"Je vous remercie, gentil monsiuer."

Bane could tell from the smile in Pamela's eyes that she found the conversation between Aunt Flossie and Marcel quite diverting.

Bradford's fierce expression suggested that, for him, the flirtatious manner of their guest was anything but amusing.

Now seemed a good time to change the topic, Bane thought.

Fortunately, Angeline did. "My brother," she said, "was recently ordained as a priest."

Her announcement quelled all other conversation as congratulations were extended by everyone, including, thanks to a gentle nudge of Lizzie's elbow into her brother's side, Ben.

Had Angeline not made her announcement, the knock at the front door might have done as well as the change of topic in quelling the quarrel that seemed certain to arise between Bradford and Marcel, despite Aunt Flossie's intervention, and ruin the evening for everyone.

Bane excused himself and returned with a telegram in hand, a look of concern on his face. "Lieutenant Governor and the prison's warden, Franklin Dawes, has sent me a message: 'Spencer Rowelings has escaped from the State Prison.'"

Badger and Luke looked at each other. In unison, they cried, "Again?"

Chapter 63

A Madman's Mind

"You who live your lives in cities or among peaceful ways cannot always tell whether your friends are the kind who would go through fire for you. But on the Plains one's friends have the opportunity to prove their mettle."
— Buffalo Bill Cody (1846-)

Excelsior, Nevada

In light of the revelation that Bane had received, the dinner party ended sooner than the hostesses had intended.

Aunt Flossie, however, had time to exchange a press of Marcel's hand after he had shaken hands with Bane, Pamela, Lizzie, Ben, and, reluctantly on Bradford's part, Flossie's brother. As she did so, she whispered, "I would be pleased should you decide to court me, Marcel."

His smile told her that he fully intended to act upon her implicit invitation.

Bane said, "Wait, Marcel!"

The deputy turned back, looking puzzled.

"I'd like to see you, Badger, Luke, and Curt privately for a moment before you leave."

They followed him into the parlor.

"I'll be brief," he said. "There was more to the telegram than I shared with the other guests at the dinner party." He pulled the folded telegram from the inside pocket of his vest, reading the part he had kept to himself until now:

Rowelings threatened to kill you and your family.

His deputies looked as horrified as Bane felt.

"Share this information with no one."

The others nodded their agreement.

"He's proven himself a man who is truly without a conscience. He has killed men and women, and I do not doubt for a second that he would—" Bane choked up for a moment, as his eyes moistened—"that he would kill Lizzie and Ben without hesitation, with whatever passes for joy in his vile heart."

"We aren't going to let that happen," Luke declared.

"No way in hell," Badger agreed.

"You can count on me; I will die before I let that bastard harm you or your family," Curt assured him.

Marcel's eyes were cold. "I have killed many men, but nothing would give me greater pleasure than to slay this monster."

"But we need a plan," Luke said.

"How can we make a plan when we don't have any idea how, or where, Rowelings might strike?" Badger asked.

"I have an idea," Bane said.

"We're listening," Luke urged.

"For some reason, or, perhaps, for no reason, Rowelings has singled me out, or, rather, me and my family. I think he believes that I'm responsible, or most responsible, for ruining whatever his own plans might have been.

"I prevented his escape from the courtroom after Judge Hawthorne rendered his verdict. I jailed the men he'd recruited to kill the judge, the district attorney, and the jury foreman. I led Badger and Luke in our pursuit of him, and we arrested him and his confederate, Matthew Lewis. We also recovered the gold he stole from the stagecoach he'd robbed, murdering all on board, and ended whatever grandiose scheme he had in mind to finance with that gold. We returned him to prison, where he was supposed to be hanged.

"In the past, others sought him and captured him, but they weren't the thorns in his side that we've been, and he blames me, as the leader of the marshal's office out this way, for his failures, particularly his failure to execute his ultimate plan. He wants vengeance, not on you, who, he may think, were just doing your jobs, but on me, the man who, he believes, in his madman's mind, is responsible for his failures, and what better way is there to avenge himself, from his warped point of view, than by killing me and my entire family?

"By killing Pamela, Lizzie, Ben, Aunt Flossie, and Bradford, probably before he killed me, Rowelings would not only get back at me for destroying his cockamamie plans, but he would, by his own twisted way of thinking, prove that, in the end, he remained undefeated, that he was the better man."

Nods showed Bane that the others agreed with his assessment.

"What are we going to do to stop him?" Curt asked.

"As U. S. marshals, we cover a lot of territory. One week, we're one place; another week, we're somewhere else. Only occasionally are we here, in Excelsior. Roweling can't be everywhere, especially since all he has left, as far as we know, is the cache of silver he stole from the stagecoach. Evidently, he knows where my family and I live."

Marcel looked alarmed. "You mean—?"

Bane nodded. "He'll strike here, in Excelsior, and his target, I believe, will be my house, here in town."

"Sacre bleu!"

"Exactly," Bane said, recognizing Marcel's tone of voice, even if he didn't understand the words themselves.

"What are we going to do to stop him?" Badger asked.

"Nothing," Bane answered.

"Nothing?" Badger repeated, staring at Bane as if the marshal, not Rowelings, were the madman.

Chapter 64

A Stroke of Good Fortune

"A tomb now suffices him for whom the whole world was not sufficient."
— Alexander the Great (356–323 BC)

Excelsior, Nevada

When?

That was the question, the same question, that had been on Bane's mind for the past week.

Would today be the day?

Tonight?

Tomorrow?

A week or a month from now?

Next year?

Not knowing when Spencer Rowelings would make his move was agonizing, just the way Rowelings probably intended it to be.

Pamela. Ever since he'd killed the man who'd abducted her, after she'd freed herself from captivity in the mountain cabin south of Excelsior, near a town as full of reprobates as any west of the Mississippi, theirs had been a rock-solid relationship, full of romance and adventure. Too much adventure, Pamela had said on more than a few occasions. She worried about him when he was away, pursuing robbers and killers and other unscrupulous fugitives or lying in wait for them to prevent them from performing additional outrages against society. He'd struck it richer with her than he'd enriched himself and the lives of his family when they'd found the gold mine on their vacation property, Lightning Hill.

Lizzie. What a precocious child! In some ways, a miniature version of her mother, the girl seemed responsible, loving, kind, and compassionate from birth, although, he realized, she'd learned to practice these attributes by observing her mother and Aunt Flossie in action every day, quietly, by example, as they showed her the social graces that many girls older than she discovered only in finishing schools. Protective of her younger brother, she sought to instruct, guide, nurture, and even correct his behavior whenever she regarded it as bordering upon impropriety. Bane smiled. Her influence over her younger brother would, he had no doubt, be long remembered and would, like his mother's and his Aunt Flossie's loving care, be a beacon to guide him for years to come.

Ben. He emulated his father and, to a lesser extent, his grandfather, and his imagination, it seemed, was big enough to hold the whole world. He lived many, sometimes contradictory, lives, for a few minutes at a time, at least, among them, cowboy, storekeeper, sheriff, and, like his father, U. S. marshal. He was also, by nature, confident, curious, courageous, and, although Ben might not think so or admit it, compassionate and considerate. He was young yet, but he was already a good man in the making.

Bradford, his father. Bane had learned to call him that, and to accept him as that, despite the fact that Bradford had abandoned him after the infant's mother had died during childbirth, in the madness of his grief blaming his newborn son for her demise. It was only years later that Bane had met the man who'd fathered him. Bradford had been a stranger to him, but Bane had saved his life when a gunfighter had held Bradford hostage. To please Bradford's sister, Aunt Flossie, and Pamela, Bane had forgiven the man who'd abandoned him and had given Bradford a second chance to become the father whom his son had never known. As usual, the advice of Aunt Flossie and Pamela had been sound, and Bane and Bradford were close now, as close as any father and son. Each had trusted the other with his life, and Bane had entrusted his family's safety to Bradford on more than one occasion. Bradford was as glad as Bane, maybe more so, for the chance to make amends, and he had succeeded in proving himself both a man of mettle and a man of great heart. It was the greatness of his heart, Bane suspected, that had resulted in the depth of grief he'd felt after the death of his wife, and it was that same greatness of heart that had allowed him to feel remorse at abandoning his son, to repent of the deed, and to become the father and grandfather he was today. From him, Bane had learned that love allows forgiveness, which has the power to heal and to bind and even to reshape the future, despite the past.

Aunt Flossie. Bane's heart melted at the thought of her love and devotion to him at a time in his life that he needed care the most. It was she who'd instilled what character he possessed, for it was she who'd taken him to church, nursed him when he was sick, saw that he attended school, corrected him when he was wrong, consoled him when he grieved, and, most of all, loved him when he'd thought that his father had abandoned him because he wasn't worth keeping—or loving. She had said that Bradford would come back to him, that they could mend fences, that they could be father and son, late, yes, but father and son, just the same. When he did find Bradford, seemingly by accident, she had told him that, with God, there are neither accidents nor coincidences, and she, like Pamela, had urged him to forgive his father and to allow Bradford, her brother, a second chance. Finally, she'd taught Bane the value of justice. "You have courage, and you don't shrink from violence when another person's rights are threatened. You don't abide bullies or bullying. You stand for right. These are your gifts, or some of them, and the good Lord has big plans for you, Bane; believe it." One of the proudest moments of her life was the moment that Bane pinned the U. S. marshal's badge to his vest.

Bane had friends, even a few whom the good citizens of his adopted home-town regarded as unsuitable, among whom was Rose O'Sharon, the madam of two brothels, who'd befriended Bane when he was friendless and had loved him, after her fashion, when he was unloved. But there were or, in one case, had been, others, also, including his deputies, Badger, Luke, Curt, and Marcel; his secretary, Angeline; the late Allan Pinkerton, founder of the famous detective agency that spanned the continent; J. D. Campbell, Luke Carver, and others, including members of the church he and his family attended. As much as they meant to Bane, he valued his family more; his friends were silver, his kin, gold.

And, now, his family's lives were threatened, as they'd been imperiled in the past.

He never doubted, but knew, that Rowelings would come, as the killer had threatened.

At present, all Bane could do was trust in his plan and wait.

And the waiting was torture to his soul.

* * *

Three weeks had passed following Rowelings's second escape from State Prison.

Again, tonight, the house was quiet.

And dark, or mostly dark, behind the thick velvet curtains hanging at the windows. Apparently, some lamps burned in some of the rooms.

It was well past midnight.

No one stirred, as far as Rowelings could tell.

No one, that is, except him and his hired guns.

The moon was a thin crescent.

The heavens seemed dim, as if the very cosmos itself were in secret alliance with the figures of darkness.

The other men shivered, but not Rowelings. Like a wolf on a winter's hunt, he had an affinity for the cold, as he did for the darkness.

Under the faint light of the distant stars, they moved silently, with precision and economy.

Wearing black, they were nearly invisible.

As they neared the residence at the south end of town, gas lanterns along the walkway between the street and the Queen Anne mansion illuminated an expanse of the lawn.

The wee hours of the early winter's morning were cold. Denuded deciduous trees wore sleeves of ice. Patches of recent snow formed white islands in the brown-green lawn. Frost rimed the house's windowpanes.

While Rowelings and four of his men waited, Ed Lear crept toward the tall, massive front door of the great house.

He was visible for the brief interval of time that it took him to ascend the wide marble steps and cross the porch to the door. He would have been illuminated longer, and more fully, had the porch light been lit.

It was not.

Still, this was a moment of risk. The interloper might be spotted.

But it was a hazard that could not be helped. The door needed to be un-locked. Breaking into the house would warn the family, and it was likely that the marshal and the other adult male in the family slept with their six-shooters close to hand. Rowelings didn't want to fight; he wanted to kill.

Standing at the edge of the street in front of the estate, with the other men he'd hired, Rowelings waited, watching and hoping.

He didn't have to wait long, nor should he. Lear was notorious for his lock picking skills, and he had all the tools of the locksmith's trade: skeleton keys, metal files, various picks, and other implements.

When he returned, Lear simply nodded. He'd been successful. He also had not heard any hint of movement within the house. Had he, he would have shaken Rowelings's shoulders. That was one of the signals they'd arranged to use in lieu of speaking.

As Lear left the premises, his role accomplished, Rowelings thought, What a stroke of good fortune! He and his men had obtained a means of ingress!

They would kill everyone in the house, men, women, and children alike.

At last, his revenge would be complete!

Rowelings gave the sign to move out.

* * *

Inside, they waited for their eyes to adjust.

As Rowelings had supposed, there were oases of light, thanks to the flames of gas lamps secured to walls, here and there, downstairs. The lights would illuminate parts of the rooms in which the lamps burned, but not extensive spaces. Consequently, some parts of the mansion were brighter than the starlit night; others, darker.

As his eyes adjusted, he better made out the hallway in which they stood and the dim shapes of furniture in the parlor to his right.

There was another room, a dark one, to his left, a library, perhaps. The kitchen, pantry, and dining room would be at the back of the house.

In the light of the parlor's lamps, more details emerged: a parquet floor, thick rugs, dim suggestions of chairs, couches, ottomans, and settees, the dark shape of a grand piano.

Most of the rest of the downstairs was dark, but the gas lamps rising from the staircase's recesses and landings to illuminate the steps revealed touches of the wealth and elegance of the house and stoked Rowelings's hatred and envy of the man who owned this splendid mansion, enjoying its comfort and splendor and, no doubt, delighting in the pleasure that the house's magnificence and comforts afforded him and the rest of his precious family.

But the bastard would not enjoy his good fortune much longer, nor would the woman he married, nor their children or the rest of his kin. Soon enough, their love and their joy, like their lives, would be naught but ashes and dust, and he, Spencer Rowelings, would prove, again, that he was the better man.

If his luck held, the sleepers would never awaken before they died.

Rowelings had trained his men for the task that lay before them now. They had rehearsed it again and again, in a two-story house that Rowelings had rented for the occasion. Now, they could carry out their assigned tasks with precision, without having to think.

He, the ablest with a gun, crept up the wide flight of stairs, leading the way to the second floor, where the bedrooms awaited them.

The stairway's carpet was another bitter reminder, as was the size of the great house itself, of the wealth that his enemy enjoyed. For Rowelings, the gold and silver he had stolen would have been enough for him. He needed no wife, no kids, no parents, no friends.

In fact, family or friends would have been a bother and a nuisance, and they'd all have had a hand out and a sob story to go with it, begging for money, not once or twice, in moments of real need, but continually. A fine house, elegantly furnished, and money in the bank were all any man needed, really. Family and friends were just annoyances.

Why a man like his enemy wanted more than a fortune and a big, beautiful home with fine furniture was a puzzle beyond Rowelings's ability to solve. As far as he was concerned, the lawdog's desire for a family and friends revealed a weakness of character. A true man neither needed nor wanted either.

At the top of the stairs, he stopped, waiting for the other gunmen, who were yet climbing the staircase that he had just ascended.

Their footfalls, like Rowelings's own, were silent. No creak of either step or leather, no rustle of fabric, no expulsion of breath among the six of them would give away their secret presence in the house. Their movements were as silent as death.

Along one wall of the hallway, two bedrooms faced another pair, opposite them, on the other side of the passageway. The fifth bedroom, no doubt the master, stood alone, opening off the end of the corridor.

Rowelings positioned himself outside the bedroom at the end of the hall. Each of the other men stationed himself at the door to one of the other chambers.

Silently, Rowelings began counting, as did his accomplices.

This was the critical part of the attack, and they had rehearsed it a hundred times, until the synchronization of their count was perfect.

Even if one of them reached sixty a moment before the rest of them, the slight discrepancy wouldn't matter. A second off would not allow enough time for any of their targets to react.

Their eyes had fully adjusted to the differences in light between the first floor and the upper story of the house.

Now that all of them were in place, each of them, in his black clothing, illuminated only dimly by the faint light of the wall lamps along the corridor, appeared little more than a silhouette.

Rowelings drew his gun. Holding the revolver in his right hand, he began turning the doorknob with his left, as slowly and carefully as the narrator of Edgar Allan Poe's "The Tell-Tale Heart."

Fifty-seven . . . .

Inch by inch, he eased the door inward, until it stood wide open.

Fifty-eight . . . .

Fortunately, its hinges had not creaked.

Fifty-nine . . . .

None of the other doors' hinges had made a sound, either.

Sixty!

He stepped into the master bedroom.

In the dimness of the spacious chamber, two forms lay beneath the blankets of the wide, long bed, the smaller figure's blonde hair a whirl upon her pillow.

The first gunshot sounded elsewhere, loud in the otherwise silent house.

One of them, the girl, perhaps, or the boy, was dead.

Almost at the same time as the initial shot, four others followed, two of which were Rowelings's.

A look of horror contorted the killer's face. No!

Impossible!

He'd shot the lawman himself, only a second ago, right after he'd killed the marshal's wife, at the same time, almost exactly, as his other men had ended the lives of the rest of his hated adversary's family!

And, yet, the bastard wasn't dead!

Rowelings hadn't killed him!

He'd failed!

The lawdog had thrust open the door to the bedroom's closet, six-shooter in hand, and shot his attacker again and again and again, and Rowelings had screamed, in pain and rage, as the bullets struck him in the heart, the gut, the groin, and Rowelings had been slammed back by the impact of each bullet; he had stumbled and fallen.

And, now, he was dying!

He couldn't believe he'd failed.

Right to his last breath, he insisted to himself that he had won, that he had avenged himself, that he had killed the man who'd ruined all his plans and all his hopes to be someone dreaded by lesser men.

* * *

"It's over," Badger declared.

Bane nodded.

"They're dead," Luke said, "all of them."

"They'll never threaten you or your family again," Marcel asserted.

Curt Hardesty nodded his agreement with the others' declarations.

Bane's cold stare would have been chilling to less hardened men.

Badger and Luke had seen the look before, the look of a killer, which, a moment ago, for an instant, Bane had been, as had they all.

Bane's suspicions had been right. Rowelings had meant to kill him and his family.

Gambling that he would be correct about Rowelings's scheme, Bane had staged each of the bedrooms to make it appear that their beds were occupied. He'd placed two of Aunt Flossie's adult mannequins, a male and a female, in his and Pamela's' bedroom; an adult female mannequin in Aunt Flossie's bedroom; an adult male mannequin in Bradford's bedroom; and child-size mannequins in the bedrooms of Lizzie and Ben.

To these figures, he'd added wigs, blonde for Pamela; brunette, sprinkled with talcum powder to create a graying effect for Aunt Flossie; and dark wigs for Bradford, Ben, and himself. He'd sprinkled some powder on Bradford's wig and had clipped the wig on Ben's wig a bit so that it, like the rest of them, had a different look than the others. Marcel, who'd had some experience in the theater, had given him a hand.

The effect, in the dim light of the hallway lamps that entered the bedrooms when their doors were opened, had aided the deception, which had fooled Rowelings and his men, whose only "victims" were the mannequins that Bane would have to replace in Aunt Flossie's collection.

Waiting in the bedrooms' closets, each of the lawmen had stepped forth as soon as a shot was fired, startling the would-be killers. As Rowelings, the gunman in the master bedroom, had spun toward him, Bane had shot the bastard.

It was a stroke of good fortune, he thought, that Aunt Flossie had taken a keen interest, years ago, in sewing and making dresses from the patterns printed in Godey's Lady's Book. Over the years, she'd made some elegant clothes for herself and her friends, including some items for their children, and Bane had taken pleasure in equipping her home studio with a hand-cranked Wheeler and Wilson sewing machine and all the fabric, needles, threads, mannequins, and other equipment and supplies she needed to pursue her art.

Her passion for sewing and his and his deputies' valor had saved the people he loved best in all the world, his family.

Chapter 65

A Short, Direct Message

"Every day, I thank God that I'm good with a gun."
— Bane Messenger (1844 -)

Lightning Hill, Nevada

As he emerged from the woods, Bane drew rein.

Although eager to reach his destination, he paused to take in the sight of the prominent mound near his family's vacation home. For a moment, he studied the burned path that zigzagged its way down the side of the hill, among the promontory's evergreens, a bolt of lightning upon the prominence. According to Shoshone lore, the Great Spirit had hidden a huge lode of silver in this area. Rumors of its presence caused much slaughter among greedy men. To punish them and to warn others against such conduct, the Great Spirit had blasted the largest hill in the area with lightning.

The name "Lightning Hill" was based upon this incident, and the name of the hundred-acre retreat that Bane and Pamela owned nearby was inspired by this legend. It was on this property that gold, rather than silver, had been found, and the mine was their chief source of wealth.

As Pamela had observed on her first visit to the retreat, the countryside surrounding the place was, indeed, beautiful. The terrain rose gradually, and the faint trail they'd followed—the same that Bane now rode alone—passed tall pines and firs. Although, during the summer and fall, the yellow leaves of quaking aspens shimmered among taller evergreens, the deciduous aspens, losing their leaves at the end of the autumn, were, as now, bare, thin, tilted columns that showed no hint of their past and approaching glory.

From the elevation of his present vantage point, he could see rolling land on every hand, and tumbling creeks flashed and glinted in the sun, as the surfaces of lakes rippled in the breeze.

From the first sight of this land, both Bane and Pamela's hearts were filled with peace and tranquility, so much so that "Serenity" had been one of the names they'd considered for their retreat.

Pamela's introduction to their rural home away from home had been anything but peaceful, though, as they'd encountered a band of toughs who'd claimed that he and his wife were trespassing on their own land.

When Pamela and he had refused to be cowed into leaving, the ruffians had laid siege to their property, with Bane and Pamela inside the Tudor house they'd just had built, and, in the ensuing gunfight, Pamela had again displayed her indomitable courage and her expertise with a rifle.

Fortunately, much-needed reinforcements in the form of Bane's friends arrived, and the battle was quelled. Of course, that incident had been only the first in a series of others, equally or more dangerous, but those times were past, and Bane had always lived very much in the present. Besides, now, as he approached their Tudor, he had other considerations on his mind.

He nudged his mare, and she resumed her walk through the sylvan splendor of the unspoiled wilderness surrounding Lightning Hill.

* * *

"Daddy!" Ben, who'd been playing with the kite that his grandfather had made for him, tossed the stick about which its string was coiled and ran across the vast lawn, to greet his father.

Bane swept him up in his arms and hugged him, the boy returning the embrace.

"I missed you, Daddy."

Bane, setting him down, ruffled his son's hair. "I've missed you, too, Ben."

The boy turned, as suddenly as he'd run toward his father, and raced toward the house, shouting, "Mommy! Daddy's here!"

The rest of the family, led by Pamela, rushed out to greet him.

Bane choked back the love, the joy, and the gratitude welling inside him, as he did the threat of tears caused by the same. He'd learned, as a child, not to show emotion, and his stoic manner had served him well, both as a soldier and as a lawman. Old habits were hard to break, especially when they had proved themselves effective.

His family knew his heart, though, and they accepted the way he suppressed even his deepest feelings. That was just one of the many reasons he loved them with all his heart; they accepted him for himself, for who he was.

After their reconciliation, Bradford had offered Bane some fatherly advice. "Count your blessings, not your sorrows," he'd told him.

At the time, Bane had not understood the steep price that Bradford must have paid, in installments of disappointment, disillusionment, heartache, pain, and suffering, to learn this bit of discernment. Since then, though, Bane had come to understand the depth of his father's anguish and of his wisdom. Bane had learned, also, that, often, the latter was born of the former.

His family had taught him something, too: sometimes, joy is so profound that it saddens the soul.

In his family, Bane knew such joy, as he did in rare moments of revelation, in which he knew, indisputably, that God not only existed but loved him, Bane Messenger, as greatly as He did the rest of His creation.

Beside such joy, the world was—the closest word he could think of was "secondary." But it did not fully capture the meaning he had in mind.

The war had hardened him. Hunting the worst of the West's outlaws had toughened him. Risking his life time after time had tempered him. What he'd seen and heard in battles and gunfights had, in some ways, formed him, shaped him, molded him, making him wary of others until they'd proven themselves and careful of committing himself in relationships with others. He felt at ease in the company of his family and friends but cautious and restrained around strangers and acquaintances.

He valued those who won his heart, and he'd lay down his life for them in an instant, as he would for the common good, in service to law and order and justice. He hadn't decided on such a course of action or the values that underlay them; he'd simply accepted them and their apparent truth.

For him, family, country, law and order, integrity, civility, justice, and God weren't simply words or ideas, but the same sort of truths of which Thomas Jefferson had written: self-evident, without any more need for proof or justification than existence itself.

Lizzie ran to him, as Ben had, and wrapped him in her arms. "Daddy," she said simply.

Bane hugged her closely. So touching was her greeting, so immediate and earnest, that he felt, again, the moisture of tears in his eyes. He blinked them away. "Lizzie," he said.

Bradford stuck out his hand.

Bane delivered a bear hug. His verbal greeting to his father, spoken in a husky voice, consisted of a single word, "Dad."

Bane smiled. He guessed that his own father had been hardened a bit, too, by the situations he'd encountered. Most men had, he reckoned.

Aunt Flossie simply clutched Bane in her arms and let her tears of joy flow openly, the greeting of a woman who'd been a mother to a motherless child. As he returned her hug, Bane felt it nearly impossible to retain his stolid air. "Aunt Flossie, I—"

She drew back, smiling up at him. "I know, Bane; I know."

Finally, it was Pamela's turn to greet him, and she, like their children, ran forward, pulling him, almost frantically, into her arms. "Bane!" She repeated his name, over and over, as she hugged him fiercely, weeping and gasping. "Bane! Bane! I'm so glad, so glad!"

Bane marveled at her, as he had many times before. She was the bravest woman he'd ever met, and the truest, and the finest, and the most loving. Somehow, most women, although they faced difficulties, challenges, and dangers equal to those of men, were able to retain a gentleness that, although it seemed delicate, was as solid and durable as any man's resolve. Certainly, Pamela was one of them, as was Aunt Flossie, and he was blessed, he thought, to have two such women in his life, the one who had raised him and the one who had married him.

This time, he could not stop the tears. He could only wipe them away.

"Daddy! What's wrong?" Ben's concern was obvious in both his shocked expression and his tone of voice.

Lizzie smiled, but she didn't giggle.

"Nothing, son," Bane said.

"Your daddy's just happy to be with us again," Pamela explained.

Ben looked confused. "Huh?"

* * *

A week later, Bane took his family back home, thankful that his deputies had cleaned the upstairs rooms of the blood of the miscreants they'd shot after Rowelings and his hired guns had come to the marshal's home to kill him and his family.

"Got this," Badger, whom Bane had left in charge while he'd been at Lightning Hill, handed Bane a telegram from the sheriff of Mason, Nevada:

Matthew Lewis was killed when he tried to escape on his way to his arraignment.

"The silver's being recovered from the cave that Rowelings collapsed after retrieving the gold he stole," Luke declared.

"And Governor Cooper sent commendations to you, Badger, Luke, Marcel, and Curt, along with his official pardons for Marcel and Curt," Angeline said. "I took the liberty of framing the commendations and hanging them on either side of the front entrance."

Bane smiled. "Seems like you've thought of everything. Maybe now we can enjoy a little peace and quiet before all hell breaks loose again."

His deputies and secretary made no reply.

"Things are peaceful and quiet, aren't they?"

"Uh, Eliot Johnson's requested an interview with you—a series of interviews, in fact—about, well, everything that's happened from the time of the prison break to now," Angeline reported.

Bane groaned.

"And Sheriff Brenner, over in Douglas County, wanted to know if you could spare a couple of your deputies to give him a hand in hunting down a few prison fugitives spotted up his way, considering the 'luck,' as he put it, you've had in capturing Rowelings," Curt informed the marshal.

Bane moaned.

"And there's been a hint that your services may be required in another investigation, the details of which haven't been divulged," said Marcel.

Bane moaned and groaned.

"It's good to be back home again, isn't, Bane?" Luke asked.

"Or back in the saddle, you could say," Badger suggested.

Afterword

A Note to the Reader

In "Fenimore Cooper's Literary Offenses" (1895), Mark Twain makes the following observation:

> In the "Deerslayer" tale Cooper has a stream which is fifty feet wide where it flows out of a lake; it presently narrows to twenty as it meanders along for no given reason, and yet when a stream acts like that it ought to be required to explain itself.

In this novel, I make use of a historical event: the Nevada State Prison break that occurred on September 17, 1871, during which twenty-nine inmates escaped. The actual break occurred thirteen years before it does in my novel. This shift in the historical space-time continuum, like Cooper's meandering stream that shrinks in width as it runs along, "ought to be required to explain itself."

My movement of the prison break thirteen years forward into the future was done to accommodate my protagonist's chronology. Having written four previous volumes of his adventures and a prequel novella, it was easier for me to perform the miracle of transplanting the prison break from its own actual period to the future of my novel's time frame than to revise Bane's turbulent chronology as it presents itself in these previous works. Why go to the mountain (time) when one can have the mountain come to oneself (the writer)?

I also have used material from an actual crime that was infamous in its day: the West's first train robbery at Verdi, Nevada. In writing of it, I used the actual names of the participants and of others who were involved in the capture of the robbers, since my descriptions of the events concerning this crime are much as they were reported in the newspapers of the time.

It's possible that, in writing of past events and activities that an author has not experienced firsthand and of which he lacks expertise, he may get a detail (or even several of them) wrong. I have performed due diligence in researching a fairly long and diverse list of topics to which I make reference or, in some cases, incorporate into the action of this novel, among which are

- Nevada's State Prison break, concerning which newspapers of the past, archived on the Library of Congress's Chronicling America website, proved invaluable;

- the train robbery at Verdi, Nevada, concerning which, again, newspapers of that period, archived on the Library of Congress's Chronicling America website, proved priceless;

- the supplies and equipment needed to make moonshine and the moonshining process itself;

- the method that Spencer Rowelings uses to lead several horses simultaneously;

- the history of Aurora, Nevada;

- the prices of whiskey per shot and by the bottle, as well as other information about saloons of the period;

- the 1881 timetable of the Central Pacific Railroad (for the sake of convenience, I assumed that the timetable was the same in 1884 as it had been in 1881);

- Bodie's glory days, for which I found the book Bodie: 1859-1962, by Terri Lynn Geissinger, especially helpful;

- the enactment of female roles by male actors during the Elizabethan Age;

- wages and cost-of-living expenses during 1884 or thereabout;

- calculations of distances within and between several locations in Nevada and California;

- Bodie mining districts;

- mining history;

- freight wagons;

- historic forts;

- nineteenth-century French cuisine;

- the history of the electrification of American towns and cities;

- locations that existed in 1884 Nevada and California, as shown on maps, including an 1873 map of Bodie, California; a map showing the railroads of 1875 Nevada; an 1879 relief map of California; an 1880 map of mining claims near Bodie, California; an 1885 map of Nevada; an 1890 map of Bodie, California; a map offering a bird's-eye view of 1875 Carson City, Nevada; a map of Bodie Hills; maps of the Central Pacific Railroad; a map of Mono Basin, California; a table showing Morse Code equivalents of Latin letters; and a Rand McNally map of the Union Pacific and the Central Pacific Railroads;

- and a variety of other topics, the specificity of which now escapes me.

Although fiction is, by nature, fictitious, it also requires verisimilitude, especially when it is set in the past, and verisimilitude requires, among other things, research into the historical times and places in which the story's action takes place. Also, by researching the past, writers learn much and are able to pass on what they've learned to their readers, many of whom are as keen about authors' genres and their settings as writers themselves.

The quotations, except for those of Bane, his family, and other fictitious persons, are authentic. The dates of the births and deaths of those who are quoted are also correct, except that, in staying true to the time frame of this novel, which takes place in 1884, I have omitted dates of death that occur after this year, since these quotes' speakers remained very much alive during Bane's current adventure, as it is recounted in Manhunt: Return to Justice, and are, in many cases, his contemporaries.

About the Author

An active member of Western Writers of America, Gary has also written four Western novels under the byline Gary L. Pullman.

He "inherited" his love of Westerns from his father, who watched many Western TV shows and Western movies with Gary and his brothers.

There are four books in Gary's series An Adventure of the Old West: *Good with a Gun*, *The Valley of the Shadow*, *Blood Mountain*, and *On the Track of Vengeance*. Gary has also written a prequel, *Bane Messenger, Bounty Hunter*, which introduces the protagonist and the series. All five of these Westerns are available on Amazon, individually and as a collection (*An Adventure of the Old West Box Set*).

Gary Lee Pullman has written an 80,000-word stand-alone urban fantasy, *A Whole World Full of Hurt*, and three novellas of paranormal suspense, *Secrets of Sea Island (A Charlotte Hastings Paranormal Expose Book 1)*, *Monsters of New York (A Charlotte Hastings Paranormal Expose Book 2)*, and *Carnage at Chesapeake Bay (A Charlotte Hastings Paranormal Expose Book 3)*.

Gary lives in Las Vegas, Nevada, with his wife Paula Darnell, the award-winning cozy mystery author of the five-book series **A Fine Art Mystery**, the three-book series, **DIY Diva Mystery**, and the stand-alone police procedural novel **The Six-Week Solution**. They share their home with their canine companion, Lindsey Lou Boo Boo, a beautiful golden retriever.

To learn more about the American West, Gary, and his work, visit Gary's Western blog, *Wild West Telegraph*.

Also by

Good with a Gun
Some are good with their hands. Others have a way with words. Still others are good at farming or ranching. Bane Messenger is good with a gun. In his line of work, that's everything—until he meets Pamela.

Valley of the Shadow
In his absence, Bane's adopted hometown comes under a reign of terror. He isn't going to stand for that, even if he has to ride through the Valley of Death—or Hell itself.

Blood Mountain
After Bane's fight with an "army" of determined mercenaries is over, his ranch, Mountain Crest, will come to be known by a new name: Blood Mountain.

On the Track of Vengeance
Bane is ready to hang up his guns for good. Then, the president calls on him to pin on the star of a U. S. marshal and end the vengeful murders of innocent men and women.

Bane Messenger, Bounty Hunter
In this prequel novella, Bane, a Union veteran, finds his calling: hunting unscrupulous outlaws who prey on veterans' widows.

An Adventure of the Old West Box Set
This collection contains a prequel novelette and four full-length novels chronicling the thrilling, action-packed career of Bane Messenger, bounty hunter, sheriff, and U. S. marshal.

www.ingramcontent.com/pod-product-compliance
Lightning Source LLC
Chambersburg PA
CBHW021211250626
47155CB00008B/2764